Panjamon

THE ISLAND OF BORNEO

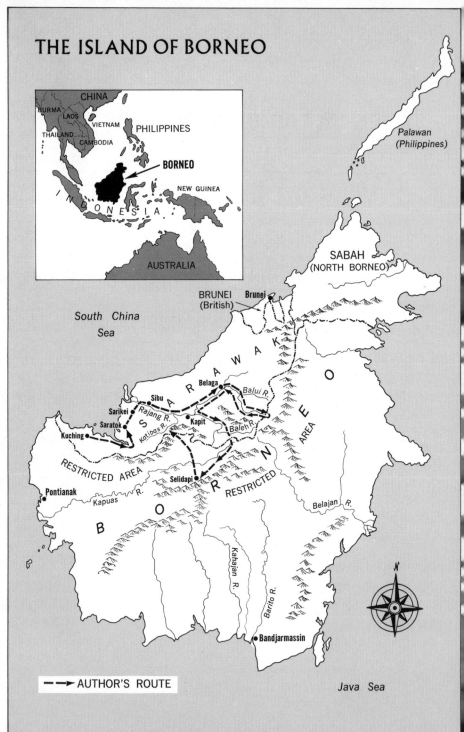

CHINA
BURMA
LAOS
VIETNAM
THAILAND
CAMBODIA
PHILIPPINES
BORNEO
NEW GUINEA
INDONESIA
AUSTRALIA

Palawan
(Philippines)

SABAH
(NORTH BORNEO)

South China
Sea

BRUNEI
(British)   Brunei

S   A   R   A   W   A   K
O

Belaga
Sibu   Balui R.
Sarikei   Rajang R.
Saratok   Kapit   Baleh R.
Kuching   Katibas R.
            B   O   R   N   E   O
RESTRICTED AREA   AREA

Pontianak   Selidapi   RESTRICTED
Kapuas   R.
                                    Belajan R.
B   O   R   N   E   O

Kahajan R.

Barito R.

Bandjarmassin

- - -► AUTHOR'S ROUTE

Java Sea

PANJAMON
I Was a Headhunter

Jean-Yves Domalain

Translated from the French
by Len Ortzen

WILLIAM MORROW & COMPANY, INC.
New York 1973

Domalain, Jean-Yves.
    Panjamon.

    1. Borneo—Description and travel. 2. Ibans (Bornean people).
3. Kayans. I. Title.
DS646.3.D6513   915.98′3   72-105
ISBN 0-688-00028-2

Author's Preface

Travel, for travel's sake, is to my mind a waste of time and energy and an unnecessary expense. It is so much better to arrive. But alas, I'm obliged to travel to satisfy my vice. Let me make this clear: My vice, for that's what it is, is the study of animals. This unreasoned passion has often taken me to remote parts of the earth.

What have I not endured in order to have a fleeting glimpse of a rare species of monkey hidden away in the foothills of the Annamite mountains? And when I think of the number of times my passport was stamped, the amount of dust I inhaled and the pounds I sweated off, before being able to observe a tribe of proboscis monkeys in Borneo . . . no, I don't like travel.

The reason for setting off this time was two strange animals, or rather reptiles. One was the Komodo lizard, a kind of antediluvian monster straight out of popular legend, which lives on a small, remote Indonesian island. About twelve feet long, it weighs all of three hundred pounds. The other was the sphenodon of Stephen Island, *Sphenodon punctatum* to the knowledgeable. It is not much to look at—thirty inches long at most, thin, little different from any ordinary lizard. But it existed in its present form 250 million years ago, long before the dinosaurs and brontosauruses appeared on earth.

More amazing still, this living fossil, which flourished during the Triassic and Jurassic periods, possesses a third eye—the parietal eye, which corresponds to the pineal gland in mammals.

These two reptiles are of great interest. Unfortunately,

they also have the great disadvantage of living thousands of miles from France.

For reasons of economy I chose to hitchhike, which is supposed to be the best means of studying the natives. But in practice this theory proved to be false.

All that was left in the kitty after buying the indispensable equipment, or what seemed indispensable, was the equivalent of about 300 dollars. And I never did get to Stephen Island.

Contents

Panjamon

ONE

Into the *Ulu*

I arrived in Singapore about a year after leaving France, having hitchhiked much of the way across Turkey, India and Pakistan. In Kashmir I had acquired a monkey of the genus *Macaca*, a young female I called "Totoche." We were used to each other by now, and when we were obliged to walk she trotted beside me until she had had enough, then climbed onto my shoulder or my pack. In Singapore I bought an old British shotgun, some cartridges and more film for my camera—and learned that Malaysia was at war with Indonesia.

This was a real disaster. There was my Komodo lizard on a little Indonesian island and here was I in Malaysian territory. A year's travel, a small fortune—for me—swallowed up, and thousands of miles covered in a variety of vehicles and on foot—all for nothing. And when I was so near to my objective.

What was I to do? On the map of Southeast Asia there was a large island which I had always been eager and yet a little reluctant to visit. Borneo seemed to me a most unhealthy part of the globe and was, I thought, inhabited by headhunters.

But I had always dreamed of going to Borneo one day, and now it was within reach. So one fine morning I bought a ticket for Kuching, the capital of Sarawak.

I found Borneo hot and sticky, full of mosquitoes and leeches, and I felt ill at ease among the millions of trees which cover a territory larger than France. Anyone used to living in open spaces is bound to feel inhibited by first

1

contact with the tropical jungle; it saps all courage and energy.

Before leaving Kuching for the interior, the *ulu* in native language, I browsed through a number of ethnographical works dealing with the different tribes that live in the forest—the Ibans or Sea Dayaks, the Land Dayaks, the Muruts, Kelabits, Punans, Kayans and Kenyas. As I couldn't visit all of them, I concentrated on the last, the Kenyas, and made copious notes about their customs, language and so on.

In order to reach their territory I had to cross a large marshy area, the home of crocodiles and snakes but also of the proboscis monkey, whose habits I was hoping to study. The going was very difficult along slippery paths that were often tree trunks placed end to end in the soggy ground, and were sometimes sunk a foot or more in stagnant water. The few villages were no more than collections of huts. But the waterways were numerous, often quite wide rivers that could be crossed only by thumbing a lift from passing canoes. And I was still in an "inhabited" area. What would it be like farther on?

The path got worse; there was less and less dry land and much more marsh. Suddenly I came to a great stretch of water, at least a mile wide. I wasn't sure whether it was the mouth of a river or an inlet of the sea. All around me there was nothing but mangroves and other exotic trees. It was beautiful and yet a bit depressing. I felt very inclined simply to wait there for some kind of river craft to come along.

After a long search I found a dry spot and slung my hammock. This wonderful invention was another purchase I had made in Singapore. It was made of good strong nylon, practically unbreakable, and was as good as a bed to sleep in. When securely slung between two branches and about a yard from the ground there was no fear of being bitten, except by mosquitoes. There were swarms of them everywhere; although smaller than the normal kind, these—which were ringed black and white—were even more aggressive, by day as well as by night. I had a mosquito net, but the difficulty was to slip into the hammock without disturbing the net, and then to avoid shifting about during the night.

Next day, as I was out of fresh food, I took my rifle and went hunting, leaving my pack and my monkey Totoche attached by her chain at the campsite. The only way of not getting lost was to follow the riverbank, but there were dozens of little streams running into the estuary, necessitating a detour to find a crossing. However, a few hundred yards from camp I saw two bands of monkeys quarreling. I crept forward, getting covered with mud, and approached near enough to an imprudent young male to shoot it. There was a general stampede as the body toppled to the ground; the monkeys that were fishing or playing in the water made for the bank with all speed, swimming like dogs.

On the way back I caught sight of an animal in the trees that seemed heavier than the macaque monkeys I had just disturbed, and from the brief glimpse I had of its color and outline it differed from most other species of its size except perhaps the *Nasalis larvatus*, the proboscis monkey that I was seeking. This was exciting, and I promised myself a closer examination of the area.

The following morning I set off with my camera, which had a telephoto lens, and the small-bore rifle; I also took some boiled water and a dozen strips of dried monkey meat. Despite walking slowly and carefully, I could not help making some noise and managed to startle a wild boar, and a little farther on a large lizard made a desperate dive for cover on sighting me. Snakes were much in evidence, and monkeys were frolicking in the trees. I was hidden in the undergrowth, quite still and silent, having heard a strange noise above me very similar to the one the previous evening. Then it came again, a little discreet cry that mingled with the lapping of the water. I twisted my neck in all directions, and then I saw them —two large, long-tailed, reddish-brown monkeys perched comfortably on the same branch and apparently having a chat. They were without doubt proboscis monkeys. Others appeared, not suspecting my presence. They looked like melancholy clowns with that great thick nose drooping over their mouths, those small, close-set eyes with a wistful expression, and a Buddha-like protruding belly. There were others disporting themselves in the water, to judge by the sounds. I crept forward a few yards and saw two of them that seemed to be fishing. They were swimming—a rather languid crawl—between the mangrove roots and even some distance from the bank. Now and again they went under and both came up with a crab, which they ate with their fingers, so to speak, spitting out the hard scaly parts and the ends of the claws. They and their kind were not as rowdy as the other monkeys.

Rain was not far off, the sky was darkening over the river, and the animals were becoming indistinguishable from the foliage or the grayish-brown muddy waters. In order to have a better view of the monkeys by the river I left my pack and gun and crawled forward, trying to remain hidden in the undergrowth.

Little is known of the habits of the proboscis monkey, so the observations I made on that and following days may be of interest. The young are kept in order with very little difficulty and hardly any brawling or scuffling takes place. They remain in one place for some time, as if making sure that they have drawn all possible sustenance from it. They are very fond of the tree *Sonneratia*, which seems to provide about four-fifths of their plant food. Crabs form part of their diet, as I saw early on, and they are by no means averse to shrimps (I should very much like to know how they catch these) or to fish, which they skillfully scooped up from the little channels and burrows along the riverbank. While doing so, they usually keep their faces just above water and grope around; but even when they duck under they must still fish by touch, for it's almost impossible to see in these miry waters.

On several occasions I betrayed my presence, and then they dived below the surface and reappeared about thirty yards away. Some, however, fled into the forest, but when these had located my position they made a wide detour and rejoined the main party in the water. It is astonishing that these monkeys should seek protection in the water when they are so well equipped for hiding away in the trees. This proclivity is sometimes disastrous for them; the natives know their habits and make them jump into the water, as it is then so much easier to kill them. The wretched monkeys do not even try to flee, nor do they bite when captured.

I made many notes and took many photographs, but I suffered a lot from the mosquitoes and the rain. Nearly every day there were heavy showers or, what was worse, a continual drizzle from a lowering sky which reduced visibility almost to nothing. Moreover, night and morning there was a sharp chill, whereas during the day the heat became stifling. I began to feel ill, and the thought of coming down with malaria in this isolated spot was not amusing. To get to the nearest doctor would probably take a fortnight's hiking, provided you knew just how to reach him and were in excellent condition.

I decided to make a strategic withdrawal in the direction of villages. After a few days' walking the going became progressively easier; there was less stagnant water and more solid ground. Finally I came upon a good path which led to Saratok, a village a little way inland. From there I followed an apology for a road to Sarikei, and then a day's boat journey landed me in Sibu, on the great Rajang River. Sibu is a town with a predominantly Chinese population and much trading goes on there, giving it a different atmosphere from the capital, Kuching.

It took a little time to readjust to town life after a few weeks alone in the jungle, but I was soon better again. I found a temple with a public room, both unusually clean; and I spent a week going round the town and gathering as much information as possible about the region I intended to visit. The Leong family, who kept the shop where I bought more film for my camera, helped greatly in this respect; and the father did me many useful services later. He was a small Chinese with a typical little pointed beard and wrinkled face, kind and friendly, and his son was his spitting image. I was to go upriver to Kapit by one of the boats—Chinese-owned, of course —that ply regularly between there and Sibu. The Rajang was very wide as far as Kapit, a placid river quite safe for navigation, I was told. The journey would last ten to fourteen hours and cost me the equivalent of thirty cents. But above Kapit where there were rapids water transport became dangerous. However, I understood there were canoes with outboard motors which maintained communications with Belaga, a small town among the mountains. Beyond there I should be in a Restricted Area. Opinions differed about the natives living in the Ulu Batang Rajang—in the interior, around the upper reaches of the Rajang. According to officials, especially British, the natives had given up the practice of headhunting; but some people maintained the contrary to be true. The best thing was to go and find out for myself.

At Kapit I got a place in a pirogue, a flat-bottomed canoe some thirty feet long. The passengers were protected from the rain and the sun by a crudely made awning of corrugated sheeting. There were two powerful outboard

motors at the stern. This and other Chinese-owned craft
linking Kapit with Belaga carried not only passengers
but the supplies needed by an up-country town—kero-
sene, gasoline, food, medicines and so on. The journey
took three to eight days, depending on the state of the
river and the number of accidents, such as the engines
breaking down or—what was most frequent—the pirogue
capsizing.

I must admit that I don't like the water; and this cruise
appealed to me even less since I had heard the Chinese
agent say that two pirogues had already capsized this
year and eight people had been drowned. And we were
only in early March. . . . The Rajang's reputation as a
"swallower of men" was well-founded. At the moment
the river was low; there could not have been much rain
up in the mountains recently. So you had to beware of
the rocks and boulders strewing the riverbed. When the
river was high the current and trees uprooted by floods
were the main dangers.

Our troubles began right at the start. The long-haired
Iban mechanic with designs tattooed on his back and
shoulders checked the outboard motors in a perfunctory
manner, wound a length of string around the starter of
one and gave a pull. There was a loud bang, a lot of
smoke and a few flames, which at once caused a fine
panic. Passengers clambered over the pigs and the chickens, the bags of rice and salt, and jumped into the pirogues alongside. A young woman jumped without
hesitation into the gray river. My first thought was for
my equipment. I heaved my pack into the craft alongside, but when I went to follow it I found that the Chinese had cast off our moorings and were pushing the
pirogue out into the river with boathooks, fearing that
the fire might spread.

However, the mechanic had remained calm and had
smothered the flames with old rags. Ten minutes later

we were all back in our places, watching somewhat anxiously as he rewound his string around the starter. There was no explosion this time, and the engine started up. The only casualty had been a hen squashed by a fat woman. Its owner, a wrinkled old lady, did not intend to let the matter rest there. Who was going to pay for her chicken? Finally the Chinese agent gave her half its price and added it to the supplies for our midday meals.

We got under way and I had a look at my fellow passengers. There were two or three Chinese returning to their shops at Belaga and about a dozen Ibans, recognizable from their tattooed designs. Nearly all were wearing shirts and shorts, though one man was clad in nothing but the traditional sarong around his loins. His wife was wearing a cotton dress such as those sold in all the bazaars. There was another small group in the bow; they were Kayans, and it was easy to see that they and the Ibans do not get on very well together. As we were still in Iban territory, the Kayans were keeping very quiet. Their women seemed well dressed and were wearing a lot of jewelry.

Our pirogue was keeping close to the bank, to avoid the strong current. At times the mechanic brought the other outboard motor into use, and then the noise became unbearable. Now and again we grazed a rock or touched a sandbank, and the pirogue heeled a little. There were uprooted tree trunks, too, floating downstream half submerged. The mechanic's mate was squatting right up in the bow and guiding him by a complicated system of arm signals, for the other could see very little of obstacles ahead from his position in the stern. As we progressed upriver the landscape gradually changed; the hillsides became steeper, the forest grew thick again (there were many clearings just above Kapit) and villages were few and far between. I saw my first longhouses of the Iban tribe, each sheltering a whole village; some were more than one hundred and fifty yards in length.

In the evening we moored at one of these villages and went ashore for the night, taking our belongings and hopping across the dried mud. We had been sitting down all day, and the benches in the pirogue were only about six inches from the bottom and far from comfortable, especially when the bailer-out dozed off and the water rose to seat level. These villagers were obviously used to such arrivals, for everything was ready for us. Several acetylene lamps were shedding a garish light along the communal verandah of the longhouse, where a good supply of canned food stood heaped in a corner. I was obviously not the first white man to set foot here, for little notice was taken of me; just a few youngsters came to chat with me for a while, before all the travelers bedded down for the night on the verandah.

As the Rajang was not in too bad a mood we reached Belaga in four days. This village was perched high above the river on a steep hill of damp clay. A long wooden verandah with a roofing of corrugated sheeting formed the "main street." Along the side overlooking the river were a few benches usually occupied by natives who had come into town to buy salt or sell blowpipes and shields to tourists. On the other side of the "street" were a dozen shops all alike and kept by Chinese, each cluttered up with an assortment of goods such as only a Chinese shopkeeper can assemble: batteries and mosquito nets, canned milk, soap, scrap iron, watches. There were three or four restaurants, too, dirty and badly lit like most in Southeast Asia, with a stove in a corner for the cooking.

I went and sat in the restaurant at the far end of the verandah, one that seemed a little cleaner than the others. Rain had been falling all afternoon and I was wet through; some hot coffee or Ovaltine would be very welcome.

It was getting dark when I left, and as I'd had enough of sleeping on verandah benches I went in search of a lodging. The British official at Sibu who had issued me a permit for travel beyond Belaga had kindly given me a note recommending me to the police chief here. So I started toward the police post, which was one of the buildings standing apart. Just then I was hailed by a tall, ginger-haired man with a beard, dressed in white shorts, shoes and socks.

"Hello there, what are you looking for?"

"The police post and a place to sleep."

"It's too late for the police, the sergeant's gone off. If you want somewhere to sleep, it's under the stars or you're welcome to come to my place."

"I'd be glad to, for I haven't a tent with me. My name's Domalain and I'm French."

"I'm Doctor D, from Sydney. I live here. What brings you to these lousy parts?"

"How about a beer? We could talk better over a glass or two than standing out here in the rain."

It had started again, a few large, gentle drops at first, but in thirty seconds it had become a torrential downpour which made an infernal din on the corrugated roofing of the restaurant we dashed into; it was pitch black outside.

An hour later we were still there, with a few empty cans in front of us. Thanks to Doctor D, I was about to complete the preparations for my expedition in two days. The most difficult part had been to find a Chinese with a pirogue and three outboard motors for hire, and then to get him to agree on a price within my means! But I still needed a mechanic.

"A mechanic and a guide, too," Doctor D advised me.

"Or better still, two guides. Though I'm not sure I'll be able to unearth them for you. There are few keen on a trip up the Rajang as high as you want to go. What a crazy idea anyway! How much money have you got left?"

"About two hundred dollars."

"Two hundred! With that you can hire half the guides in the district."

In fact it was the food supplies that cost me most. I was taking four hundred pounds of rice, some of it to distribute to villagers I met (this was the doctor's idea, and it turned out to be a good one), some cooking oil, hens, four pigs and a lot of other provisions. The day before setting out I counted how much money I had left. It was less than fifty dollars. I had no need of pencil and paper to know that I wouldn't have enough for my return ticket to Singapore. But all that was a long way in the future. . . .

"Check your supplies once more," said the doctor. "What medicines are you taking?"

I showed him the two phials and a tube of quinine tablets.

"Are you joking?" He looked at me as if I were completely mad. "As a doctor I've a long experience of these regions. There are epidemics all the year round, and whole villages get wiped out without anyone knowing just why. That's not counting the more common cholera and typhus . . . and malaria is an endemic disease. So for God's sake take a good supply of quinine, sulfonamides and antibiotics."

As I discovered later, the mortality rate among the Ibans in the mountainous interior is indeed terrible; the average life expectancy is twenty-five years. Seventy percent of the babies die in their first year. Since the Second World War the population of this tribe has dropped from ten to three thousand.

The doctor gave me a small crate containing thirty pounds of medical supplies.

"And what do you expect me to do with all this?"

"Think of the natives! Hand some out in the villages you visit. I'll explain to your guides what to do with it. And now, good luck!"

The outboard motors sounded like dogs howling at the moon. It was impossible to hear oneself speak. But at least we were moving fairly quickly. Only two of the motors were being used; the third, a yard astern at the end of a shaft, had its propeller out of the water and would only be brought into action when we came to the big rapids. The pirogue was specially adapted for the upper reaches but otherwise was similar to the one that had brought me to Belaga—flat-bottomed and thirty feet long with an awning of corrugated sheeting. We were well laden with fuel and supplies. This "expedition" of mine looked a bit ramshackle, but I didn't mind that.

We kept near the bank as much as possible, to avoid the strong current and have some shade from the trees. At the end of the first day we left the Rajang and went up the Balui River, which is just as treacherous. There were rocks everywhere, some of them standing more than thirty feet out of the water, but more dangerous were those just below the surface that only a native eye could detect. And uprooted tree trunks came swirling down toward us now and again.

It rained every day, either heavy downpours or a fine drizzle that got on my nerves. In betweentimes the sun blazed down. As we moved upstream the mountains rose higher and closed in, becoming more and more rugged. There were fantastic landscapes, narrow gorges and colossal falls of rock, against the background of the thousand and one greens of the jungle.

When the rain became too violent we drew into the bank and waited patiently, protecting ourselves as best we could and remaining quite still in the hope that this would save us from the worst of it. My three companions were all Kayans, honest, willing and stouthearted. We made a good team; they made up for my lack of experience with the river and the jungle, and I helped them as well as I could and tried to imitate them. I was not at all sure what had induced them to come with me; it was certainly not the small amount of money I was paying them.

Our progress became slower and slower. Several times we had to unload the pirogue and manhandle it through a dangerous stretch, then go back to collect the bundles. This took a long time and was very exhausting. Sometimes we could not take the pirogue into the bank, so had to carry our burdens over smooth, slippery rocks, at the risk of falling into one of the treacherous races.

Hauling our craft along was less of an effort, but the bank was seldom clear enough for this. The pleasant cruise watching the banks slide past had come to an end. I was beginning to understand the significance of the dotted lines representing the course of the river on my map. And higher on the map were some hachures indicating rapids. We'd have to take our chances.

We sweltered in the hot, sticky atmosphere; sunshine and rain alternated, the latter a fine drizzle. But it turned very cold at night, and I was glad that I had not carried out my intention of exchanging my warm quilt for a light woolen blanket. We had passed a few villages on the first two or three days, but now there was a complete absence of any habitation. But our days were far from being dull. Whenever we touched a rock or the propeller-guard caught on some obstacle, the pirogue suddenly heeled or the bow reared up and a few gallons of water came aboard. Would we capsize or not? The engines raced in a deafening crescendo—and each time our hearts were in our mouths.

"One pig, Tuan."

A boar was swimming madly across the river. We turned toward it as the mechanic throttled down and the two guides seized their spears. The poor animal had no chance; it was threshing about in the foaming water with three spear wounds in its hide. The blood gushed out and was carried away by the current. Then it was still, the spears still sticking in it. Not even three of us were able to hoist it on board, so we towed it by its tail and ears toward a sandy bank. My companions were very pleased; it meant three hundred pounds of excellent meat for us. The wild boars of Borneo are said to be the biggest in the world, and certainly I've seen some that were colossal.

We stayed on the little beach to deal with the carcass. Half a day's rest wouldn't do us any harm. While three of us cut up the meat, the mechanic overhauled the outboards. He stripped one engine down, spreading the parts on an oily rag. I only hoped he could assemble it again, for I couldn't be of much assistance, as I told him. This disturbed and even shocked him, for everyone knows that white men can do everything, except walk through the jungle. That evening, while sitting around the campfire, stuffing ourselves with hot fat meat, we talked in bad English and a few words of Malay, helped out by gestures and signs. We managed to understand one another without much difficulty.

"What do you work at, Tuan? The doctor told us that you were an animal doctor. He explained it to us, but we did not understand very well."

I tried to explain, too, but it was a bit difficult. "I'm not a doctor and I don't cure animals."

It took a long time to convince them that all I did was watch animals.

"How can you watch them if you can't see them?" And they roared with laughter.

They had shown that they could sight game in the

forest far quicker than I could. But I came back at them. "Can you catch live snakes, Kaio?"

"No," said Kaio, "that's dangerous. I kill them."

I asked the mechanic; he was the one who had teased me a moment ago. He scratched his head and looked at me askance.

"When I see a snake, if it's black and crosses my path from left to right, I leave it alone and go back to the village. But if it crosses from right to left I cut off its head, unless it's going too fast."

I explained that I caught them alive, black or white, and whatever the direction they were going.

"Even the snake that rears up?"

"Cobras, you mean? Yes, I catch them, too."

They obviously didn't believe a word of it. To their minds, all snakes were dangerous.

"The Kayans say that the only good snake is a dead one."

"We'll catch some later on, you'll see."

"Yes, Tuan." They were polite as usual, but I could see they took me for a blatant liar.

The next day we came to the rapids and had no time for snakes.

This, said the guide, was the critical point of the journey. The mechanic stopped the engines and we ran gently onto a small sandy beach. A little way ahead towered a steep cliff about 150 feet high, partly covered with thick creeper and scraggy bushes. We could see nothing of the rapids, for the river took a right-hand bend just here; but now that the engines were silent we could hear a loud roar, seeming to issue from the bowels of the earth. We tied up and set off in single file to climb the cliff.

We reached the top after a long struggle, and from there we could see the foaming waters careering down amid a chaos of rocks. The noise was deafening. There

were two steep chutes with about fifty yards of comparatively calm water between them. The lower presented
less of a problem, but the upper was much narrower and
steeper, with a race of indescribable ferocity.

I was completely stunned and looked at the others,
hoping they would say that it was impossible. They
stared in silence for a moment or two, then the mechanic
spoke up. "We can't get through now, the river is too
high. But perhaps in a few days. . . ."

That was a relief; but the fear of showing panic in
front of my companions was stronger than my fear of the
rapids, so I said nothing. I gave a sidelong glance at the
others; their faces were blank. The mechanic seemed to
be memorizing the positions of the rocks showing just
above the raging waters, which would not be visible
from below. One of the guides was looking very unde-
cided; he half turned toward me, and I winked and gave
the "thumbs-up" sign. He nodded. When I was asked
my opinion I gave an optimistic "Okay," which was far
from corresponding to what I really felt.

We climbed down again in silence. We would just have
to wait. In order to prevent the pirogue from being
carried away by a sudden flood, we hauled it well up
the beach and tied it securely. The boar we had killed
the previous morning was beginning to smell, but we
grilled a few slices. I found it distasteful, and after the
meal I asked Mayok, the other guide, if he would like to
go hunting with me. He agreed at once, because it would
give him the opportunity to show his superior skill—
which I'd never denied—in spotting game. So we set off,
I with my gun and he with a hunting parang at his side
and a wicker basket on his back. I shot a wild boar,
which Mayok cut up, and we managed to stagger back
to camp with it; fortunately he had carried by far the
heavier part. We all ate well that evening.

Next day the river was still too high to attempt the

rapids. I tried to think of some way of deriving benefit from our enforced stay. As my three natives were endowed with exceptional vision, I enrolled them in helping me to collect insects. They were not very enthusiastic, but I had another idea in mind. While scratching around for insects it often happens that a snake or two comes out of hiding, and I should not at all mind showing these fellows how to catch a cobra alive. I gave each of them a pair of tweezers and took my gun under my arm, for one never knew what might come within range. In the course of our prospecting we came upon many things—a variety of spiders, whose venom was a much greater danger in this climate than in Europe; some scorpions and a great variety of scolopendrids; and, as I expected, reptiles of all sizes and markings. The three Kayans showed an unholy fear of the snakes, which was surprising when I thought how little impressed they were—or seemed to be—by the rapids.

We stumbled upon a thick tree trunk lying halfway down a small ravine, and I thought we might find a variety of little creatures sheltering under it. The four of us just managed to roll it over and were preparing to collect the panic-stricken insects when a magnificent cobra suddenly reared up a foot or so away from the mechanic. Without looking to see if it was black or not, or going from left to right, all three Kayans leapt back and ran off.

Now nothing is easier than capturing a cobra. It can be done with the bare hands if you've had a little experience and have good reflexes. But if you're not sure of yourself it's advisable to carry a tube of serum. The technique is to pin the snake's head to the ground with a stick so that you can grasp it by the neck with thumb and forefinger. Of course, the cobra does not wait for this to happen; either it attempts to escape or it attacks. But it can always be held back by grabbing its tail, provided your hands are kept out of reach of its fangs. When you hold it up high in the air, head downward, it is helpless. Contrary to popular belief, cobras are not particularly swift or aggressive.

I have handled hundreds and been bitten only twice, and then not while capturing them. You begin to get your eye in after capturing a dozen or so, and then the sport becomes as tame as collecting coleopterous beetles. Few people would agree, but it's true.

In my opinion the small snakes are most difficult to capture: they are very swift and dart up trees or slip into cracks; and when you manage to corner one, great care is needed not to damage it. As for pythons, it all depends on the size. Only one species of large python is found in Borneo, the very common reticulated python, usually between ten and twelve feet long. The smaller can be captured without any difficulty; even if it gets its coils around you there are ways of extricating yourself despite its relative strength. Nor is there very much danger from those twelve feet and more in length, unless you are alone. Help is needed to uncoil a python of this size, and three is the ideal number for capturing one.

However, to get back to the cobra in front of me. No help could be expected from the Kayans so I seized it behind the hood and chopped off its head, having first checked that it belonged to a common species. In these remote areas one not infrequently discovers a rare subspecies that can easily be mistaken for an ordinary specimen unless closely inspected. This little incident improved my prestige with the Kayans.

After a week of waiting for the waters to go down, my guides suggested continuing on our way upstream.

"Will the waters go down any more?" I asked.

The mechanic appeared to be the most decisive and was certainly the most experienced—after all, he was in charge of the boat—and he answered that they might go down but he was not sure. Although I was still very doubtful about the chances of ascending the rapids safely, I gave a confident "Let's go."

We lashed down all the baggage as securely as possible. During the week of waiting we had carried the fuel and food supplies to a point above the rapids, to give ourselves every chance; we would pick them up when we reached the spot.

I tied my pack to an upright of the boat and attached my best camera to my chest, so that my arms would be free. We had previously cut some long bamboo poles, one for each man, to keep the pirogue clear of the rocks. Everything seemed ready. However, we decided to eat as much as we could before setting off; we would need all our strength for the effort ahead. That meal was more like a ritual; we were all silent, each with his own thoughts. Kaio, in view of the occasion, opened a small, untouched jar of *borak*, the strong rice wine of the Kayans.

Right until the last I had hoped that something would happen to delay the start. A kingfisher crossing our path from left to right, for instance—a very bad omen which would give us at least a day's grace. But no, the gods of the river and the forest seemed to be on our side . . . let them remain so.

All three motors started up; everything was in order, and we slowly drew away from the restful bank. As soon as we reached the bend and were out in the middle of the river, the struggle against the current began. Even before the rapids came in sight we were zigzagging between dangerous rocks. A tree trunk came spinning swiftly past, hit a rock and bounced back into the water, raising a great foaming splash.

Kaio was right up in the bow, head stretched forward and his pole at hand. Every so often he flung an arm wide to signal an obstacle to the rest of us farther aft.

Mayok was standing next to me, ready with his bamboo pole. Whenever the pirogue seemed about to hit a rock he leaned over and gave a vigorous thrust, helping the mechanic at the helm to swing the boat away.

As we drew near the rapids we began to be tossed, sometimes heeling dangerously and shipping a lot of water. The ominous high cliffs on either side seemed to be scoffing at our rashness. Suddenly we were in the midst of it; all around was a confusion of great rocks with wild waters battering madly against them, careering past us at gunwale level in a never-ending silvery stream. The din was infernal. All three of us were up forward now, fending the boat away from the boulders, staggering and falling to our knees when the poles slithered off the smooth stone. A sudden heavy thud made me drop my pole and I instinctively clutched at the awning as the bows rose up. Quick as a flash, Kaio pushed hard with his pole and we slid off the rock, smacking heavily into the water and taking a lot aboard. A few yards higher we went aground again and had greater difficulty in getting off an almost flat rock just below the surface. But finally we were beyond the first of the rapids. The struggle had lasted about half an hour and we were exhausted, not only by the physical exertion but by the nervous strain. And already we had to prepare to meet the second obstacle, a steep chute of racing, seething water, more fearful than the chaos of rocks below us.

It was no more than fifty yards away, looking from our lowly level like an enormous, overwhelming mass. Even a novice in river navigation could tell that we would never make the ascent. With the engines at full speed we were making practically no headway against the current. I felt helpless. "Go up in reverse?" I shouted to the mechanic in the stern. He shook his head. It was impossible. If we went only slightly broadside on to the current, it would capsize us before we knew where we were.

Then it happened: a great smash, water everywhere, and everything was wiped out. I had the feeling of falling into a washing machine, being soaked and pummeled, wrung and scraped. I was thrown against rocks, turned upside down, had the air forced from my lungs . . . the next moment I shot upward, but had no time to draw breath. . . .

There were three of us washed up on a sandy beach, lying stunned and still, not very far apart from one another. Only Kaio and the pirogue were missing. We had no idea what had happened to them and, unnatural though it may seem, we were too exhausted to care.

The sun woke us the following morning. We were all bruised and aching. About eighteen inches of skin had been torn from my back, and this was beginning to hurt. If it became infected I would be in a bad way, for the medical supplies had not been unloaded with the rest as they took up little space. The fish were probably having the benefit of them.

After walking along the bank for about an hour we saw Kaio sitting dejectedly on a rock. He had thought he was the only survivor, having looked for the rest of us all the previous afternoon. He had suffered less than any of us; while searching around he had spotted the pirogue a little lower down on the opposite bank. It did not appear greatly damaged, apart from one of the outboards being wrenched off. But we could not tell from our side of the river, as the stern was buried in a tangle of roots and plants. The propellers had probably caught in this, which was lucky for us.

The river was comparatively calm at this point and it seemed possible for someone to swim across to the pirogue. The three Kayans discussed who should make the attempt and finally Kaio settled the matter. He stripped and plunged in, and although he entered the water a hundred yards above the pirogue the current carried him well down beyond it. The three of us followed his progress from the bank; he swam as all the natives do, a crawl with his arms while his legs did the movement for the breast stroke. He swam steadily, saving his breath. In any case, it was no great difficulty for a Kayan used to these dangerous waters since childhood; the only real risk was from crocodiles. There were quite a few in the length of the river, although we had not seen many coming up; they had been scared away by the din we made. But Kaio reached the opposite bank without incident, after half an hour's effort, and made his way back to the pirogue.

The three of us went and stood opposite and waited impatiently for the verdict. It could be disastrous for me. My pack was very likely at the bottom of the river, not to mention all my photographic material.

Kaio was going over the pirogue thoroughly. We saw him nodding his head now and again, tapping the outboards and shaking the structure.

"If only he'd say something!"

"Kaio! How is it?"

"One engine gone, one broken, one still good. The rest of it is all right."

He must have found a small axe in the tool locker, for he began cutting away the tangle of roots to free the stern. As this seemed to be taking a long time my two companions went foraging for food in the forest. None of us could face climbing the cliff to fetch the rice which we had left with the other supplies above the rapids.

I stayed sitting on the ground; my back was hurting so much that I dared not venture into the forest. A branch or a creeper brushing against my spine made me grit my teeth, and I did not move about very much that day. In any case it was soon dark, and the three of us huddled together to keep warm, after swallowing a few handfuls of insects and some fern shoots. We ate it all raw—the insects alive. It was the first time I had done that.

In the middle of the night I felt feverish and light-headed, and wondered how much worse things could get. Suddenly a flame flickered on the opposite bank. Kaio had found a light, and there was only one place where he could have got it from—in a side pocket of my pack where I had put a score of boxes of matches wrapped in plastic bags. They were intended to be presents for any natives we met. I had an old lighter for my own use, but it had, alas, slipped from my pocket during our aquatic rodeo. For my pack not to have been thrown out of the pirogue seemed too good to be true! I mentally went through its contents. All the little things suddenly acquired an exaggerated importance—the string, fishhooks, pocketknife . . . even some antibiotic ointment.

In the morning Kaio brought the pirogue across, using a makeshift paddle and taking a slanting course. Now the moment of decision was upon us—to go on or turn back?

The day before I had felt overcome by disappointment and bitter about all my bad luck. But I had been thinking things over during the night, despite the fever, and I'd reached the conclusion that it was better to take the bull by the horns and press on, rather like a tired runner who continues from sheer doggedness.

However, I asked the three Kayans what they thought. Were they prepared to go on? None made any answer at first; they just stood looking at the ground, the mechanic poking at the sand with his bare foot. As I expected, it was Kaio who looked up first.

"I'll go, Tuan."

He had spoken for them all. They suddenly burst out laughing, looking at me until I joined in.

We decided to bypass the rapids by portage. Although not dangerous, it was going to be very difficult to get the pirogue up the cliff and to a point beyond the rapids. The wound on my back healed more quickly than I had dared hope, thanks to the antibiotic ointment so miraculously salvaged; but for the time being I could not be of much assistance. I gathered wood for the fire and did the cooking, not in the saucepans—which were now at the bottom of the river—but in hollow bamboos which were just as good; better even, as there was no washing up to do.

You choose a nice big hollow bamboo and cut off a portion with its partition. You put the food in, with some water, then cover it with a turf and place it directly on the fire. There is no need of a whistle to announce when the food is cooked; the bamboo bursts open, spilling the boiling water which douses the fire. Then all you have to do is to eat. The curious thing is that the food is always cooked exactly right whether it is meat, vegetable shoots or fish. We sometimes wrapped the fish in leaves and cooked it on the glowing embers. This is a method used by all primitive tribes in the tropical jungle.

My companions undertook the hard work of clearing a path through the forest for the pirogue and of repairing the outboards, if possible. We could use paddles if necessary, but we would then lose a lot of time. While the mechanic tried to revive the engines, Mayok and Kaio made rollers for the pirogue. This was laborious work, for one man had to climb the trees to disentangle the cane shoots, then bend them over while the man on the ground pulled as hard as he could. But my companions were used to it; before the days of outboard motors this was the way they had always got past the rapids. When they had collected enough canes to make rollers they climbed the cliff and started to cut a clearing through the forest, beginning with the thorny bushes and bam-

boos that formed thick impenetrable clumps. The task
was made more difficult by the uneven terrain.

The mechanic stripped down the engines, hammered
at the buckled propellers with stones, straightened a
shaft and gave everything a liberal dose of oil; I was
skeptical of their ever functioning again after such a
dousing. However, I let him get on with it.

After a week of hard work the three Kayans began to
get tired of a diet of grasshoppers and fern shoots, and
temporarily abandoned their tasks to make traps. We had
little to make them from, other than what the forest itself
provided. We set some rudimentary traps of the deadfall
type, and in order to have large quantities of meat
quickly three of the traps released tree trunks heavy
enough to break the back of a wild boar. But luck never
came our way. We also laid a number of snares and with
these caught a lot of birds and small animals—jungle
fowl, pheasants, mongooses, badgers and ferrets.

I set my own snare, one that was new to my Kayan
friends. I still had a supply of fishhooks, about a hundred
of all sizes and a score of large three-pronged ones. I also
had three balls of nylon string, each three hundred feet
long, which I had intended to give to villagers I met. I
stretched a length of string between two stout supports
—a couple of trees or rocks—and above a run if possible,
then attached a great number of hooks by short lines and
camouflaged the hooks with mud. Animals that got
caught in the hooks became more entangled the more
they tried to free themselves. Depending on the size of
the hooks, squirrels, jungle fowl and civet cats could be
caught in this way, sometimes—as happened on this occasion—even a young macaque monkey.

The mechanic had twice tried to start up one of the
outboards, but without success; there was not even a hic-
cup from it, just the starter spinning around like a top.
He wound his piece of string around it again, put one

foot on the gunwale to get more leverage and gave a sharp pull. The engine leapt into life, smoking and making a peculiar noise.

I have never seen such a delighted face as the mechanic's. With his hands on his hips, he listened to "his" engine and proudly walked all around it.

The two guides congratulated him and thumped him on the back and, as I expected, it ended in roars of laughter and a dip in the river, all splashing one another. For some odd reason they seemed to think everything would be all right now, and I let myself be carried away by their optimism. The mechanic, considering his own job finished, turned his attention to the system he had thought out for hauling the pirogue up the cliff. And by means of his crazy "block and tackle" assemblage we got the pirogue to the top in only half a day, whereas we had taken ten days to prepare the way through the forest.

Then we put some rollers under the pirogue and all we had to do was push. But we had to go back on our tracks a short distance at one point, because of a mistake in our direction, and clear a fresh path. It was no easy matter to edge the thirty-foot craft between the tree trunks, but after two days of effort she was once again afloat above the rapids. It took one more day to fetch and mount the outboards, which we had left behind during the hauling operation, to reload the rice and the gasoline and to get everything trim. Then we were ready to cut through the water again, though at no great speed as only one outboard was working. The other we had salvaged maintained a stubborn silence.

So we had been held up for twenty-five days solely on account of those rapids. The immigration officer who had given me a permit for the Restricted Area valid for only fifteen days must have been joking.

TWO

Among the Kayans

As we rounded another bend in the river a village came in sight, perched on a rounded hilltop. All about were the pointed summits of mountains standing out sharply against a clear blue sky. In the clearings surrounding the village were a few fields of maize, a score or so of banana trees and checkered patches of rice. Around the long-house was a haphazard array of huts built on piles, some square, others rectangular, which all served for storing the rice. The whole formed an oasis of calm in the midst of the jungle, giving me an impression of serenity and simplicity such as I have rarely experienced anywhere else.

The noisy outboard motor had given warning of our approach, and the whole village was waiting for us, assembled along the top of the clayey, sloping bank. The few women still washing clothes or bathing in the river hastily climbed the slippery steps to join the crowd. I felt sure that never before had a combustion engine shattered the tranquillity of these surroundings.

When we nosed into the bank some of the men dashed down to take a line and make us fast, but without displaying very much curiosity. It was a little as if a group of their hunters were returning after a lengthy absence. Only the women and children betrayed their deep surprise.

The mechanic proudly demonstrated his importance by revving up the engine with the propeller out of the water. I left the two guides to do the explaining, limiting myself to taking my pack ashore and smiling at one and all; there must have been at least a hundred people swarming around us.

The village chief, as he seemed to be, came over to me, took both my hands and shook them warmly. Then we all walked in single file up to the village, with the children running around us shouting and laughing. Some of the men had taken charge of our baggage. The women had gone running on ahead and when we reached the longhouse the mats were already spread out, and the intense activity going on gave the impression that some celebration in our honor was being prepared.

The chief seemed anxious to welcome us with all due respect. I realized later why he was so eager to establish his clan's reputation for hospitality. There on the threshold he favored me with a speech of welcome which lasted a good half-hour, and of which I didn't understand a word. From time to time the men standing around nodded wisely, gave vigorous sounds of approval or commented in a low voice or with a laugh. When the chief finished there were shouts and yells and long applause. Courtesy required me to make a reply. I called the mechanic over, he being the one of my three companions who best understood my English.

"Tell him that I thank him for his welcome, that I am terribly sorry not to speak Kayan . . . that he's a great chief . . . well, you know what to say."

Just what he did say, I've no idea, but his first words were greeted with an outburst of laughter. These people weren't difficult to amuse.

While this exchange of fine words had been going on, the women had brought some tall jars, and I could see that we were about to have our reward in the form of rice wine, which flowed in abundance whenever the clan had reason for celebrating. The chief asked for a calabash, squatted down on his heels and dipped it into the first jar, took a few sips of the whitish liquid, pulled a face

and spat noisily over his shoulder; then he handed me
the calabash. I was puzzled as to what to do. If it was as
bad as all that, why did he want me to drink it?

Kaio came to my aid. "You make out that it's very
strong, just as the chief did. And you drink the lot, you
must drink the lot."

I had no need to make an effort to pull a face. It was
not very strong but tasted downright vile, a poor brew
that had turned sour. I imitated the chief and finished
by spitting over my shoulder.

My three friends submitted to the same formality, and
as soon as they had finished the chief pushed the first
jar aside and dipped his calabash in the second. This was
a much better brew, sweeter and with some taste to it;
the alcoholic content was higher, too. I was making ac-
quaintance with genuine *borak*, the real thing. I would
drink a lot more of it yet. . . .

Great activity was going on all around me. Women and
girls were seeing to the cooking, without any screaming
or jostling; everyone knew what had to be done. The
men seemed very busy, too, but it was more difficult to
tell what they were busy at, though I noticed that they
had time for a large gulp of *borak* as they passed. We
were guests of the entire longhouse, for these people
live as a real community. However, the chief had taken
charge of us and given us a luxurious room next to his
own apartment—luxurious, that is, for a jungle village.

The longhouse was strongly made and built on many
piles of hardwood. As the ground was very uneven, some
of the flooring was fifteen to twenty feet above it while
in other places it was no more than three or four. All the
flooring was made of hollow bamboo, split into lengths
and attached to the joists with twists of rattan or cane.
There were gaps between these bamboo floorboards
varying from two to four inches, so that at first you felt
insecure walking over them, especially as they were very

springy; you were in constant fear of twisting your ankle or even of falling through and finding yourself among the dogs and the pigs. Sometimes a length of bamboo, worm-eaten or of poor quality, did give way under someone's weight, and this caused a great outburst of laughter that almost shook the longhouse. I saw an instance of this, later on, when one poor woman, obviously pregnant, went right through the floor to the mucky ground fifteen feet below. Everyone laughed until they cried, including the woman concerned, although she had broken her foot in the fall.

The communal verandah was 230 feet long and 25 feet wide. Hanging along the wall were fishing nets, rudimentary tools—and some human heads. All the communal activities took place here, the ceremonies, feasting and dancing. There were wide openings letting in plenty of light, but no means of closing them against the elements. The interior was a long line of private rooms, each the home of a family where they ate, slept and made love. There was a door to each room but without lock or bolts. Everyone trusted the others, and the door was merely to provide a minimum of privacy.

Hammocks were unknown and everyone slept on plaited matting with a single covering against the chilly nights. The family's ceremonial dress was kept in a wooden chest; and in another corner of the room was the hearth, raised about six inches from the floor with soil spread underneath as a protection. Branches for the fire were hung on the walls, as were the cooking implements, the bowls and ladles and spits, made of wood or iron and all finely finished, showing a mastery of working with these materials.

The chief's apartment was larger than the others and was situated in the middle of the longhouse; this is invariably the case in Kayan communities, and the chief's room is often decorated with ritualistic designs and paintings. The nobility lived on either side of the chief, in order of rank, while the lowest in the social scale, the serfs, were right at the ends of the longhouse. The roof was made of hardwood tiles which could withstand the effects of the damp and heat and especially the attacks of termites and other insects for twenty or thirty years. The steep pitch, too, helped to keep the roof watertight.

However, for the moment there we were on the verandah still drinking *borak*, and its quality seemed to improve with each mouthful.

Then the women arrived with masses of food. There were very few vegetables in this feast of welcome, as meat dishes are signs of nobility and wealth and so are served to honor a guest; the meat depends on the success of the hunters, but there is always the local produce of chicken and pork.

As the afternoon progressed the atmosphere became livelier and more friendly, but much noisier, too, and there were the first signs of drunkenness. Fortunately there was plenty to eat. We dipped into the contents of large green leaves, taking handfuls if the food was not too hot and using our fingers to pick out slices of hot fat pork, which was everyone's favorite. My own tastes were by now much the same as the Kayans'. I sometimes feel nostalgic for those primitive orgies when we stuffed ourselves with local food with no frills to it but a taste and flavor beyond compare. . . .

The celebrations reached their height as night began to fall. We could hear more pigs and hens being slaughtered down below. There was no halt in the supply of dishes and no pause in the drinking; when my calabash was full it had to be emptied, and when empty was refilled. My two guides and the mechanic were the center of an attentive and lively audience who never stopped commenting on their tales or joyfully keeping the calabashes circulating. I wondered what they could have been talking about all this time—and what they were saying about me.

"Eat up, Tuan!"

The chicken that I started to eat tasted as if it had been beaten to death with an iron bar; it was full of splinters which stuck in my teeth or pricked my throat. The rice, however, was good; it was very fine, grayish, and sticky when hot. This was the only vegetable served during the feast, and it had been steamed. The way of eating it was to gather up a little and press it into a ball with your fingers, adding a piece of meat or fish. The Kayans season their food very little, unlike most of the peoples of Southeast Asia; yet there were plenty of pimientos growing in a half-wild state around the longhouse.

The women gradually came and joined the men when the cooking was finished. When a plate was empty they just went and filled it from the big iron pots simmering on a low fire. Everyone ate where and with whom he pleased; social differences did not seem to matter at these communal feasts.

Totoche, my monkey, had been playing with the children all evening, biting some of them now and again. But at the moment she was flat on her back, arms outstretched and her big belly looking fit to burst; she had never been so drunk.

My own head was not feeling too good. For several hours we had not stopped eating and drinking; we had demolished mountains of meat, and some of my neighbors were starting to vomit. Fortunately there were nice, handy gaps in the floor, and only a slight movement was necessary. . . . Down below the pigs were waiting, grunting contentedly.

I thought how ridiculous was the evil reputation given to these "terrible headhunters" by popular magazines. I had never felt so safe, so much at home, as with these

Kayans. Admittedly, there were a few lugubrious trophies hanging from the beams just above me; but they
were thick with soot from resin candles, old heads dating
from very many years ago. I certainly had no fear of
mine going to join them.

When I managed to catch Kaio's attention—he was
drunk and kept telling stories that he lost the gist of—I
asked him whose heads they were.

"Mostly Punans," he said, gathering his wits together
for a moment. He obviously had no desire to talk of such
things this evening, so I left it for another time.

The evening was far advanced and I thought that the
festivities would not last much longer. But nothing of
the kind—they were only just beginning! I was at my
second vomit when there was great applause and a procession of girls arrived with a fresh supply of large jars.
These had lids on, and I wondered what could be in
them.

"*Borak*, Tuan!"

What, more drink? A gong sounded but had no effect
on the chatter and the laughing, if that was the intent.
The gong boomed again, and the hubbub slowly dimin-
ished. A third stroke on the gong, and silence was
finally obtained. But not entirely; here and there a few
whose tongues had been loosened by drink went on talking. And a young girl just behind me had the giggles;
she put her hands over her mouth and the people around
her dug her in the ribs, but all to no avail. It was then
I noticed that everyone was present, even little boys and
girls and old women, anyone who could toddle along
(not the best of definitions that evening).

The chief had staggered to his feet when the gong
sounded for a third time, clung to a friendly shoulder and
then drawn himself up, making a show of dignity. The
speech he began to make was obviously not an im-

promptu one, for all the listeners appeared to know what it was about—except me, to whom it was addressed. My mechanic came and sat next to me and explained.

Two girls placed one of the large jars in front of me. I was interested to see that it was of Chinese origin, to judge from the dragons carved on the handles.

"Look, Tuan!" The mechanic showed me that the wooden lid had two holes in the top, one with a cork in it and the other with a long hollow stem sticking through it. He lifted the lid, delighted once again to take something to pieces, and explained what was expected of me.

The long stem had a float to it and was marked to show the level of the liquid in the jar, which held about ten gallons of *borak*. The amount one drank through the stalk was shown on the gauge, and whoever lowered it the most was the winner. But this was more than just a drinking bout. It would have an important bearing on my future relations with the Kayans. To them, a guest should have no fear of drinking more than is good for him for fear his hosts poison or kill him while incapacitated; nor should he be afraid of revealing his real thoughts and feelings while under the influence, if they are good and honest. So I had to stand the test of my true feelings toward these new friends.

"And that's why, Tuan, you must drink as much as possible."

"Yes, of course. But, tell me—you know these people—how much do I have to drink to make a good showing?"

"How can friendship be measured?"

Those were my sentiments.

I let out my breath, concentrated on the task ahead, then put the drinking stalk to my lips and started to draw. . . .

I could hear men murmuring all around me; there was no laughing now. I had the impression that bets were being made. After swallowing steadily for what seemed a very long time, I understood why this kind of torture was so effective. When I got out of breath I opened my mouth, took a gulp of air, then went on sucking up *borak*, gazing at the float. It did not seem to be going down the mark very quickly, and if I wasn't to pass out before reaching an honorable level I had to drink much faster. But I've never been a great drinker and my capacity is somewhat limited. The stalk was jerking about . . . going up and down . . . I couldn't see very well.

Enough! I couldn't take any more. I leaned back to the sound of great acclaim, and through a mist saw my mechanic come and embrace me, while the two guides were pushing their way over to me. I felt I'd come out of it quite well.

Then it was the chief's turn. He crouched down by the same jar, which had been filled to the original level again, and looking as if this was the most important thing in the world, put the stalk to his lips, let out his breath through his nose and started to draw.

My eyes were clouding over and I felt I was going to pass out at any moment. I hung on long enough to see the chief open his mouth, flap his arms and collapse. A moment later I went the same way. For us at least, the party had ended.

I woke up twenty-four hours later. The mechanic was sitting beside me, rolling a cigarette. His first words were: "Number one, Tuan, very good."

The Kayans and I were now on very friendly terms and I knew I could stay with them as long as I wished without being viewed with suspicion or having a watch kept on me. So I was in a position to take full advantage of my stay. But as I had lost practically all my films and photographic material there was little chance of obtaining pictures that I could sell later. But at least I had a marvelous opportunity to find out what I could about the way of life of these Kayans.

I don't know the date of the first expeditions into Kayan territory but I do know that in the Sarawak Museum at Kuching there is a report made in 1913 on the country and its inhabitants. Since then the Kayans have developed considerably through contact with "civilized" people. The great majority of them live in communities in the Belaga region and lead as simple an existence as did previous generations. Their customs have changed very little. The jungle and the river are still much the same. And yet they are no longer true Kayans, such as those I had just met. The true Kayans are found in these few remote communities which have refused contact with the modern world.

Before the arrival of the "White Rajah," Sir James Brooke, in 1842, the Kayans were a powerful people leading an independent life beyond their unnegotiable rapids, and for a long time they flouted the authority of the white governor. At that time their traditional enemy was a tribe originating in Sumatra, the Ibans, who had gradually penetrated into Borneo from the south and crossed Kalimantan (now Indonesian Borneo). There has never been peace between the Ibans and the Kayans, not even today. Brooke took advantage of this animosity; the supposedly inaccessible territory of the Kayans was invaded with the help of the Ibans and by a combination of cunning and boldness. A great many Kayans, men and women, were massacred; most of the survivors were forced to adopt the kind of life imposed on them by the white men. Even today, more than a hundred years after that merciless "mopping up" operation, the Kayans are a minority group, still politically and physically oppressed by the swaggering and formidable Ibans, who are undisputed masters of that part of Borneo. They number about 250,000, whereas the Kayans, including related tribes such as the Kenyas, Kejamans, Skapans, Berawans and Sebops, are no more than 15,000. For as often happens, the massacre had been followed by a series of epidemics which decimated the Kayan population and left them with no hope of recovering their former importance.

They seem bound to die out before many years have passed, for although no longer massacred they are gradually disappearing as a tribe through amalgamation with others, and so are losing their ethnic characteristics. The Kayans are intelligent and ingenious, and want nothing better than to educate themselves and to learn about the new techniques (one had only to see the way my mechanic coped with the outboard motors), but this leads them to abandon not only their traditional way of life but also their ancient customs.

The Kayans, who are easily recognizable in the towns of Sarawak, have achieved an artistry in weaving and decorative clothing. Their craftsmen make weapons whose finish would stand comparison with any produced by European artisans, and which are in keen demand. In fact, their old enemies try more or less successfully to imitate their techniques, and occasionally a Kayan craftsman is found in an Iban village. In short, it can be said that the Kayans constitute the intellectual and artistic élite of the Borneo tribes.

The men are of average height, about five feet eight, but this is tall for people living in such a climate and in such conditions; they are well built with muscles strongly developed by their constant activities in the jungle and on the river. Their faces are rather flat with high cheekbones, sometimes with slanting eyes like the Mongol races. Some of the men even wear a moustache, which is most exceptional among the natives of Borneo.

The women are often very beautiful, slender but strong and with delicately jointed limbs. Around their hips they wear two wide strips of material, usually dark but with a bright, light edging, and this is their only garment. Their high, full breasts are perfectly shaped, and they have the fine skin of all Asiatic women. The intricate designs tattooed on their arms vary from one clan to another; some tattoo their thighs and calves, but never their knees.

Little girls have their ears pierced and wear heavy nickel-silver or iron jewelry which over the years pulls the lobes down to their shoulders. Many women also wear an elegant band of finely woven straw around their foreheads. Both sexes neatly pluck their eyebrows, using tweezers or wax.

The men's clothing is even simpler, and they tattoo their shoulders and sometimes their biceps, the designs being neat and unobtrusive, at least in the villages I visited around Belaga and in the mountains. They wear their hair short, in a sort of "pudding-bowl" cut, except that they let it grow very long at the back. When they go into the jungle they tie this long tail of hair into a bun, to avoid catching it on branches or bushes. They pierce the top of the ear in order to insert a panther's tooth, an ornament much prized by warriors; the lobes are often elongated in the same manner as the women's. They wear thin black bracelets around their wrists and sometimes their biceps, and loose necklaces—altogether a discreet adornment. A mere loincloth is their only garment on most occasions, whether in the jungle or the longhouse; but on ceremonial occasions they wear a sarong with the ends hanging front and back almost to the knees.

They are handsome men with a fine bearing and a natural ease of movement, full of laughter, with an enjoyment of life difficult to imagine. They are brave and proud, hospitable, generous and intelligent.

Although I am not an ethnologist I found these people very interesting to observe at work and play. I did not really understand and appreciate them until a short time before leaving; and now I think of them with nostalgia. I needed to stay a whole year to get to know them properly, for in spite of an apparent ease of familiarity it is not in their nature to betray their feelings readily. How could they, after the way they have been treated? Their ordeals have taught them to beware of contacts with outsiders and to stay on their guard. Great ingenuity is needed to obtain information, especially when one does not speak their language. However, I did learn something of their social structure.

The title of village chief is hereditary; he lives, as already mentioned, in the middle of the longhouse. He has powers of life and death over the members of the clan; no one can query his decision, whether it is a matter of moving the site of the village, organizing a hunt or declaring war. His subjects have to till his land and pay him tithes in either meat (the best portions are his by right) or rice wine.

There are practically no slaves or serfs; the few that remain live like the other villagers and take part in festivities and ceremonies, although they are considered a lower class. Originally most of them were prisoners of war; they used to be Ibans but are now Punans, in the remote areas where the custom still exists. In any case, there were never very many slaves; it was the number of heads rather than of prisoners which made a warrior's reputation. In the village where I was staying there was only one family of serfs, though the word hardly applied to the second generation, who lived just as their masters did, dressed the same and followed their customs. In fact, marriages were permitted between serfs or their offspring and other young people of the clan, at least if the latter belonged to the lower classes.

The Kayans are extremely superstitious and their taboos are legion. This leads them to quit the village for several days at certain times of the year, thus leaving their domestic animals free to forage among the stocks of food and allowing birds to feed on the rice fields.

Their main activities are hunting and fishing. Rice cultivation is left to the women; this makes few demands once the ground has been cleared and burned, and then only during a certain time of the year. Repairs to the longhouse are scrupulously carried out without any orders needing to be given, as everyone knows the job he has to do.

It is a rather idle life and gives them plenty of time to exercise their artistic—and gastronomic—talents. Although the Kayans do not devote the whole of their leisure time to feasting and drinking, they undoubtedly attach great importance to these activities. Their orgies are famed, and the slightest pretext (as I well know) is enough to start one—planting out the rice, the start or finish of a big hunt, a birth or a wedding, the arrival of a foreign visitor. . . . In addition there are the many religious festivals, each an excellent reason for opening the heavy jars of *borak* and bringing out the *sakés*, which are rather primitive guitars, or the *keluri*, a little organ made of bamboo pipes with a peculiar blowing system.

And so the days slip by, with life governed by unchanging customs, under an undisputed but genial chief, in the middle of a dreadful jungle and in a cruel climate. Danger is ever present, death and disease are frequent visitors.

A cock crew and another nearby answered the strident call. A moment or two later a score of them were crowing away. I felt I had been sleeping in a hen house, which was not far from the truth. What I could hear were the fighting cocks, scrupulously looked after in the chief's apartment, attached by their legs. These stupid and disgracefully spoiled birds were the participants in brief

and bloody fights which the whole village watched with
intense excitement. It was also their duty to awaken
everyone. So I got up. The cocks had stopped crowing
but now loud yawns were coming from next door. Privacy was not exactly well preserved here.

There was a thick mist outside, making it impossible
to see for more than a yard or two. It was distinctly chilly
and I literally shivered, but that was not sufficient reason
for evading the ordeal of the bath. Little groups were
silently going down to the river carrying calabashes,
halves of coconut shells and towels. Even the youngest
were not excused because of the cold. A few people who
slithered and fell on the muddy path raised the first
laughs of the day.

Daily life begins again after this early-morning bathe,
when the cold water has washed away the unrealities of
the night and especially the effects of the wine. The men
roll their first cigarette of red tobacco, which is damp
and stains the fingers like henna, while the women warm
up some food left over from the previous day, a piece of
meat that is already going bad and some shoots which
have gone bitter, or perhaps a few portions of fish that
have been pickling in brine in hollow bamboos. This fish
has a horrible smell and taste, but the Kayans seem particularly fond of it for their breakfast. This is not a family
meal—everyone eats when ready, without waiting for the
others. Then the men finish their toilet, that is to say,
they trim their nails, pluck the hair from their faces with
a little pair of iron tweezers, choose which bracelet to
wear and so on.

The sun has by now cleared away the mist; the tall
trees and the shape of the mountains beyond are beginning to emerge. It is time to go into the forest to clear
the traps or snares and down to the river to empty the
nets or pots. Fathers take their sons if they are old enough
and feel inclined, for the children enjoy complete free-

dom; they can play all day long if they wish. When they grow tired of bathing or fighting, they go off on little hunting expeditions of their own with weapons suitable to their size. They bring back squirrels, rats, insects, etc., which they either give to their mothers or cook themselves for their own "play" meals.

That day I went with the chief. He took only his hunting parang and blowpipe, and carried a wicker basket on his back. I walked behind him, empty-handed. We went at a fast pace in the dim light, and the wet from the trees rained down on our chilly bodies. Since arriving at the village I had been wearing only shorts and my old rubber shoes, without socks. The Kayans could see absolutely no point in my shoes and wondered what on earth made me wear such things.

We climbed for about an hour up a narrow, ill-defined path which I would have had difficulty finding if I had been on my own. We had to reach the chief's traps just before daybreak, before the wounded animals escaped or the dead ones were attacked by red ants.

The first trap was a deadfall, made for a boar; it was empty. A hundred yards away was another trap, primitive but apparently effective; it consisted of two heavy logs placed about eighteen inches apart above a run, and a thick branch in the run joined to the logs by a thin creeper. An animal running into the creeper brought down the two logs, and in theory had its back broken. Most of our morning was taken up in visiting the other traps, which were smaller and varied according to their prospective victims. In a hunting ground such as this, with which the owner is thoroughly familiar, the amount of game snared should be considerably more than that of an itinerant trapper. We soon came upon an argus pheasant dangling by a leg from a springy branch, about eighteen inches off the ground. It was a very large female, a magnificent specimen. A little farther on two jungle fowl had suffered the same fate, though both their heads had been eaten away by an early-morning visitor, probably one of the many forest rats.

The chief's family consisted of a dozen people, so he needed plenty of meat. There were times when he returned empty-handed several days in succession. Fortunately his position and the privileges that went with it assured that he and his family would not starve, but some days they did not have enough to eat.

I remember reading in geography books at school that "the inhabitants of the tropical forest have no cattle and no arable land, and they live on wild fruit and by hunting. . . ." That is not only false but ridiculous. Practically no edible fruit is found in the primary forest, except the wild durian, which weighs several pounds and has a prickly rind and a fetid smell, and one or two others that hang a hundred feet from the ground and fall only when overripe; a man would need to be very fortunate to gather them before the wild boars, the monkeys and orangoutans got at them; the last, in any case, gather them from the branches without any difficulty when they are just ripe. Failing fruit, the natives make do with shoots of all kinds. Hunting is uncertain, for game is wary and never abundant. A man has to be a very good and experienced hunter and trapper to get enough food to satisfy the needs of a family. He may well return home with no more than a few rats and lizards in his basket for as many as ten consecutive days. Hard times are fairly frequent in these jungle villages, but they seldom last long enough to become disastrous. There is always something to nibble at, be it only a few insects. But the tropical forest is far from being a hunter's paradise.

By the time we got back to the village the heat of the day was upon us. The chief was tired out, and he decided not to go hunting later; there was almost enough meat for everyone. So he settled down comfortably on the communal verandah, got out his tobacco box and day-dreamed as he smoked.

Everyone in the village smoked. Tobacco could be taken as a gauge of wealth; the rich man had a large plantation of it, the poor man grew just enough to satisfy his vice. Tobacco is very useful for bartering. The neighboring tribes and especially the nomadic Punans always ask for payment in tobacco.

The Kayans smoke two kinds of cigarette—a very thin one made of a long, stiff dry leaf with only a tiny pinch of tobacco in it, and a fat one, something like a cigar but much shorter, made of a green tobacco leaf rolled around red tobacco, and all horribly damp. This Borneo tobacco is very strong; it rasps at your throat and takes some time to get used to. The fat cigarettes have a particularly harsh flavor and the smoke almost made me choke the first time I tried one; but I quite took to them eventually.

The women, who are more active than the men, about the house at least, do not smoke so much and prefer chewing tobacco or betel. As for the children, I often saw three- and four-year-olds drawing on a cigarette.

The life of the children, in fact, soon becomes similar to that of their parents. Many of our own children would doubtless envy them—they have almost complete freedom and nothing is forbidden them, and there is no school other than that of the jungle. But transgressors quickly pay the penalty. A child who ventures too far afield runs the risk of getting drowned or eaten by a crocodile. I was most impressed by the manner in which these little youngsters soon assume the serious business of life. They begin by playing at going hunting and before very long are helping their parents in the struggle for subsistence.

The chief had given the women of the family the game we had brought back, and they were preparing it for the pot. The midday meal is usually lighter than the evening one and much less is drunk with it. The cuisine, if one can call it that, is very restricted, without any fancy dishes or sauces. There are just two methods of cooking —food is either boiled in a hollow bamboo or in an iron pot, or it is grilled on hot embers, sometimes wrapped in leaves. Variety comes from the raw material: snakes, bats, pangolins (scaly anteaters), tortoises and turtles, frogs, rats, monkeys—all these are eaten and rarely does anyone refuse. Fishing provides a fair amount of food, too. I went with the chief's son in a small, slender pirogue, a most unsteady craft, to haul in the fishing nets; we returned with several fish eight to twelve inches long. But downstream where the river is much deeper the Kayans would sometimes catch huge fish weighing over two hundred pounds. Such a catch would be a godsend, and the wife would pickle some in brine for when times were hard.

The women's work in a longhouse extends little beyond the preparation and cooking of meals, probably for economic reasons or through a habit of idleness, unless it is the result of elaborate organization. In any case, cleaning is greatly simplified by the wide gaps in the bamboo floor; all that is required to dispose of the remains of a meal is to push it down below where, like other matter dropped from above, all of it is devoured by the dogs and the pigs.

In the afternoon everyone takes a siesta, either in the family apartment or on the communal verandah. Then the men go hunting in the forest until nightfall—if they feel in good form, if the gods are not opposed to it and weather conditions are favorable. . . . No one is compelled to go; a man sets off if and when he feels like it, and can return half an hour later without needing to give any explanation. Or you might hear him say, "Aie, a snake crossed my path"—and everyone understands.

I had a slight suspicion that such superstitious beliefs

encouraged laziness. But who could blame them? In any case, necessity soon puts a stop to idleness. When the family has not eaten meat for some time and the wife starts giving the man a nasty look, he gets down his blowpipe, whistles his dogs, attaches his parang to his side, horizontally, puts up his back hair, takes his wicker basket and goes bravely off into the jungle.

I found myself more or less debarred from joining in the hunting, and for some time I was puzzled by this. The reason, however, was quite simple—they were all afraid of my meeting with an accident. The whole village was concerned for my safety: I mustn't swim in the river because of the crocodiles, I mustn't go into the jungle because something might kill me, and so on.

Did they take me for a child or someone incapable of looking after himself? I discovered eventually that it was nothing like that, but that the villagers feared the authorities in Belaga would conduct an inquiry if anything happened to me, and would impose severe sanctions. The village was not far enough from civilization for these Kayans to defy the laws of the Federation of Malaysia. They were well aware that the police force was quite capable of carrying out punitive measures against a village responsible for the death of a foreigner. It is because of this policy that one can travel without fear almost anywhere in Sarawak.

So as I was not allowed to go very far by myself, I spent much of my time wandering along the verandah, chatting with the girls and playing with the children, and endeavoring to puzzle out the meaning or origin of various unusual or unexpected objects.

There were, for instance, some slabs of wood covered with hieroglyphics that were supposed to tell the story of the gods and the history of the Kayans. It must all have been greatly abridged, for on the four slabs in the possession of the village I could count only fifty or so signs and symbols. Then there were the large jars obviously of Chinese origin which I had seen during the festivities, and a strange ceremonial garment made from the skin of an animal not found in Borneo. And there were some tobacco boxes made of bronze, a metal unknown to the Kayans, and a few large seashells used for drinking *borak* at particular festivities. I asked my guides, but they were of no help.

"Kaio, where do all these things come from? They weren't made by the Kayans?"

"I don't know, Tuan, except that they come from a long way away."

"Don't you even know what this animal is with long white hair?"

I had to wait until I was back in Belaga to have the explanations. Before the time of the White Rajah, Chinese merchants had penetrated into the interior and sold their usual curios to the Kayans. So widespread had been the sales of these commercial travelers that the Chinese could well claim to be the first explorers of Borneo. But what dangers they must have run! At that time the head of a foreigner was a great attraction to the Kayans and the Dayaks and was not very safe on his shoulders.

The seashells came from the China Sea and the garment with long white hair was Nepalese, made from the skin of a yak. And I had been congratulating myself on finding a new species native to Borneo!

Now and again I sat down in a group of Kayans and made notes, and this caused them some astonishment. I had salvaged a few sheets of paper and a couple of ballpoints from the wrecking of the pirogue. The Kayans were ignorant of a means of expression other than the spoken word and the signs left in the jungle to indicate the presence of a trap or snare or of some danger. Kaio and the mechanic tried to explain that white men and the Chinese have a writing which can say as much as

speech. I could tell from the villagers' suspicious looks
that they didn't believe a word of this. They have never
for a moment thought that the hieroglyphics on the
wooden slabs I mentioned are anything but a decoration similar to their own tattooed designs.

After a few days I ventured to say to my mechanic:
"Will you ask the chief if I can go hunting with him?"
    "Yes, I'll try, Tuan."
    If the chief gave a negative reply to the mechanic it
would not be so annoying for me as if I had asked directly, and in any case he could explain more easily to
the mechanic. However, the chief agreed, despite all the
handicaps implicit in dragging me around with him; for
one thing, he was bound to return emptyhanded.
    We set off very early next morning but did not go up
the hill that was the chief's trapping ground; his son
would be going to visit the traps today. The chief was
carrying his long thin blowpipe (about eight feet in
length), which had an iron spearhead securely attached
to the end by a thin piece of cane, and at his side was
a small bamboo quiver containing half-a-dozen poisoned
darts. Their points were smeared with a dark gluey substance that has an even more powerful action than the
notorious curare of the South American Indians.
    We followed the narrow track for an hour and then
plunged into the thick of the jungle. I had become familiar with this kind of walking during the past months
—over steep slopes covered with slimy mud under a canopy of trees, in a stifling atmosphere amid hordes of
mosquitoes. In the north as in the south of Borneo, and
to the east and west, it's everywhere the same—just thousands of square miles of unchanging jungle, sheer hell.
    There are two sensible ways of progressing in such a
confused and distorted topography: along the ridges or,

as we were doing, by following the riverbeds. Anyone who tries to go straight ahead by following a compass course is either mad or ignorant; he would not get very far or be able to continue for very long. Even along the riverbeds progress was far from easy; we were constantly caught up on brambles and thorny bushes, but the worst was being attacked by leeches. In the end, however, one becomes used to these parasites and a jungle-dweller makes light of them. Apparently I was not yet a jungle-dweller, for I found them an abominable nuisance.

The most difficult was walking over the slippery stones and pebbles, which were often covered with a thin mossy slime. I kept slithering and stumbling and made a terrible din, enough to scare away the most dim-witted monkey in the forest. The chief, on the other hand, was striding silently along with assured step, glancing at the trees and peering into every thicket, more from habit than anything else, I felt sure, for in my company he had very little chance of surprising any game, except perhaps a deaf snake. I admired his patience; he never once looked around at me or made any comment. I know that in his place I should have sent an idiot packing who could not walk properly.

He was going slowly now and seemed even more watchful; and I almost managed, by taking infinite precautions, to make myself unobtrusive. All around was an eruption of greenery, an absolute blaze of foliage and plant life, as is often seen near rivers and streams. To our left a small squirrel was staring at us, having suddenly halted as it ran down a tree. Rimau—that was the chief's name—slipped a dart into his blowpipe, carefully avoiding any abrupt movement, put it to his lips and gave a silent puff. The squirrel was literally impaled on the tree trunk. Before its struggles could break the dart, a blow with the flat of the chief's parang finished it for good. One in the bag. It hardly weighed a couple of ounces, skin and bone included, but here one never lets an opportunity pass; everything is good for the pot.

A little farther on some hornbills were disporting themselves. I had great difficulty in spotting them, despite their large size. They were of the helmeted species, *Rhinoplax vigil*, which are found only in southern Thailand, Malaysia and Indonesia. It is probably the most handsome and stately of all hornbills, with its large red-and-yellow bill, deep-red head and neck, dark-brown back sometimes verging on violet, white breast and white, very long tail (about four feet) with black quills. This bird, with its large bill and tail, gives the impression of being as big as a peacock. Its bill is valued as an ornament by the Kayans, and they carve graceful designs on the upper part. Alas, these hornbills made off when we were almost within blowpipe distance. For a few moments we followed their noisy flight.

We continued for a long time without sighting anything except squirrels, and they were always too quick or too far away for us. Then Rimau espied some shreds of fruit on the ground; they were acid berries much favored by monkeys and wild boars. These had been chewed by monkeys, but none was to be seen in the nearby trees. The chief, with a skill that baffled me, followed the track of the monkeys guided only by the minute traces of their frugal meal and some occasional droppings—a pip or two here, a fragment of green skin there, so tiny as to be almost invisible in all this vegetation.

We twisted and turned among the trees just as the monkeys had while following their tastes and inclination.

Rimau pointed to a tree. *"Kara."*

Macaque monkeys, and many of them. We could hear the branches bending as they jumped about, and now and again their cautious cries reached our ears. A whole band of them seemed to be busy eating their fill. What an opportunity!

They were of the *irus* species, identifiable by their long tail and prominent muzzle. One jumped into the tree just above us and calmly began examining this larder, parting the leaves and throwing aside unwanted fruits, making a great mess. Rimu had a dart in position and was waiting for the animal to appear within range. He and I were crouching down, hidden under a clump of ferns.

A female, easily recognizable by her huge red behind, started to tear a thick piece of bark from the tree. It refused to come, but she went on prizing at it with her strong fingers and suddenly the whole patch came away and fell to the ground, revealing a colony of insects. They were probably termites or ants, or perhaps the little blackbeetles which monkeys find delicious, for Lady Irus fumbled greedily at this food store, casting anxious glances at rest of the band now and again, as if fearing some might come and rob her of her find.

She was so intent on her selfish enjoyment that she did not notice the slim wooden tube veering in her direction. There was a barely audible *pfft*, and the dart hit her in the middle of the back, half-burying itself. The monkey gave a *"Craa"* of surprise and pain, lost her hold and fell right through the branches to the ground.

We stayed still. The other monkeys had heard the cry and scattered in all directions; but soon, as everything seemed calm, they cautiously returned to see what it was all about.

The wounded monkey on the ground was struggling frantically to pull out the dart, but the head had broken off in the fall. The poison quickly had effect, and the monkey's movements became spasmodic; half a minute later they ceased altogether.

Some monkeys had returned to their foraging, but

others were still suspicious. One large male inspected a little too closely, and received a poisoned dart in his throat for his pains. He managed to make a couple of bounds and reach a branch, where he hung for a few moments, then fell paralyzed to the ground.

The two monkeys were still alive and Rimau had no intention of finishing them off. The reason, cruel though it may seem, was quite understandable—living meat would not deteriorate while being carried back to the village. A poisoned monkey would remain in a coma for anything from half an hour to several hours, depending on the quantity of the lethal dose. On one occasion the villagers had waited several days for a wounded fawn to die, so that they could eat it. In the meantime it represented a store of fresh meat, a sort of live refrigerator.

Life here is far from being easy; the people are used to pain from early childhood. There are no medicines available, and the slightest wound or illness can be dangerous. The most elementary needs of life are obtained only through many daily efforts. Difficulties and suffering are a part of life. So why feel pity for an animal? When a village woman gives birth the mother washes herself, with water that has not been boiled, of course, and then squats down cross-legged by the fire; and the following day she resumes her household tasks as if nothing had happened.

Rimau and I arrived back at the village with our bag just before nightfall, at the time when the shrill chirpings of the cicadas were at their height—brightly colored red or yellow cicadas, and three times the size of the European kind. Our ears were full of their strident sounds. We got rid of our burdens and after a long drink of *borak* went and sat on the verandah to smoke a thick green cigarette.

The groups of men around us were all very lively, some telling jokes and others commenting on their day's hunting. One man had been lucky enough to kill a wild boar, and he had a thick fat slice to give to the chief, who merely nodded toward his apartment when the man approached him with it. No word of thanks, not even a grateful look—and none was expected. The successful hunter had the obligation of sharing his meat with the community, and it was only natural for the chief to have the best portion. Community life had a real meaning here. The selfishness of our modern world, with everyone doing down the next man, had no place.

There was an unusually calm atmosphere about the longhouse this evening, but it did not prevent people from laughing and talking and taking little mouthfuls of *borak* from time to time, just like the men with their bowls of cider back home in my native Brittany. The dogs roamed around the groups that were eating, on the lookout for a bone or two, getting a kick or a blow when they came too close. The resin candles gave only a flickering, smoky light but had the great advantage of keeping away mosquitoes.

Such evenings were wonderful, giving an unbelievable feeling of deep relaxation. It was like being on another planet.

But alas, these moments were coming to an end. I had told the chief that my three companions and I would be leaving in a couple of days. Back at Belaga, people must be wondering what had happened to me—the Chinese who had rented me the pirogue and outboards, the police who had given me a limited permit, and Doctor D, to whom I had promised to be back in three weeks.

Another day was drawing to a close. This was the last night I should spend here. Suddenly a gong began to sound and its low rumbling spread through the village. Then another gong joined in, and another, until the longhouse seemed to quiver on its piles. The women had

been making little ricecakes all afternoon, while the
youngsters cut bamboos to decorate the big house. The
men had all gone hunting, for much meat was needed
this evening, many wild boars, deer if possible, monkeys
anyway, anything, provided it was meat; this was the
evening of the big party, our farewell party.

The hunters came back in ones and twos, some with a
monkey, others with squirrels for roasting. Chief Rimau
had killed a young boar, and his son had caught three
small rodent-like animals (*Tragulus kanchil*, incorrectly
called agoutis or guinea pigs). And by a lucky chance a
fine rusa, a stag weighing more than two hundred pounds,
had fallen victim to the darts of the Punan slave. When
everyone had returned we spread out the whole bag on
the verandah, just for the fun of it. A day's hunting by
thirty-two men had resulted in: a full-grown stag, two
boars, four monkeys, three rodents, half-a-dozen squirrels
and a twenty-pound tortoise.

When the men had smoked a well-earned cigarette
they retired to their apartments and took their precious
gala garments from the chests; one man shook out his
yak-skin cloak, another brushed his panther-skin jacket,
and out, too, came the headdresses of hornbill feathers
and the bracelets, and each man decked himself out,
preened himself and practiced a few dance steps.

Then the *borak* began to flow. The special drinking
shell had been brought out for the occasion, and the girl
who handed it to me made me empty it to the last drop.
The girls behaved quite freely with the men and there
was often a rough and tumble. Most of them are lovely,
with delicate features which look a little odd with their
thin, plucked eyebrows. They have perfect figures and
wear only the double length of black material with a
bright hem, which reveals their thighs in the same way
as a Chinese dress with long slits. The garment, which is

really a reduced form of sarong, is quite graceful and
delightfully feminine. Nothing unnatural degrades the
beautiful, splendid spectacle of these young women
strolling about half naked and with an elegant bearing
on these festive evenings. In the longhouse there are no
taboos on sex; everyone is free. The girls are fond of flirt-
ing and are very forthcoming, at least with unattached
men. As a consequence, or through indifference, virginity
is not an indispensable condition for marriage; but on
the other hand, once married the women are models of
faithfulness.

Of course, as soon as I knew that these fruits were not
forbidden to me (having taken the precaution of en-
quiring, which gave rise to many bawdy remarks), I
went a step further with several charming girls in whose
good graces I was already; and without going into de-
tails, I can report that lovemaking among the Kayans is
a very pleasant experience and that the desire to perform
well is aided by a technique that surprised and delighted
me.

As it is wine that gives vigor to the festivities, the girls
have the task of going around the groups with bowls
filled to the brim and ensuring that every guest is drinking. A girl sits down beside the man she has selected and
offers him the bowl. It is good manners to refuse the
borak at first—but who could refuse for long when
pressed by such a charming hostess?

The festivities soon became very lively this evening.
We had eaten a considerable amount of meat; and then
the musical instruments made their appearance—the
primitive guitars and the gongs; xylophone-like instruments made of different-sized gongs, which were very
melodious; and miniature organs made of bladders with
bamboo pipes, which produced sounds that seemed to
come from the very bowels of the jungle. These instru-

ments gradually combined and responded to one another until they united in a strange, powerful music, strongly rhythmical, with a weird resonance.

But how can anyone describe the atmosphere of these Kayan concerts? You have to feel the village around you, smell the sickly whiffs from the candles, see above your head the sinister trophies quivering in the light; you need to have been adopted by this splendid, proud and violent tribe, seen its warriors moving around in their plumed headdresses and cloaks of yak skin, wearing ivory earrings and nickel-silver jewelry, and admired and desired these women whose beauty blossoming in the heart of the jungle seems a touching miracle.

Now and again I automatically sipped some *borak*, unaware of what I was drinking. I felt a profound happiness of a kind seldom experienced in a lifetime.

But suddenly there was a disturbance and the music stopped. I saw a young woman stand up in the middle of a group. I recognized her; she was courted by all the young men in search of a wife and was undoubtedly the most beautiful girl in the village. After being repeatedly called on to dance, she had at last consented and risen slowly to her feet, pretending to be bashful; and she now went and fetched six hornbill feathers which she slipped between her slim fingers, then took her place again in the middle of the group.

She stayed like a statue for a few seconds, then slowly, imperceptibly, her wrists drooped and her fingers arched, her tall supple body swayed like a forest liana. Just as warily, she took a little step forward; and the dance began. Her subdued, slow, infinitely graceful movements were in perfect harmony with the music.

After about ten minutes another girl joined her, then another, until there was a long line of them weaving among the spectators like some legendary serpent. Gradually the men joined in, too, and soon it was no longer a dancing performance but a joyful round of the whole company. Some men who were already drunk held on to the shoulders of the person in front and sometimes stumbled over the mats on the floor.

I hoped that they would not make me join in—but alas, those who remained seated had to drink for the others. The spectators were soon thin on the ground and I had no option but to join the merry throng, urged forward by two or three bold young women. There were still a few sitting it out; the girls pulled their heads back by the hair and made them drink a full calabash of *borak*, amid much laughter. The wine was circulating among the dancers, too, who found it more and more difficult to keep on their feet. The fine serpent that had turned into a round dance began to break up, and soon everyone had returned to his or her place again—or someone else's —on the verandah.

The night was now long spent. A magnificently clad warrior stepped forth to perform the famous Kayan war dance. He had put on the chief's cloak of yak skin, which was open in front and swung free from his shoulders, so that the long white hairs hanging down his back were like some uncanny fleece, rippling with his every movement. There were three great hornbill feathers stuck proudly in his cane headdress and curving outward. He wore dark bracelets around his biceps and wrists, a sky-blue loincloth, and at his side a splendid sword in a precarious wooden scabbard set in boars' tusks. He began twisting his hands and slowly his body started to twitch and move, then he gave a series of quick turns and wild springs, before suddenly resuming his slow movements. His hand crept to the sword hilt and closed over it, then suddenly drew the sword, flashing in the light from the dozens of lamps, and he began to mime a fight to the rhythm of the music—attacking, countering, thrusting and fending. Then he seemed to go into a trance; as the

Kayans say, the spirits entered his soul and body to protect him against the spirits of his enemy. And so came the final act, of religious and high symbolic significance: the beheading. The blade slashed the air and severed the enemy's head with a single blow. The whole audience, galvanized and hysterical, gave a great shout of victory. It was savage and terrifying. The dancer was crouching on the ground, exhausted; he recovered gradually, while the festivities were resumed.

Cockcrow. . . . I had slumped into sleep just before dawn, still on the verandah. I wasn't the only one; practically the whole village had fallen asleep where they sat, too drunk with wine and song to drag themselves into their family apartments.

I had already packed and had only to carry my things down to the pirogue. All the villagers had assembled on the riverbank. The chief came over to me, laden with presents—a long hunting blowpipe, two finely worked swords and a Chinese bronze tobacco box. Other men came and gave me baskets, headgear and lengths of cloth; the poorest threw a hen or two or a piglet into the pirogue. The village slave, the Punan, ceremoniously presented me with his fighting cock.

I hastily opened my pack, brought out the hammock, the fishhooks and the gourd, and placed them all on the wet sand. A girl came forward with a bowl of *borak*, the last for me. I drank it slowly and reverently, as if it were the last drink of a condemned man. My two guides and the mechanic were also included in this last round.

As soon as we had finished, a band of young women dashed toward us with handfuls of black soot and daubed us all over, while the crowd roared with laughter. This is the Kayan way of saying farewell.

I was very sad and the chief wanted to know why. "Why are you looking sad?" Kaio translated.

"Tell the chief that I'm sad because I'm leaving him."

"If you liked being in the village, you must look pleased and laugh. Only if you didn't like it must you look sad."

"In that case, tell him I'm very pleased."

I gave a warm smile. I couldn't do better than that. We have different ways of showing feeling at home. If I had had a little more courage I'd have told my three men to go off without me, but. . . .

I took a last look at the village, at the chief and his subjects, a last look at. . . . It was over.

The motor spluttered, smoke poured out—we had lost the oil while attempting the rapids—and then we slowly drew away from the bank. There was a bend in the river, and then all I could see was a corner of the village and a part of the longhouse roof; then that vanished, too. My eyes were moist.

THREE

More Plans

I was in a bed, a real one, in the best hotel in town, as a guest of the *Sarawak Tribune*. This paper had snapped up my account of my travels and produced a wonderful and terrifying adventure story in which I found it hard to recognize myself.

Lying comfortably in bed between clean white sheets, I relived the final episode of that journey back from the interior, down the Rajang River.

We were speeding along with the current. In the afternoon we came to the rapids, but I hardly recognized the place. The surroundings were the same, of course, but the water was much lower than before and although the current was still very strong we did not have to unload and haul the long canoe around, as we had greatly feared.

However, while taking a bend a little too fine we hit a rock, the galvanized-iron awning folded in like cardboard and we shipped a full load of water. But nothing worse—luck was with us.

Alas, next day it left us. While going along an almost calm stretch we struck a rock flush with the water, and capsized. Kaio, who was right up in the bow, was thrown head first onto the rock. We were all thrown into the water, too, but the mechanic, the other guide and I were the only ones to reach the muddy bank. Kaio never came to the surface again.

I had no plans for the future. One idea after another went through my mind. Return home to France? I had neither the courage nor the desire to resume a way of life I'd deliberately given up more than a year ago. Even if I had not discovered very much during my travels, I'd at least learned that I could no longer live "normally" outside Asia, or at any rate away from the tropics, the hot sun and copper-colored women. The East is no myth.

Stay in Borneo then? I'd sure like to, but all my equipment had been lost—tape recorder and cameras, rifle and the rest. I'd got back to civilization with seventy-two photographs. But what was chiefly missing was that little shot of optimism that gives you the necessary incentive.

In the event, Doctor D provided it.

Knock, knock . . . "Come in!"

The doctor's ruddy face appeared in the doorway. "Hi there!"

We went and ate in one of those picturesque Chinese restaurants, dirty and badly lit, cheap, but where the food is much better than in the tourist joints.

"Well, what's your program?"

"I haven't made up my mind yet."

"Do the Ibans interest you?"

"Yes, but I don't want to make the same mistake as before. I went off to stay with the Kayans without a clue, without any technical preparation or ethnological knowledge. That expedition was a failure, even without the boat capsizing.

"You could go and have a look around, and start to learn the language in a village on the Rajang. Ethnologically, the Ibans are amazing. They're certainly the last headhunters in Borneo."

"Yet I've been told all that's a thing of the past."

"It's a bit like cannibalism in Africa—it's ended, but every year a number of people are arrested for it."

The mountain Ibans were apparently the first to invade Borneo, coming originally from Sumatra, and they moved up the Kapuas River to its source, spreading terror as they went. They finally came to a halt in the middle of Kalimantan.

Later a second invasion descended on Sarawak. These Ibans, also called Sea Dayaks, were known to practice headhunting as well as piracy in the Sunda archipelago.

The former activity has practically ended but a few islands still have the unpleasant reputation of sheltering some persistent pirates, now motorized, who frequent the waters between Borneo and the Philippines.

These Ibans, having massacred or driven the Kayans and the Land Dayaks inland, now live in the first three Divisions of Sarawak. Their villages are always sited on rivers or along the coast; as a seagoing race, they dislike pushing inland. Although most hospitable, they are nevertheless people it is best not to upset or offend.

The doctor was beginning to arouse my interest.

"And how can I get in touch with the mountain Ibans? Those along the coast and the Rajang River leave me cold—they want money to be photographed!"

"You go up the Baleh River as far as you can, then take to the jungle. Their villages are scattered about here and there. But the population is quite small. From aerial observations during the war the total number of these Ibans is now estimated at little more than a thousand."

There were already five empty beer cans on the table between us, and my eyes were getting blurred.

"Whatever you do, don't go asking the District Officer for a permit, as this region is still a restricted area. The Indonesians make punitive raids now and again, and besides, the people there don't like having visitors. To avoid diplomatic incidents, the government has forbidden tourism in the region."

"Well, if they're so unfriendly, how am I going to manage to make contact with them?"

"My advice is to take some presents with you—little beads, nylon string and fishhooks. So long as you don't

shock them or violate their customs, you'll be okay. But
before you leave, check up thoroughly on their ways and
customs, so that you don't make any blunders."

We went on discussing the idea all evening. I gradually came around to it, as the Tiger beers slipped down.
This region was new, virgin ground probably, or at any
rate hardly touched by civilization. Just what I had been
despairingly seeking ever since starting out. I was under
no illusion that I should be exploring the country; the
Ibans have long been known about, even those in the
mountains. Their customs have been described in several
books published in the late nineteenth century, and I
did not think there was much to be learned on that score.
What interested me, though, was the human experience.

"What language do they speak?"

"Probably the same Iban as down here, but with certain differences, for they left their native country a long
time ago and must have their own dialect by now. I'm
sorry I can't tell you more, but I only know the Kayans."

It was very late, and we parted after downing a long
cool drink.

Next day I nosed around all the local bookstores but
found very little—a few magazines with articles about
the Dayaks, but nothing specific about the Ibans I was
interested in. However, I had better luck when I went
to see my friend Leong. He lent me a camera and let me
have several rolls of color film without any trouble. I
didn't ask for more as I wasn't reckoning on being away
very long, a couple of weeks at most, just long enough
to get to know the natives and learn a few words of their
language, to find out what was the sort of thing to do—
and, more important, what not to do. In short, this would
be a reconnaissance, a trip just to make contact. Later on,
I would go back better equipped and with more technical knowledge of cinecameras and photography.

I bought a heap of tiny, many-colored beads from a

few Chinese shops. Apparently they have to be tiny to give most pleasure to the Ibans, and they are the best things to take in the way of gifts and barter. I had more than ten pounds of them, which ought to do the trick.

I was taking about thirty-five pounds of luggage, as I didn't want to overload myself. There were at least five pounds of medicines, a gift from the Doc, most of which would end up in the bushes, as before, when I got tired of carrying them.

I had bought a parang of Chinese make, one with a long handle and comparatively short blade, and at the bottom of my pack were a mosquito net and a hammock. I'd had to pay a high price for the latter, in the bazaar. It was simple but strong and waterproof, just the right utility article for this kind of trip.

I didn't think I'd forgotten very much. I was just a little anxious about the rolls of film, which were of different makes, and about not having any photoelectric cell. However, all this preparation had sent my morale shooting up again. I had enquired about sailings to Singapore; there would be a ship at the end of the month, in a couple of weeks' time—which left me long enough for my trip upriver.

I had no idea what was in store for me. . . .

FOUR

How to Get Lost in the Jungle

One of the big Chinese motor barges, shuddering violently as it churned slowly along, took me up the broad Rajang River to Kapit. These tubby wooden vessels run a shuttle service between Sibu and Kapit, each carrying about one hundred passengers. On the journey upriver the cargo consists mainly of food, spare parts for automobiles and for the many outboard motorboats running about these rivers. On the journey back the hold and deck are stacked with bales of rubber.

The rubber comes from small and often badly tended plantations belonging to the Ibans of the region. Packed in bundles of one hundred pieces, it fetches very little when sold to the shrewd Chinese who are found almost everywhere in the region, often quite far from towns. They too own rubber plantations, but better kept and with a high yield. The Ibans have no love for these "yellow faces" who exploit them, and the Chinese despise the "savages." However, there are not too many clashes, for each has need of the other.

Kapit is farther from the sea than any other town in Sarawak. The whole region is inhabited by Ibans who still live in their traditional longhouses, which instead of being surrounded by the jungle are shaded by rubber trees. Some of the older Ibans are still tattooed, but the young ones prefer shirt and shorts to a pattern on their skin. Quite a few go to school and can converse in broken English. There are a number of missions of rival sects that do their best to instill some kind of Christianity by distributing copies of the Bible or the New Testament.

A well-organized tourist service offers visits to a few longhouses just outside the town. Tourists are taken for an hour's cruise in a canoe with an outboard motor, or bolder spirits can go on foot, following well-defined paths. The village chief, who is paid for his services by the tourist office, welcomes you dressed in traditional costume and makes no objection if you wish to take some photos of him and any occupants of the longhouse. It is usual to leave him a few Malaysian dollars. If the amount is reasonable you are invited to drink some of the renowned *tuak*, the rice wine of the Dayaks—which in my opinion is not so good as the *borak* of the Kayans.

I find all this tourism somewhat distasteful. But the Ibans are not to blame; in their natural state they are a most likable people, not particularly hard workers or so ambitious as their neighbors and enemies, the Kayans. But these are minor failings which bloom easily in the sunshine. Moreover, the Ibans are very hospitable, which shows how they must have been got at in order to accept money for showing tourists their village.

However, it should not be forgotten that a few decades ago the bravest of them were headhunters and gave Borneo its sinister reputation, or that most of them lived —as a few still do—by downright piracy at sea or pillage on land. Very stringent measures must have been taken to restrain these instincts. They are, then, very hospitable people but quick-tempered and easily roused, and who then take a long time to calm down. But as I spent only a week in Kapit, I cannot claim to know these Ibans well.

On the outskirts of the town I met a good-looking girl who suggested that I spend a few days in her longhouse. I jumped at the offer. It would give me a chance to live among the Ibans and get to know their customs. Biniou— that was the girl's name—had already taught me a few words of their language. When I penetrated more into the interior there would, of course, be no one who could speak English.

Biniou and I took our places in a small pirogue, a dugout canoe with an outboard motor having a long propeller shaft, not at all easy to steer for anyone not used to it. Biniou had settled the fare with the mechanic. For ten Malaysian dollars we were going to be taken half a day's journey upriver to her village. Some of her friends who lived in the same longhouse had come aboard, too. We left the majestic Rajang River and its succession of rapids and turned into the calm Baleh River. For about an hour after leaving Kapit there was practically no sign of what had once been a great forest; in places the trees had been felled to sell as timber, elsewhere they had made way for miserable little plantations of rubber trees. As we passed I noticed that many of the rubber trees were diseased or in bad condition. The Ibans are obviously not cut out for that kind of work.

We stopped frequently to disembark or take aboard passengers, which slowed down the journey considerably but made it more interesting. Eventually, as the sun was setting, we landed at the foot of a cliff, and Biniou pointed out her longhouse perched on the top like a convent on Mount Athos.

We had a warm, spontaneous welcome. Biniou, quite proud of her capture, led me by the hand to the far end of the village.

"And what do you call that?"

"Acé. . . ."

In Biniou's company I amused myself by learning about thirty words a day. Then in the course of conversations I tried to form sentences. It is not a difficult language; there is practically no grammar, and the order of words is about the same as in French. The Iban language has none of those difficult intonations which charac-

terize the other languages of Southeast Asia. It sounds
rather like Arabic without being so guttural.

Daily life was not so very different from what I had
known among the Kayans. Nevertheless closer contact
with civilization has brought certain changes. Hunting
has lost its primitive character and its vital importance;
these Ibans go off into the jungle armed with rifles and
buckshot. Their blowpipes no longer hang in the racks;
most of them have been sold to tourists in Kapit. The
collecting of rubber occupies some of the villagers for a
few hours a day, at dawn and then in the afternoon. But
often there is no rubber to collect, owing to idleness and
neglect of the plantations.

Each family owns a few patches of rice, of the same
variety that grows round Belaga. As the Ibans make
clearings by a scorched-earth technique, these small
fields are very scattered. The older the village, the farther
away they are—sometimes half a day's walk. The Ibans
eat a great deal of rice at every meal. It has become their
main dish, whereas the Kayans use it more for making
an alcoholic drink. This does not mean that the Ibans
never touch alcohol; on the contrary, and they drink to
excess during their festivals, which are still quite numerous. But there are not the spontaneous, cheerful drinking
parties that I had enjoyed among the Kayans. I felt sorry
about this, not because I had suddenly become a drunk-
ard but because I liked that good company. Happy
drinking sessions help to break down barriers, no doubt
about it. I hoped to find the same convivial atmosphere
farther inland.

I went hunting once or twice with my hosts, but we
came back empty-handed except for one night when,
with the help of the reflector of an acetylene lamp, we
shot a cervulus, a small barking deer.

After a stay of ten days I told my friends that I was

going to continue my journey upriver. By then we were able to communicate without difficulty; a few of the young ones spoke a little English and I had more than three hundred Iban words in my head or written down.

"Why don't you stay with us? The Ibans up there aren't the same as us, and there aren't many villages."

"How long will it take to get to the head of the river?"

"Five or six days."

I did not have much money left, but the following day I gave the chief a few Malaysian dollars. I gave Biniou a playful smack on the bottom, shouldered my pack and went down to the river. For one hundred local dollars (about thirty American dollars) one of the boatmen had agreed to take me as far as the river was navigable. It was a small fortune for him, certainly more than he could earn in three months of working on the plantations.

Each evening we stopped at one of the longhouses by the river. They were in touch with the towns and civilization by water, yet the higher upstream we went, the fewer oil lamps there were and far fewer rubber plantations; consequently the people had less money and fewer possibilities to buy modern equipment. Another difference I noticed was that the farther we went the more welcoming people were. After the fourth day I think I should have left a bad impression if I had offered the slightest payment for the hospitality given me.

The river became narrower, and we were not making much speed with the wheezy old motor. But at each bend the hills rose higher and lifted their tangled green summits to become real mountains, steep and rugged. Several times a day we had to push the canoe over sandbanks or reefs of rock just below the surface. On one of these sandbanks we encountered a full-grown crocodile, its jaws agape. When it noticed us it moved unhurriedly to the water and slid in. Later the same day a python about thirteen feet long emerged from the jungle and dipped into the river. We could see it swimming just under the surface but it disappeared when we drew near.

The jungle became thicker, and monkeys appeared all along its edge, sitting on rocks or perched on branches. They watched us until we came within gunshot, then in a few bounds they disappeared into the greenery. Most of them were of the genus *Macaca irus,* which usually live near water. But I also noticed a few of the "pigtail" variety, more thickset and with short tails; these stay on land more than do the others. The noisiest and the shyest of those I saw were the silver gibbons; several times, on rounding a bend in the river, we caused a chattering group of them to scatter.

There were a great many animals, which meant a great deal of game; but to go hunting on those steep slopes one would need to be a mountaineer. A wonderful, untouchable game reserve. Who knows how many interesting species it holds, perhaps even unknown species?

Toward the end of the sixth day my boatman put in to the bank, for no apparent reason.

"What's the matter?"

"Cannot go anymore!"

"Yes you can." The river was not very wide, but I was sure that we could still go higher. "A little more," I said.

"Not enough gas."

That was not true; he would have the current with him going downstream and wouldn't use much gas. The fact of the matter was that he did not want to go any farther; and I had already paid him. I could not get him to change his mind. On the way up he had taken paying passengers and filled his pockets, so was pleased with himself. If I wasn't so pleased, that was all the same to him—unless I turned nasty.

Cursing and swearing, I put my pack and my monkey

on the sandy bank. But he must have thought it was all too easy. "Fifty dollars more, very far, Tuan!"

I answered that with a gesture known the world over, which did not seem to his liking.

"Fifty dollars or you don't go!"

The canoe had its nose on the sand, a couple of yards from my pack, and he was in the stern. His parang was under the seat in the bow.

I started to open my pack, muttering, "Okay, okay" while he watched me, doubtless thinking that I was getting out the money. My parang was at the side.

In a second I had it in my hand, and as quickly reached for his and hurled it into the river. He only had time to take one step forward—and I must have looked pretty vicious, for he didn't continue.

"You can come now!"

I don't think he appreciated the situation, but I'm sure he had no desire to get near my knife. Before he could think anything up, I got hold of the boathook and threw it on to the bank.

"And now clear off!"

I pushed the canoe off with my foot, and there I was alone. That was one man I'd better not meet on the way back. I listened to the engine growing fainter in the distance before shouldering my pack.

I had not expected to be landed like this in the middle of the jungle, and it was not going to make my task any easier. If I could follow along the bank of the river without too much climbing I should be all right, but I feared that the obstacles would be too great in places.

"Well, what shall we do, Totoche?"

"*Broo . . . bro.*"

So we set off along the bank. After a quarter of an hour's plodding I came to a point where, just as I had feared, the steep rocky face came right down to the water. I had either to climb the cliff or work around it by plunging through the jungle—which didn't exactly fill me with enthusiasm. But in view of the late hour and my lack of climbing skill, I decided on the latter course, especially as I had—or thought I had—some experience with making my way through forests. But before I had gone fifty yards through the dense undergrowth I felt completely lost. I had never known such a thick tangle of foliage and branches, all dripping water, nor was I used to such hilly terrain. Every half-hour or so I scrambled to the left to make sure I was not getting away from the river, my only guide mark. I did not make much progress that way, and I'd soon had enough.

From time to time I managed to reach the river, but in that mass of vegetation there was no telling how the ground rose and fell, so that I sometimes found myself a hundred feet above the water.

When night fell I was worn out. Suddenly the treetops dimmed and darkened, and five minutes later I could not see my hand in front of my face. I only just had time before it became quite dark to find a place to sling my hammock. This I did in complete blackness, not wanting to use my torch unless it was absolutely necessary. Grouping about, I tied the nylon cord around a tree trunk, adjusted the pegs at either end, put my parang within reach and hoisted myself fully dressed into the hammock—which promptly slipped down a stage and left me lying on the spongy ground. Nylon cords are certainly strong, but knots must be pulled very tight. Made wiser by this experience, I slung the hammock again and fastened the cords with a whole series of tight and complicated knots.

From all around came the nightly fantasia of the jungle. I was used to it, but this was the first time I had slept in such surroundings alone and without a gun—which makes a tremendous difference to morale. I had tied Totoche to the base of the tree; if anything happened she would be able to warn me, and I should at least have time to seize my parang.

In the middle of the night we were treated to a torrential downpour. In a matter of seconds I was completely drenched; luckily I had automatically closed the top flap of my pack the moment it started. Lightning flashed all around and thunder rumbled like the gods in their wrath, echoing around the high hills and resounding strangely under the canopy of the jungle. It was undoubtedly impressive, to anyone under shelter. But I was soaked through and little inclined to appreciate this apocalypse of sulfur and water. Then the rain eased off, the noise died away and the lightning scattered its fury elsewhere. The rain continued falling steadily for the rest of the night, and I could hear the drops slipping from the leaves and splashing on the ground.

I had not brought any protective covering with me because I did not want too much to carry and had thought I could put up a bamboo awning just as quickly as a ready-made but complicated shelter.

Next day I met with the same difficulties. The going was just as hard and I wondered how far I should get in these conditions. The headwaters of the Baleh River had to be reached before I could hope to meet any mountain Ibans, and that was still a few days' walk away. But how many, at the rate I was going?

Food was beginning to be a problem, too. I had about seven pounds of rice and some salt with me, but something more than that was needed. It had been agreed that the "guide" would take me as far as possible up the river and, more particularly, would leave me in a village where I could obtain some useful information and be given directions. There were undoubtedly ways through the mountains, if only one knew them. But in this wild, confused landscape there was little chance of finding a way through, and much more of going around in circles—until one dropped from exhaustion, which would soon happen.

I know of nothing so frightening as realizing you are lost. I was once lost in southern Morocco and I well remember the panic I was in when I could not find any landmarks. Here it was worse, for there were no landmarks—only trees, all alike and all around, as enclosing as prison bars. Even from the hilltops one could see nothing that helped to indicate one's bearings. Where a tree had been blown down and there was some sort of clearing on a hilltop, still nothing could be seen but, all around, an ocean of greenery stretching to the horizon. However, I was not completely lost yet; the river, I knew, was somewhere over to my left. But I had only to turn around a couple of times and I shouldn't know which was the left.

In the afternoon of my second day in the forest I came to a tributary of the Baleh River. There did in fact seem to be a wide gap in the mountains ahead, and down this valley flowed a peaceful, fairly shallow river with a muddy bottom here and there. This was a godsend to me. I gave up trying to keep to the Baleh River and followed this more accessible waterway.

Most of the time I was able to walk at a good pace between the water and the trees, occasionally making my way around a patch of quicksands, fortunately easily distinguishable. But sometimes I had to make a detour through the jungle. The canopy of leaves and branches kept out the sun, but it was still possible to see clearly. The air was stifling, and with the heat and humidity it was like being in a Turkish bath. I was constantly being stroked or scratched by creepers, brambles and bamboo canes as I slithered and slipped on the carpet of rotting leaves and mud, and stumbled over half-buried tree trunks and broken branches; and then there was the parasitic fauna. The tropical forest has nothing beautiful about it; it is just dreadful.

Night could not be far off, and I wasn't going to be caught napping this time. I began cutting down some bamboo canes to make myself an awning. Just then, I heard voices approaching. I looked around and saw two natives paddling a canoe upstream.

"Hoo-oo!"

Overcoming their surprise, they paddled hard toward me.

"Is there a village near, a *rumah?*"

"Rumah Pacou."

Quickly packing up the few things I had spread on the bank, I got into their canoe. It was so narrow that I had a job to squeeze my bottom into it. The two paddled when the river was fairly deep, but most of the time they poled the canoe along. It was quite dark when we reached the village. A Tuan arriving without warning was a great event. And the villagers rivaled each other in being the most helpful and the most hospitable. I had no need to ask for a drink; hardly had I sat down when a girl brought me some *tuak* in a coconut shell. The two men wanted me to stay with them, but the chief indicated that it was more seemly for him to invite me.

While we were trying to make ourselves understood in an unbelievable mixture of Malay, Iban and a few words of English, I heard the squeals of a wretched pig being slaughtered; and all about the village hens were being killed. I had an idea there would be celebrations this evening in honor of my arrival.

"Where have you come from, Tuan?"

"Kapit."

"That's a long way! All on foot?"

"No, not all the way. But I'll have to go on foot now to cross the mountains into Indonesia."

"But there's nothing beyond here, no villages, only Punans perhaps. It's very dangerous, because the people there aren't like us. *Panjamon,* Tuan."

"*Panjamon?* What does that mean?"

"Cut off heads. They kill strangers—as we did, before the English came."

"Do you know Kapit?"

"I've been there several times."

"What, without an outboard motor?"

"*Nadaï motor*, we aren't rich."

The first dish was served in a big enamel plate such as those sold in bazaars. Thick slices of pork lay in boiling hot fat. Disregarding the miserable little fork, I picked daintily with my thumb and forefinger. It was delicious.

"You eat like the Ibans, Tuan."

"I've been among the Kayans; there weren't any plates."

"Are the Kayans a nice people?"

To please him, I answered that the Kayans were nice but that I liked the Ibans better.

"*Djamaï, djamaï*, the Kayans are a bad people, they're headhunters. You mustn't go back there."

To hear him talk, the only safe place for me was at Rumah Pacou.

As the *tuak* slipped down, the party warmed up. This wine was not bad, a little on the sharp side perhaps, but very comforting after a wet night in the jungle. We were drinking it from glasses, and I was curious to know where they came from. I looked for the make and to my surprise read "Duralex, made in France." The glasses were not the only evidence of relations between these "savages" and the civilized world. The courses did not all arrive on banana leaves or other large leaves but generally and more prosaically on trays from a bazaar. Even, so, I felt I was at the ends of the earth.

The food—pork, chicken, vegetables from the forest—and the ambience were much the same as among the Kayans, but this longhouse was not so roomy or so pleasant as Chief Rimau's. It was very dim and rather dirty, and there were many dusty old objects hanging from the rafters and along the walls. There were a few bunches of heads, too, hanging over the doors to the rooms. But these were very ancient, blackened by candle smoke and made grotesque by being capped with dust and cobwebs.

"Where did those heads come from?"

"*Ipoun* [Japanese]."

"Did the Japs come as far as this?"

"Oh no, we went to look for them."

I got the impression that the Ibans must have had a good time a few decades ago. One man who could speak some English told me that he had served in the famous Sarawak Rangers, a native force raised by the British and used against the Indonesians. Once, after a successful ambush, he had taken his officer a fine head dripping with blood, expecting to be decorated or, at the very least, commended. But the British major swore at him roundly and put him in detention. He still hadn't got over it. However, it did not stop him from proudly showing me half-a-dozen dog-eared photographs of himself—hardly recognizable in his uniform—with a group of comrades in the Sarawak Rangers. Born fighters like the Ibans, well led, made first-class soldiers and served the British and Australians very well during the Second World War. But when hostilities ended the authorities hastened to call in their weapons, for the Ibans would never have resisted the temptation to use them against neighboring tribes, the Kenyas, the Kayans and the Punans, for whom they have an age-old hatred. However, in recent years they have been allowed to buy shotguns to go hunting, and as the police are well organized and the "bamboo radio" works perfectly, incidents are few and far between. This bamboo radio, a variant of the "bush telegraph," is the means by which the authorities receive speedy reports from their informers in the villages.

Between mouthfuls of pork and gulps of *tuak* I tried

to glean some information about the inhabitants of neighboring areas. There didn't appear to be any. There was just one more village a little higher up the same river and a few *rumahs* scattered along the upper reaches of the Baleh River. If these people were to be believed, the mountains were almost deserted.

"But there are other Ibans, surely?"

"Yes, but they aren't like us, and we've never seen them. The Punans have told us about them. They don't speak Iban like us, they're bad Ibans. *Panjamon.*"

"Panjamon" is a word that often comes into conversations. There obviously exist strong animosities not only between races or tribes, but even between clans. One village often envies a neighboring one, and the warriors ask for nothing better than to have it out; and if one man has the bad taste not to speak the same language or practice the same customs he must be "wicked." Nevertheless, it must not be thought that the natives go slaughtering one another. On the whole there are only minor incidents, violations of territory, thefts, etc., and in such cases the aggrieved man takes his blowpipe or shotgun and goes to seek vengeance, if the portents are favorable.

Far be it from me to sit in judgment on them, and to be truthful, I think it's no bad way of doing things. It livens up the daily round, and at least prevents any problem of overpopulation.

I stayed only one night in this longhouse. There was nothing to be gained by staying any longer. I thought I could reach the last Iban *rumah* on the river before nightfall. After that, it seemed, there was nothing, except the river which soon became a stream and then disappeared. So I should have to climb the mountains or find a way around them. When they said there was nothing beyond, they meant no villages. But there were roaming bands of Punans in those parts, wild, shy people but not at all aggressive, if I had understood correctly. They are real forest nomads, the best trackers and hunters in the whole country. Little is known of their way of life, but they are very likely the last wild men of Borneo.

Before setting out in the morning I bought three hens and a supply of rice. But I had to pay in Malaysian dollars, for my hosts were only mildly interested in the tiny beads and fishhooks. I hadn't gone far enough yet.

After spending a night in the next village, where I was just as well received, I set off again, this time into the unknown. It was easy going up the long valley which wound its way between mountain slopes. Now and again I increased my rate of progress and refreshed myself by cutting across a bend in the river. It was not very deep and the risks were slight—so I mistakenly thought. I had innocently deduced that there could be no large crocodiles in a river about sixty feet wide and only three to six feet deep. I changed my mind in the afternoon when a scaly monster reared up less than ten feet away from me, scurried into the water and disappeared, After that I changed my tactics at once: I looked more carefully where I was walking and became even more selective as to where I bathed.

I made very little sound walking on the sand or in the mud, and so the jungle seemed all the more alive. I could see birds and monkeys, though not very many of the former, and I saw the tracks of boars and deer. It was a great pity that I had not bought a gun in Kapit, but as foreigners are prohibited from hunting it would have been a costly and complicated business.

As was to be expected, this pleasant walking did not last long. The river soon narrowed and divided into a number of mountain torrents rumbling down toward me. The slopes became much steeper. The real difficulties were about to begin.

Drawing on my small yet useful experience with the jungle, I did not try to take a straight course but went along the beds or banks of streams, and when that was no longer possible I followed the ridges.

In this part of Borneo, where a mountain chain runs from east to west and the landscape is wild and tormented, it is impossible to see where one is going; the next hundred yards might lead to anything, a gentle slope, a rock face that has to be laboriously climbed, or a ravine whose depth is hidden in dense vegetation. I never saw the sun, though some mornings I had a vague idea of where it rose.

On the first day I had the silly idea that I could always turn back. In fact I blazed my trail every score of paces by slashing a tree trunk or breaking a branch. As an experiment I tried retracing my steps. Before I had gone fifty yards I knew just what the situation was—I couldn't find the trail I had marked. This technique, which is obviously not the invention of writers of adventure stories, is used by natives with success. But as for me—!

It was still not too late to turn back but, strangely enough, I didn't want to, not then. Even today I can't explain my reactions and decisions in the heart of that jungle. I can only think I must have been slightly off my rocker, with a good deal of fatalism as well.

It would be difficult to write in detail about that fortnight in the jungle and still more difficult to describe my feelings. You need to know the Borneo climate, the jungle and everything connected with it—the cold and the rain, the heat, fatigue and loneliness.

I don't claim that the crossing of those mountains was a great feat. I was in excellent health, I had enough to eat—or almost—but it was hard nevertheless, very hard. The loneliness was the worst. No one to talk to, no one to share my fear or on whom I could vent my irritation or bad temper. I was lonelier than if I were in the middle of the Gobi Desert or the Pacific Ocean.

I soon lost all notion of time and events. The first evening I had still not realized that things might turn out
badly. After a few days my shirt was in tatters, ripped
by brambles and thorny bamboo. It fell away from me
bit by bit, leaving little khaki flags hanging from
branches or on the ground, pathetically marking my
progress. On the fifth day I discarded this shapeless rag
and put on my other shirt, a serviceable garment but too
thin for the damp and cold. My new shorts were cut-
down jeans and stood up well to the rough treatment.
Until then I had kept myself as clean as possible, that
is to say, I washed and shaved every morning. But now
I let my beard grow. It pricked and felt very uncomfortable with the heat and the sweat, but I hadn't the
courage to get out my razor. Later will do, I thought—
the first sign that I was slipping. . . .

I was living chiefly on the rice I had with me, though
I spent quite a lot of time searching the undergrowth
for edible plants. My experiences with the Kayans
proved very useful, but I was still not confident enough
to make full use of that source of food. I kept to bamboo
shoots and a certain kind of fern that was easily recognizable. But I needed all my concentration to gather
some, for the right kind did not leap to the eye; and
then I had to find the places where it was most abundant.
The natives are accustomed from childhood to notice
everything edible as they walk along. Even before sighting it they can tell, or rather sense, that behind this
thicket there will be some *paco,* that promising clump
of bamboo is not really up to much, these plants have
roots like bits of string but a few yards farther on there
are some with succulent, nourishing tubers.

To live off the jungle you need a nose like a truffle
pig's. It is a matter of instinct as much as experience, an
instinct to cultivate and develop with practice. I had
thought there was nothing I didn't know about living on
what nature provided, but now I began to realize I was

in fact less capable than a Kayan child of subsisting in these conditions. I only had to come to the end of my rice, or lose it, to find myself at once in a desperate situation. This reminded me of some of Doctor D's war stories: of the many Japanese who got lost, accidentally or deliberately, in these regions and were followed at a distance by Dayaks, who watched them die of exhaustion; and the many wounded men who were finished off and eaten by their starving comrades! Numbers of Japanese soldiers were driven mad by hunger and fear. Many hanged themselves or put a bullet through their heads, but the most to be pitied were those caught in poisoned traps or hit by poisoned darts; they died slowly, paralyzed, while ants ate at their wounds, swarmed over their faces, up their nostrils and into their ears. . . .

Every now and then I found myself dwelling on these somber images. But my morale was not too low; I just felt surfeited. My consciousness didn't seem to be functioning properly either; there were times when things went blank. Totoche was blithely unaware of these problems. I had decided to let her run loose, so that she could forage for herself. In this way I was able to glean some of her secrets and also some of her gatherings. But after I had helped myself to one of the grasshoppers she had collected, there was no chance of getting near her when she had something in her paws or mouth.

Every evening I slung my hammock and built an awning to shelter me from the rain; it was good enough provided the rain was not too heavy or did not last too long. After a few discouraging attempts I found the right kind of leaves to use. Other leaves had the great disadvantage of curling up as soon as they got wet, which turned the flat roofing into a grill of greenery—a line of rolled leaves, then a space, more rolled leaves and so on. On the whole my nights were quiet and restful, thanks to the mosquito net; I wondered what state I should have been in without it. After a few days of pushing aside branches, catching myself on thorns and being struck by canes springing back, my body became covered with scratches, weals and blisters, all excellent places for harboring germs. I had thrown away the medical supplies that the Doc had taken so much trouble to get for me; they took up space and were useless(!). But I had kept the vitamin tablets and took two a day regularly.

One evening, just before slinging my hammock, I came upon a splendid red-headed krait, one of the most venomous snakes that exist, a member of the *Elapidae* family. It is also one of the most beautiful: a small red head with very little neck, a gleaming dark-blue back with two distinct bluish-white stripes on either side. It has a thin red tail, unlike that of the other elapids. This was the first time I had seen one, but with those markings there was no mistaking it. Unfortunately for the poor creature I did not then know that it is practically inedible. Since then I have tried them several times with different sauces, but without much success. This one paid for my ignorance, for I chopped it in two before it could escape into the undergrowth. Cleaned and skinned, it ended up in the hollow bamboo I used as a cooking pot. But it was hard and rubbery, with a great many bones and a nasty taste. After two mouthfuls I left it for the ants.

On the seventh or eighth evening I happened upon a small cave at the foot of a huge cliff. There was no need to look for leaves to make a roof; the rain held no fears for me that night. It was wonderful. All I had to do was to clear the entrance and level the ground inside. But I was not free of all my worries, for my supply of rice was dangerously low. I still had a few handfuls, which represented so many days' food. After that it would be a matter of surviving on what the jungle cared to provide. However, I decided not to ration myself, perhaps because I was not strong-minded enough, perhaps through a kind of instinct not entirely illogical. If I did ration myself, would I remain strong enough? I might as well keep fit and with all my faculties as long as possible. The days that followed seemed endless. I got up at sunrise, and the chilly dampness of the early morning was most unpleasant; then it gradually became hot, unbearably hot. Which was worse? The one was as bad as the other.

I was getting tired, too, or rather weary, and in the sort of daze which turns a man into an automaton putting one foot mechanically in front of the other, stepping over a rotting tree trunk without even noticing it. The fear of getting lost, that fluttering of the stomach, had given way to a fatalistic resignation. I went on only because that gave the one hope of meeting human beings. Some day I was bound to come upon a watercourse, a fairly wide river, and then it would be the devil's own luck if I didn't reach a village.

By the end of a fortnight I was completely done in. I hardly had the strength to sling my hammock—it would have been so much easier just to stretch out on the ground. My morale must have been at a low ebb, for after all a fortnight alone, even walking for seven or eight hours a day, was no great exploit. Many men have done as much and in far worse conditions, yet there I was feeling lost and at the end of my tether.

On the fifteenth day I stopped keeping a diary and started just ticking off the days. And that morning, for some unaccountable reason, I felt a little better. It was just as cold as usual, the dewdrops falling from the leaves were just as unpleasant, and there was still a gray sky as on any other dull morning. So much better was I that I even had a wash and shave. Then I breakfasted on the water I had cooked my rice in the evening before—the last handful of rice.

My rubber shoes had at last given out, and the mere act of throwing them away had a dreadful effect on me —it was as though I had come to the point of committing suicide. In the jungle without any shoes! Fortunately I soon realized that the ground was not the carpet of thorns that I had imagined, and that the insects were not especially set on my delicate feet; and I quickly found that my big toes gave me a very useful grip on slippery slopes.

Suddenly I stopped in my tracks—I had heard the sound of running water. I was always hearing running water, and every day I followed or cut across a dozen small streams. There's no lack of water in Borneo. The higher one goes, the noisier the streams and more frequent the cascades; the gurgling of water over stony beds had become a very familiar sound. But now this was a quite different sound. Could it be a river? Another fifty yards and I had reached the bank—and there indeed was a river, a lovely river at least sixty feet wide. It was oddly like the one I had left a fortnight ago; so much so that I thought for a moment I was back where I had started. It was a ridiculous idea that I dismissed at once. I had been heading south all the time, and even with the many detours I had made I could not possibly have gone round in a circle.

Where there's a river, there's a village; at least, every chance of one. But how far away—two days' journey or ten? In any case, there would be a village. And that was a great thing for me. I no longer felt lost. I knew that of all the directions I could take, here was the right one; by following it I should be going toward other men. Never for a moment did I reflect on the reception I might get.

FIVE

The Welcome from the Dayaks

I danced for joy on that small sandy bank. My monkey, Totoche, was scared by this sudden change of humor and kept at a safe distance—"You never know, with this man." It was not yet full day; the surrounding mountains were only just appearing through the morning mist. White clouds were drifting past, so low that they seemed to catch on the rocks and the crests of the trees. From close by came the first call of a silver gibbon, that strange lament of the Borneo jungle—a long, rather high-pitched howl which ceased suddenly only to start again almost at once. Now other gibbons were joining in. It was magnificent. There were very few mornings when I did not hear this wonderful animal reveille.

Suddenly there came a different call, seemingly from the other side of the mountains, a more syncopated call, "*Ouii . . . ouii*," followed by a long plaintive sound. This, too, was a gibbon, but of a different species; and for me that was something new which had its importance. Although the silver gibbon *funereus* is found all over north and northeast Borneo (Sarawak, Brunei, Sabah), the regions south of the mountain chain (Indonesia or Kalimantan) are the domain of the gibbon *moloch abbotti*. And it was the call of the latter which I had just heard. Any doubts I had about my position were swept away. I was well across the mountain frontier.

I was now completely isolated but—idiotic though it may seem—I laughed long and loud, and called Totoche to witness: "We're there, Totoche, we're there." It was quite insane; I was in about the same situation as a shipwrecked man alone on a raft who realizes he is exactly in the center of the Pacific and who rejoices over it. Yet that's how it was. I felt happy, so happy that I forgot for the moment the difficulties into which the situation was leading me. I must have scared the nearby acrobats, for their waking calls had turned into shrieks of alarm; they were less than a hundred feet away, but the mist prevented me from seeing them. The other gibbons, though, the *moloch abbotti*, were still at matins.

I had stayed there long enough, and moved off again, following the river. It was still fairly easy going, except for a few muddy places or where I had to clamber over fallen trees, helped by broken branches and trailing creepers.

Shortly before midday I stopped to sling my hammock for a siesta, and had a look around for anything eatable. The last of the rice had gone the previous day, and I wasn't keen on continuing on an empty stomach. I gleaned a few shoots here and there, but they were far from making a meal. On the other side of the river a band of monkeys of the genus *Macaca* were chattering away as if making fun of me. I gulped down the soup I'd made and then stretched out in the hammock. It was most unusual for me to break up a day's march like this, but the spot was pleasant for once and the heat was less stifling than in the jungle. Failing food, a short rest would do me good.

The food problem was getting really serious. I could try making snares with the nylon thread and fishhooks, but that would mean staying here for a day or two, to place the snares and collect the trapped animals, supposing there were any. Or I could go fishing. It was possible here even without a line, just a fishhook on the end of nylon thread; there were plenty of worms in the mud. However, I decided to push on, and to think again about trapping if I found nothing to get my teeth into this afternoon. I would search the undergrowth more carefully; sometimes one surprises a scared or sleeping animal, though very seldom. Once before, however, I had come upon a pangolin, a scaly anteater, rolled up asleep under a fallen tree trunk.

I picked up my pack and called to Totoche, who was hurling abuse at her cousins across the way, and we set off. I soon came to a brook and went up it on the chance of its harboring some frogs or tortoises, and to my great surprise I found a cane fishing basket blocking almost the whole width of the water. It was a typical native device —a tiny entrance with spikes pointing inward and a short neck to the cage, in which there were now two fishes swimming about. When I recovered from my surprise, my first impulse was to pounce on this fresh food. But I remembered just in time that it would be the worst possible mistake to make. Although the natives are very hospitable, they are most particular about ownership, and the slightest pilfering in a neighbor's hunting ground is tantamount to a declaration of war. In the villages farther down it results in a permanent break between the two families concerned; up here in these isolated regions it must lead to someone's losing his head. I valued mine too much to risk it for a couple of catfish twelve inches long.

One thing was certain, I was not far from a village. Snares or nets are never set more than two or three hours' travel from a longhouse. So I felt there would be some new development before the end of the afternoon. As I had carefully avoided touching the fish, there was nothing to worry about—but who could tell? I set off again, wondering uneasily about the welcome I would have.

Voices! It was more than a fortnight since I had heard a human voice. My immediate reaction, stupidly, was to dive into the forest and crouch down behind some tall ferns. Two men came along, talking together. Each was carrying a long blowtube and had a small wicker basket over his shoulder. They were naked except for the usual loincloth, and tattooed all over; they passed close enough for me to see that one had a particularly intricate design on his left hand. The other designs, especially those on the neck and shoulders, showed that the two were Dayak Ibans.

As soon as they reached the sandy riverbank they stopped dead—there were my footprints showing distinctly. The men realized at once that they belonged to a stranger; there was no mistaking these long, slender footprints for those made by a native's splayed foot with the big toe turned outward. The prints left by Totoche must have added to the men's astonishment. By common accord, without exchanging a word, they dashed for the trees, bent double, and hid about ten yards from where I was. I couldn't see them, but I heard the leaves rustling.

There was no point in my remaining hidden, in fact it was dangerous to do so. If they came upon me they were quite likely to shoot a dart at me before I could explain who I was.

"Hey, you fellows! Hoo-oo!"

Silence all around.

"*Salama, salama!*"

Among the Sea Dayaks to the north *salama* is a greeting; *salama pagui* means "good morning," *salama malam* "good evening." I learned later that these Ibans have not quite the same language and that what I had called out was the name of a fish.

Ten feet away from me a man was crouched with his long blowpipe pointing in my direction. I had not heard him approach; his companion had been rustling the leaves while the other worked his way around to me. Now the second man sprang out from the undergrowth, his weapon at the ready. They were as surprised as I was, and exchanged a few rapid, guttural phrases without taking their eyes off me. Their language has similar intonations to Malay and the Iban spoken in Sarawak, but it has a harsh, grating sound with a staccato delivery. They sounded as if they were arguing.

They came nearer, pointing their long blowpipes at me. These weapons had iron points and for a moment I thought they were going to spear me in the stomach. But they just pressed the points against my chest, hard enough to break the skin. My God! Then one put down his weapon, pulled my parang from its sheath and opened my pack. The next moment he had emptied all the contents onto the damp ground. The sight of all this caused them to relax a little, but the pressure of the point on my chest increased, if anything. I stood like a statue, hardly daring to breathe. I could see more plainly the design tattooed on the man's left hand, which meant that he was a headhunter. They exchanged a few more words; then one of them bundled everything back into my pack, tossed it to me and roughly pushed me forward.

"Pulaï rumah."

Totoche decided to make her appearance, and after some hesitation followed on behind. The two Ibans could hardly believe their eyes. I was certainly setting them problems, but I had worse ones. Later, they admitted to me that they had thought of making an end of me on the spot, but finally decided to take me back alive, for the glory.

The longhouse was not far distant; before an hour had passed I began to hear the barking of dogs and the snorting of pigs. A few minutes later we came to the village. The longhouse was built on stilts and stood a little way back from the river. Some children on the outer verandah caught sight of us and quickly roused the village.

Men and women came running behind the children and in a moment we were the center of a crowd of about fifty.

My escort, obviously very proud of themselves, prodded me along with an important air. Questions were rained at them, but none of the crowd was aggressive; there were no hostile shouts, merely expressions of great surprise, and perhaps a little fear, on the part of some women. Totoche took shelter between my legs, but when the dogs came trotting up she sought safety on my shoulder, which caused some laughter. We mounted the ladder, a sloping tree trunk with roughly hewn steps, to the longhouse verandah and then to the *ruaï*, the long, inside verandah which is a kind of village street. There it was dim and cool. The pitch of the longhouse roof was very steep because of the torrential rains, and each side came so low that I had to bend my head, whereas the ridge piece was sixteen feet above the floor. On the other side of the *ruaï* were the family apartments, each a little private domain.

I was left to myself in the *ruaï*, and as no one gave me any orders I slipped off my pack and sat on the floor. The two warriors who had captured me had abandoned their threatening attitude, but they never stopped glancing at me from where they were standing. I kept hearing the words *hantou, hantou* coming from a chattering group a few yards away, from the women in particular. *Hantou* means "ghost," and in Dyak mythology the spirits of the ancestors—when the fancy takes them to visit the living—take on a human form with a milky, almost transparent, complexion.

The people seemed to be waiting for someone, the village chief, I supposed. He did not appear to be in the longhouse.

Suddenly a gong sounded—two long booms and then many quick short ones. It was presumably the alarm signal, for in a few minutes a score of men came running up, weapons in hand, and some scared-looking women; they had probably been tending plots or gathering food in the forest.

The chief was among these new arrivals. He seemed completely nonplused by this event, and it took my two captors no less than three-quarters of an hour to explain what had happened. They both began speaking at the same time, and after a while the chief indicated which one was to make the report. Now and again the chief gave a deep "*Aau*" like the bark of a dog; and when the other had finished he looked hard at me, then spoke roughly. I couldn't understand more than two or three words such as *rumah* and *barappa*.

"*Nadaï jako iban!*"

My Iban was very poor but the chief had evidently understood, for his face cleared.

In the meantime, Totoche had been up to her tricks and had pinched a cigarette from a man squatting near me. It made everyone laugh. I handed the cigarette back and the man thanked me with a hearty "*Trimakassit!*" It was a word I knew. We might manage to understand one another if I could refer to my notes.

I attached Totoche by her chain and got out my notebook. With two fingers I imitated a man walking and added "*Dua poulo,*" meaning that I'd walked for twenty days. The natives understood at once. Then I pointed in the direction I'd come from, not forgetting to indicate that I had crossed the mountains, and ended by jabbing a finger at my stomach. "*Maccan,*" I said.

"*Maccan, maccan,*" they all nodded.

"*Acé kara orang Tuan!*"

The chief ordered some rice to be brought to me. The atmosphere was beginning to thaw. The children were teasing Totoche and had almost forgotten about me; there was a burst of laughter from them now and again.

I'd taught Totoche a number of tricks during the year
we had been together, and at a sign from me she would
give a back somersault or dance on her paws, pretend to
be dead, march about with a stick on her shoulder, cover
her head with a hat or clap her paws, and so on, all in a
comic manner that never failed to amuse her audience.
Now she had all the onlookers holding their sides with
laughter, and the chief and his group had to move away
in order to continue their discussion.

The rice arrived, with a little chicken and some bamboo shoots. It was a good, tasty helping and I soon swallowed the lot; that felt better. I had been really hungry.
Two or three women smiled at me and said I must eat
more than that.

The chief and about a dozen men, probably the village
elders, had gone into a *bilek,* one of the family apartments. I guessed they were still discussing what to do
about me, but I felt that matters were going the right
way. These people were not so aggressive as I had
feared, and they had given me some food. That might
not mean very much; a well-fed man's head is distress-
ingly like a thin man's once it's hanging from the ceiling.
Still, I didn't think mine would be going that way, not
now.

The sun began to set, and still the council continued.
Now and again they sounded as if they were arguing;
but it was more likely because of the harshness and em-
phasis of their language. I spent my enforced idleness
in looking about me and counted thirty or so *bileks,*
which probably meant that the population of the longhouse was between one hundred and fifty and two hundred. The floor of the communal verandah was not very
level and the gaps between the bamboo slats were even
wider than in Kayan longhouses—a real man trap! There
did not appear to be very many bunches of heads, but
then I couldn't see the whole of the verandah. I did

notice, however, two heads which were far from being old; in fact they looked more like this year's crop! They were still quite clean and without a spot of dust on them. Some of the other heads, though, certainly went back a generation or two; they were blackened by soot and smoke, and there were spider's webs in the eye sockets and between the jaws.

On the outside verandah I could see rice spread out on matting to dry in the sun; this was what remained of the harvest after making *tuak*. Chickens that went near were relentlessly chased away by women or children. Some of the children were amusing themselves by shooting mud pellets at the chickens through blowpipes. A game like any other. . . . Daily life had returned to normal; there was still a group of people near me, but most of the villagers had gone down to the river to bathe or had returned to their occupations in the forest.

At last, just before nightfall, the heavy door of the *bilek* opened and the councilors emerged. It had been a good session, for I'd seen one jar of *tuak* taken into the room and to judge by the state of some of them there couldn't be much of it left. The chief was steady on his feet and still very dignified; but there was a little old man with a wrinkled face and only a few bad teeth left who could hardly stagger along. It looked as though I'd found another jovial band of natives. What remained to be seen was whether their wine pacified them.

I did not know enough about the Ibans at that time, neither about their lively curiosity nor their keen sense of hospitality. But in fact they had discussed my case for so long in order to decide what rank to give me. The Ibans do not have an aristocratic or feudal society as the Kayans do; rather the opposite, as they are much more democratic. Nevertheless, there are certain social differences, and the arrival of a stranger like me had, understandably enough, thrown them into some confusion.

If my two captors had got nervous or excited I'd have had my head chopped off, that's for sure; and if I'd stolen the two fishes I'd have met with the same fate, or else been held as a slave for the rest of my life. Just thinking about it sent cold shivers down my back. However, nothing like that had happened, and after some wavering at first it had been decided that I was a welcome guest. And now this was made clear to me.

The Tuaï Rumah, or village chief, whose name was Tangale, came over to me and launched into a long speech that seemed never-ending, especially as I didn't understand a word of it. But I listened respectfully, still seated. The people around us paid very little attention, talking loudly among themselves. The chief got annoyed now and again and bellowed for silence. It became embarrassing at times. At last he finished and took me by both hands. I stood up and he shook my hands hard and at length. Then all the others, all the men anyway, did the same. No doubt about it, I was accepted.

When this little ceremony was over, the chief took my pack and led me to his family apartment at the far end of the longhouse (an Iban chief, unlike a Kayan, does not necessarily live in the middle). He introduced me to his family, beginning with his wife, a little wizened old woman who gave me a smile that showed all her stumps. I wondered how old she was. The Tuaï was not a young man but was still vigorous, with a broad, well-developed chest—probably from long years of canoeing—and muscular arms and hard, knotty thighs, able to carry very heavy loads, as I was to see later. He had a flat face with hardly a wrinkle on it, and his long, broad nose was rather unusual for a Dayak. His jet-black eyes were very prominent, almost protruding, and most expressive. When he was angry, they became quite terrifying. His wife was followed by two boys of ten or twelve and a grown girl; she was married to a gaunt, sad-faced indi-

vidual, who was in fact the wag of the village. He had a
soft voice, unlike everyone else, and never stopped telling jokes. When he got drunk, which happened most
evenings, half the population collected around him and
roared with laughter at his jests and banter. He became
my Iban teacher; a good friend. There was an old man
dumped in a corner of the room—the grandfather, paralyzed. He didn't seem long for this world. Throughout
the night I heard his difficult breathing, rasping cough-
ing and noisy spitting. The chief had another daughter,
about fifteen, whom I came to know very well later. At
this time she was living with other members of the family
in a neighboring *bilek*.

The chief's room was about twenty feet square, the
same size as all the others. The hearth was in one corner,
with a supply of wood stacked above; a small window
looked out on the nearby forest. Hanging all about the
room, from the rafters and along the walls, were a vast
number of things—parangs and blowpipes, pots of all
shapes and sizes, horns, boars' tusks, etc., a lot of junk
fit for an attic, most of it draped with dusty spider's
webs. Then there was all the wickerwork, at which the
Ibans excel: the baskets and the fishing pots, wide-
brimmed hats and matting. In another corner was a
large, crudely made wooden chest which contained all
the wealth of the family. And at the far end, carefully
lined up in order of size, were a dozen large jars of *tuak*,
the second blood of the Ibans and their peerless companion at evening get-togethers. It all reminded me very
much of the longhouses on the upper reaches of the Rajang.

We tried to converse, but as we were getting nowhere
I started to unpack. A neighbor looked in, then another,
then some children entered . . . Five minutes later
there was a small crowd passing my things from hand

to hand. I was frightened they might steal or break something, but there again I did not know these Ibans. However, when they started handling the camera I showed them that it was fragile and that they were not to touch any of the little things sticking out. They commented on the objects as they passed them around, the stick of shaving soap, the bottle of quinine tablets—which I was careful to prove did not contain poison by taking out a tablet and swallowing it. But at once everybody wanted to try one. Now these tablets had a bitter, unpleasant taste, especially when crunched in the mouth; and in a moment the people who had tried them were spitting them out all over the place, to the great amusement of the others. At least I could now be sure that my quinine tablets were safe.

It was the hammock that aroused their curiosity most of all. Three or four of them tried to discover the use of this peculiar length of netting with a stick at each end. It could not be for trapping, as the mesh was too wide. They tried putting it on their heads, but no, that didn't seem to solve the problem either. One of them left the room with the hammock, probably to seek advice next door or from people on the verandah. When he came back he had some more people with him but was still as puzzled as ever. So I slung the hammock between two pillars and got into it. This caused a sensation. Everyone present went to admire and try out the hammock. During the next few days several men started making themselves a rope hammock, but when it was finished none of them ever used it.

We all left the chief's room and went back to the communal verandah. A gourd filled with *tuak* was brought to me, but the chief tasted it first. "*Tsss—*" He pulled a face, then shook his head as he handed me the brown drinking bowl. It was of average quality—had probably been left to ferment a little too long—but I had to take a good long drink, about a pint of it. They didn't do things by halves here.

"Oua, bagous!" I exclaimed appreciatively. Actually *bagous* does not mean anything in Iban, I discovered; the word for "good" is *badas*, which is Malaysian or Indonesian in origin. However, they understood what I meant. Then we started on a round of the *bileks*, tasting each family's concoction—sweet, bitter, vinegary, all kinds of *tuak*—and I had a gulp each time as a pledge of friendship.

Suddenly there came a dreadful yell from the chief's *bilek* and we all dashed back. My flashlight was lying on the floor. I had purposely said nothing about how it worked so that they wouldn't use up the batteries. But this inquisitive lad had fiddled about with it, pressed the button, and to his astonishment a beam of light had struck him in the face. Some of the others, having overcome their own fright, picked up the flashlight and examined it all over, tapped the glass and felt to see if it burned. Finally I took the flashlight from them and gave a demonstration, then put it away in a side pocket of my pack after partly unscrewing the bottom to disconnect the batteries. That would stop them from playing about with it and working it.

Although some of them found my equipment odd and mysterious, they were all very kind and friendly—except one man, who had been giving me a dirty look ever since I arrived. When we were all back on the verandah again I tried to be friendly and get him to unbend, but without success. I even heard him utter a few words which must have been very disagreeable, for they at once brought some murmurs of disapproval from the people next to him. Had I an enemy already?

All the upset caused by my arrival had prevented the women from preparing the customary dishes for a celebration, and apparently the hunting that day had not produced very much. So a couple of fat pigs and a dozen hens paid the price. But the *tuak* flowed as on the best of occasions and the level in the jars dropped considerably. The Kayans were dedicated drinkers, too, but at least they had paused now and again to nibble at some food. Here the bowls of wine were constantly being refilled and then had to be emptied at one go. Despite cheating—which wasn't easy—the time came when I just could not swallow any more of the gourdfuls of *tuak* that kept coming my way. Fortunately there was the vomitorium close at hand. All that anyone needed to do when overflowing was to rise slightly, turn the head and bend over a gap in the floor . . . a wipe of the face with the end of one's sarong, and off to a fresh start.

All along the verandah there were family groups eating and drinking outside the doors to their *bileks*, with a certain amount of visiting from one group to another. The group I was in was the largest and included, at first anyway, all the village elders, the chief and the guy who did not seem to approve of my presence—the witch doctor! Luckily, the witch doctors here do not have the same powers as those of African tribes. They are really quack doctors, confining their activities to curing ailments—they undoubtedly possess a wide knowledge of local herbs and drugs—and to being intermediaries with the spirit world. They have much less authority than a chief, but are listened to with respect and play an important part in traditional ceremonies.

I thought it would be best to try and coax this one with some presents—if he would accept them—and to be careful not to intrude into his domain by offering anyone tablets or ointments. Every man to his job.

The celebrations were reaching their height. I was treated to a succession of speeches and an inconsiderate number of bowls of *tuak*. Now and then someone started up a drinking song and everyone joined in. Apparently it is usual, as with the Kayans, at such convivial gatherings for some woman to go and sit next to the man of the hour—the chief guest, as it might be—and holding a large bowl of *tuak*, improvise a song in his praise, sometimes with a touch of humor. For instance, if the warrior has had a heavy branch fall on his head while out hunting, the woman's *panthom*—song—might well refer to his having a head like iron.

A buxom woman with splendid breasts came and sat by me. I enjoyed just looking at her more than listening to her chanting away. At last she came to the end and handed me the bowl. I drank the lot and then, not wanting to pass out just yet, spewed it all down below without further ado, which did not prevent me from then showing great pleasure at the attentions paid me, as custom demanded.

This evening the guest of honor was being pampered. After giving me so much to drink, they now wanted me to sing. "*Panthom, panthom!*" they were all calling.

All eyes were on me, there was no way out of it. What could I give them? I let them press me a little, for form's sake, then rose unsteadily to my feet, putting a hand on a helpful shoulder. I waited for silence, then launched into that hearty drinking song "Chevaliers de la Table Ronde."

Before I reached the end of the first verse their eyes were as round as bowls of *tuak*, and when I came to the refrain,

> *Goutons voir, oui, oui, oui,*
> *Goutons voir, non, non, non,*
> *Si le vin est bon,*

they all burst into loud and uncontrollable laughter, holding their sides and rolling about. It was impossible to continue, and anyway I couldn't stop laughing myself. When they recovered they got me to start again. At the fourth attempt I just managed the first two lines, and that was as far as I got. Never in living memory had the Ibans laughed so much.

In future, every time there was a celebration, and especially when there were guests from other villages, I was called on to sing the irresistible "Chevaliers de la Table Ronde."

SIX

Hooked!

I had no intention of staying long in the village. I had left Kapit with the idea of making a reconnaissance for a later and more elaborate expedition, of confirming what the doctor had told me and making sure that this region was worth exploring. I now knew that it was possible to cross the mountain chain and reach the native population, and that I could live among them and study their way of life. So the wisest thing would be to set off back, to return to France; first to have a rest, then to find a traveling companion and organize a more lengthy expedition. But I was up against the immediate difficulty of finding a way back from this remote village situated I knew not where. I could of course follow the same procedure that had brought me here and walk at hazard but roughly in the opposite direction, north-northwest. But it would not be easy—in fact my experiences of the past couple of weeks had shown that it would be decidedly dangerous.

I was wondering what to do, and after a fortnight in the village my easygoing nature decided for me—I would stay another fortnight. In any case, I was not wasting my time. I was taking photos of the village and its inhabitants and was noting down everything of interest. The joker who lived in the chief's *bilek* kindly gave me lessons in Iban, just half an hour to an hour every day. It was very easy. I liked this rather guttural language and made rapid progress by taking part in conversations. The vocabulary is fairly limited except on the subjects of hunting, fishing and the jungle; then it is rich with shades of staggering precision. For instance, there is not just one word for "tree," but one for the trunk up to a man's height, then another for the rest of the trunk to the first branches and yet another for the top part. Similarly, a distinction is made among the branches, with different words for the lower ones, the large and the small and for those in the sunlight. *Shoula lotong ari Kate* does not just mean "There is a monkey in the tree," but "There is a young monkey on a large branch in the second upper part of the tree." There is one word for cooked meat and another for meat on the hoof; wild animals of the same species are given different names according to their age, size and sex (especially deer). And so on. This is quite understandable for people who live off the jungle and only off the jungle; they have to express themselves clearly and with exactitude. On the other hand, a month is ample time in which to learn enough to follow an ordinary fireside conversation. A vocabulary of two hundred words is sufficient.

I went hunting and fishing with the men, but more often I accompanied the women and children when they went foraging in the forest. I was more interested in this activity, because on my way back to Kapit a knowledge of which plants were edible and which were poisonous would be extremely useful. Besides it was less tiring and demanded less skill than trapping or stalking.

I learned a fair number of useful things, especially that the little streams are veritable larders. Under most of the stones are found delicious snails with black or dark-brown ridged shells, some as big as your thumb. You just prize them from the stones and boil them. If you haven't a pin or a pointed instrument to get them out of the shells, you can break the top and suck them out. And under the dark rocks are found frogs of all sizes —really tasty—as well as shrimps, other tiny batrachians, small crabs, etc. In the forest I could recognize a dozen or so plants that were edible though not all delectable. Tastes differ!

We sometimes went on a day's outing, a sort of picnic by the river. The whole village took part. At midday we sat on rocks or on the sand to have our food, then bathed and played about in the water. The men went off into the forest with their blowpipes, and if they were successful we ate the game there and then. It was usually a monkey or a small musk deer, occasionally a shy muntjac which had been concealed in a bamboo thicket and been put up by the dogs. In the latter case the animal was not even cleaned but thrown straight onto the glowing embers; before it was properly cooked the men started to cut it up, leaving the rest to finish cooking. When they got to the offal, they threw it to the dogs.

I had made a few friends, old and not so old, among the latter being two young ladies. One was a tall slender girl, a little thin even, but nicely curved in the right places and very graceful; the other was shorter, just as pleasant, and seemed a nice cuddlesome piece. I didn't know how old they were—maybe fifteen or sixteen. I had the impression of being among a fairly permissive society, and if the opportunity occurred I wouldn't be averse to improving relations with one or the other girl, or even both of them—why not? I wasn't after exclusive rights, far from it, but I didn't know how a young man here set about courting a girl while not committing himself to a definite attachment. Obviously the best thing was to ask the young men I knew to enlighten me on the subject. Explanations were soon forthcoming and without the slightest reticence. Sex among the Ibans of Kalimantan is an easy, uninhibited matter, as among the Kayans. Unmarried girls and widows can have affairs with unattached men, and no one takes exception. Professional prostitutes are unknown, though some women have an evident inclination for the oldest profession in the world. Young men act more familiarly with them than with the other girls, and it sometimes happens that they meet married men deep in the forest. Otherwise, adultery seems to be extremely rare; indeed, communal living does not lend itself to such behavior. Besides, I had the impression that if the guilty parties are caught, there is trouble. I heard of a married woman who had almost killed her unfaithful husband with a parang, and he had been forced to leave the village, badly wounded as he was. He was then living in a longhouse ten days' walk distant.

During one of our long evening gatherings over bowls of *tuak,* by the light of candles, the young men gave me a detailed explanation of how to convey one's feelings to a girl. Beginning with an exchange of glances and a joke or two, you followed up with more direct allusions but cloaked in double meanings. If the girl slipped away and happened to go into her *bilek,* you followed after her—a move which was bound to draw bawdy comments from people round about. The girl pretended to be busy around the hearth, putting away pots and so on, so you sat down and waited. If she came across and sat down with her legs drawn to one side, a sign of submission, that meant the answer was "Yes." If, on the other hand, she continued busying herself about the room, or even went out again, then you had the wrong idea and there was nothing for it but to sneak back to the verandah and submit to the jeers of your friends.

But if the girl was willing, the suitor carried on openly. It was advisable, however, not to spend three consecutive nights with the girl, for that was tantamount to a request for her hand in marriage. So if the man had no such intention he spaced out his visits. And if the relationship continued there was no need to go through the preliminaries each time, as described above; the couple knew what they were about.

Thus briefed, one fine evening I tried my luck with the tall girl. For the past few days she had been more than friendly, especially when we were bathing in the river. The knowing winks of my companions were additional encouragement. I was a little afraid that I might have gotten the wrong ideas, for the young people fooled about quite a lot, especially in the water. But it was worth a try. That evening I was sitting with a group of young men chatting quietly and waiting for the evening meal, puffing slowly at our big cigarettes of damp tobacco, when some young women came and sat near us. My girl friend was one of them. We exchanged looks and smiles once or twice, then she pointedly got up, bestowing her sweetest smile on me, and went toward her *bilek* at the far end of the longhouse. I watched to see which door she entered, then I got to my feet, too.

"Hey! Where are you going?"

The question was followed by several laughs.

I went along the verandah, treading carefully on the springy bamboo flooring and followed her into the room. Her parents were there, too. That complicated things, but I could hardly draw back now. I sat down in the middle of the room, and the father came to join me. I hoped this move was not intended to be as suggestive as mine with regard to his daughter. You never know in Asia!

But no, Papa was perfectly normal. A minute or so later his daughter sat down beside me.

"*Sapa nama?*"

"Jean-Yves."

"*Na badas* [not very nice]."

She thought for a moment, then announced her choice. "Dioudi."

So I was baptized. We exchanged a few trivial remarks; my limited vocabulary did not allow me to make grand speeches, but that was of no importance.

When the evening meal was announced I left to go to the chief's *bilek,* and on my way out the girl secretly pressed my hand. There'd be no problem, I thought.

She rejoined our group when the evening meal was over, and after no more than two drinks of *tuak* we both went to her room. Her parents courteously gave me a big bowl of wine and then left us in peace. A little later we found ourselves alone in the room and could blow out the candle. . . .

I avoided spending a third evening with her, not wishing to lose my bachelor status, and remained drinking and joking with my friends until a late hour. Not long afterward I got to know the other girl, Kobe, intimately, too. She was one of the prettiest girls in the village and certainly the most graceful. She was always smiling, and when we came to know each other better she would cling tenderly to me whenever we were alone. I can still remember the day when Kobe joined me in the forest, where I had gone to look for shoots. We made love on the damp ground behind a clump of tree fern, with mosquitoes swarming around and a procession of red ants passing by.

When I had been living in the longhouse for nearly three weeks I decided it was about time to leave, but put off telling my hosts. I should have liked to remain longer but I was afraid of overstaying my welcome. Nothing had given me cause to suppose this, but I did not want to become a burden. I was almost a dead loss to the family I was living with: I did little else but eat their food and drink their *tuak.* Besides, one day or other I should have to think of going home. But I had to admit that I should be sorry to part from Kobe and her friend.

One evening there was a pleasant little party in progress, nothing very special, just to celebrate the chief's having killed a splendid deer with magnificent antlers, which would soon adorn his *bilek*. We ate and drank copiously, as is usual in the circumstances. I was beginning to get used to *tuak*, and I took part in the conversation; I was even able to understand some jokes and puns —and there are plenty of them in Iban.

The main topics of conversation at these convivial gatherings were hunting and women. The jokes were spicy and on the crude side, and the women contributed their share. Probably because of the communal life, one and all were quite prepared to describe their nocturnal romps; everyone was well aware of what went on next door. Kobe and her friend were quick to tell all the ladies of the longhouse about their experiences with me and to describe in detail certain anatomical differences—apparently very slight—between the Iban and the European male.

If someone should inadvertently burst into a "bedroom" where a couple is occupied at something other than threading beads, he goes off laughing and may even frankly inquire how the matter is progressing.

"*Niamaï bampot, Kobe?*" Which might be translated as "Everything going well?"

"*Niamaï*—but we haven't finished yet."

Just another instance, if one were still needed, of how free of inhibitions the Ibans are.

The gathering this particular evening was a kind of family party and we were watching some impromptu dancing. A girl of about fifteen danced first. She was not very big but had a perfect figure and delicate features, a face of sweet, pure beauty and a truly noble bearing. I had noticed her on several previous occasions, but she rarely joined our joyful group; she was probably rather shy or at least more reserved than the others. She gave a wonderful exhibition of Dayak dancing; her slow rhythmic movements were very lithe and graceful, but her face remained impassive and grave. She was a very beautiful girl.

"Tangale, she dances the *inau* very well," I said to the chief.

"*Ao!* She's the best dancer in the whole village," he agreed.

"Yes, she dances very well indeed," I went on enthusiastically. "Who is she?"

"You think she's pretty?"

"Yes, she's very pretty, Tangale."

The chief looked at me and said, "She's my daughter."

I couldn't take my eyes off her; but she seemed to be dancing without paying the slightest attention to what was going on around her. She was absorbed in her art.

"You didn't tell me that you had such a pretty daughter. I've never seen her in your *bilek*."

"You really think she's pretty?"

"*Niamai!*"

The people around seemed to be taking an unusually keen interest in our conversation, although there was nothing remarkable about it to me.

The chief said again, "She's pretty, isn't she?"

Had he suddenly gone gaga? His daughter was certainly a nice piece, but I saw no reason to keep on telling him so all night long. Perhaps he was a little drunk, though we hadn't really started drinking seriously at that stage. However, if it kept him happy. . . .

"Yes," I said, "she's very, very pretty. I think she's the loveliest girl in the village."

"*Ao! Ao!*"

He broke it off then, but I noticed that people were looking at me in an odd sort of way.

The chief's daughter finished her dance and was applauded, and she went to sit among a group of young people at the other end of the verandah. For some unknown reason I had a vague feeling that something had happened and that it affected me. But what?

However, after one or two more bowls of *tuak* I had almost forgotten about it; but then my curiosity was aroused again when I saw a man in the group at the other end pointing at me. They must have been telling the chief's daughter that I had said she was beautiful. It was true, and there was no harm in that. When she looked toward me I smiled, but there was no response. Never mind, Kobe was sitting nearby and I winked at her. But to my surprise she looked quite put out.

The party ended as usual with quite a number of drunks and a few falls amid the smell of vomit. I went to bed. The wizened grandfather was still huddled in his corner.

The following morning I told my Iban teacher that I was thinking of leaving in a day or two. He would let the others know. I hate all the business of saying good-bye. Yes, I said, I'd be leaving tomorrow.

"Tomorrow? But when are you coming back?"

"Oh, later. I have to go back to my own country now."

He obviously couldn't believe his ears and seemed quite stunned.

"But what about the wedding?"

"What wedding? Nobody told me there's going to be a wedding."

"But the chief's daughter!"

"The girl who was dancing last evening?"

"Why, of course!"

"All right, if there's a wedding, I'll stay a little longer." That would enable me to take a few more good photos.

My Iban friend looked completely taken aback by my remark. He got up and went from the room, to return a minute later with Tangale.

"Why do you want to go away?" the chief said. He seemed very annoyed and his dark eyes flashed angrily.

What was all this about? Did they want to keep me prisoner? I wondered, beginning to feel uneasy.

"I want to go back to my own country. I've been away a long time and my parents will be getting anxious."

"I don't believe there can be a country where every-body is like you. There's no place where people go off on such long journeys."

I had already realized that they had not been con-vinced by my stories of the sea and the snow. But that was no reason for keeping me here.

"And what about my daughter?"

"Your daughter? What about her?"

He began to get really worked up at that. Some men looked in to see what the trouble was; they seemed sud-denly hostile, and yet up to then we had been good friends.

We could not be on the same wavelength, the chief and I. "Look, Tuaï Rumah, I don't speak Iban very well. You must explain what's going on. I'm very fond of this village and all the people who live here. I'm afraid I've annoyed you without knowing it."

My inadequate knowledge of the language was a handicap to expressing myself, and I had to keep trying to find the right word, but finally I managed to make him understand.

So the chief explained. "Yesterday you asked for my daughter's hand in marriage, and today you want to go away! She was already betrothed to someone else and I had to give three pigs to have her back. Her fiancé isn't very pleased. I did all that for you, and now you're talk-ing of going away!"

So that was it! My throat went dry. I realized that I had been hooked, Dayak style.

"Give me some *tuak*."

According to them, I had made a marriage proposal in due and proper form. Had I not stated three times that the girl was very pretty and danced well, and said it in front of her father? The facts were there, I had uttered the fateful words.

I tried nevertheless to find a way of coming to some

arrangement. But there was no way. The chief did not want to lose face, and he had already upset the fiancé's family. To him it was a very important matter; as the Iban village chiefs are elected, he had to keep his popularity in mind. So I tried another argument—that I couldn't play such a trick on the poor fiancé. That was no good either. In any case, the poor fiancé was so disgusted that he wanted nothing more to do with the daughter, the chief or me.

Well then, how about the daughter, what did she say? She didn't love me, and I had no wish to marry her against her will. That carried no weight at all.

"She has no say in the matter. Besides, I'm sure she'll come to love you. Kobe and her friend like you very much, and so do other girls."

That was flattering, but quite calamitous. We had been discussing the matter for some time, and I could still not believe what had happened to me. What could I do? I had the feeling that it would be wise to give way, so I pretended that there had been a misunderstanding.

"Ah, now I see, Tangale. I thought you'd refused me and I was annoyed. That's why I wanted to go away in such a hurry. You know I don't speak Iban very well. I'm very pleased to know that you agree to my marrying your daughter. She is very, very pretty and she dances beautifully."

An angel passed and cleared away the clouds in the Rumah Selidapi longhouse deep in the Kalimantan mountains, and at the same time put a rope around my neck.

For the rest of the day I communed with a jar of *tuak*. For once I had an understanding companion.

I was awakened by the booming of gongs. The chief's was the first to go into action, making a deafening din. It was taken up by all the other gongs in the longhouse, each family beating at the large bronze sheet hanging from the beams. In a few seconds the whole village was athrob. The cocks joined in, then the dogs, making one unholy row.

Since I had become "engaged" I had slept alone, without Kobe, in the family apartment. My future wife was still next door with her uncle and his family. I happened to see her once or twice, but our meetings were never very romantic. I had the distinct impression that she did not at all appreciate this forced and hurried marriage. I was very sorry about this and fully shared her feelings; we were at least agreed that we had both been taken in. I tried not to dramatize the affair and to be philosophical about it all. I only hoped she would not maintain that attitude.

This was the great day. The village had been decorated and enormous quantities of meat prepared, including a few boars that luckily were still reasonably fresh. And this morning and on the following days there would be a great massacre of pigs and hens.

But first of all, everybody went down to bathe, a long line of silent little groups in the chilly mist.

"*Mané, mané.*" The children dashed gaily into the water, but I went in slowly and gingerly; it was very, very cold.

There was no breakfast for us; the women were far too busy preparing the other meals and especially the traditional and inevitable flat rice cakes, which are not particularly good anyway.

Some guests from the next village had already arrived during the previous two days. In the course of the morning we welcomed another dozen pirogues, filled with men and women in ceremonial dress, all very curious to see the strange biped who had appeared at Rumah Selidapi.

Time sped by, for we all had a great deal to do, and

some of the villagers never stopped brushing or mending their ceremonial garments or plucking their hairs.

Toward midday I had to put on a big *sirat*, a kind of long loincloth made of a dozen yards of material. The ends hung down in front and behind almost to the ground. They put black, very thin bracelets on my wrists, nickel-silver bracelets around my biceps and still more rings just above my calves. An enormous headdress of hornbill feathers and a sort of cope made of long fine feathers completed my bridegroom's costume. Pity I couldn't admire myself in a mirror. There was just one discordant note to my splendid local color—my spectacles.

Just before the ceremony began I was allowed to see my bride. She was certainly a charming girl, but very young—fifteen at most! I got the feeling that she, too, had decided to make the best of it, for this time she gave me a smile and asked if I was pleased. Well . . . in one sense, yes.

The chief gave me a rough outline of the ceremony. The wedding itself would take only a few seconds.

A gong boomed, and out of the forest appeared the witch doctor, clad in a magnificent garment made entirely of tiny colored beads. He came toward the village brandishing a long war parang in one hand and a human head with a mane of raffia in the other. He climbed the ladder to the outer verandah and entered the longhouse. Each family was waiting in front of its *bilek;* outside the door they had erected a tent of straw mats, where the evil spirits were supposed to be sheltering. The witch doctor went to the first *bilek* and walked around the tent, sipped a little *tuak* offered him by the lady of the house, then passed on to the next *bilek*, followed by the family from the first.

The witch doctor chanted magic spells in front of each tent and slashed with his parang as though engaging in a fierce combat. And so, followed by an ever-increasing throng, he purified and exorcised all the apartments and all the families in the village.

Once the evil spirits were dead, or at least expelled, we went into the bright sunshine on the outer verandah. The finest matting, lengths of cloth and branches of greenery were spread along the side, and everywhere stood bamboo poles with tufts of colored rags at the top. The gongs kept booming out every few seconds.

The chief's family, myself included, took up position in the middle of the verandah, with the witch doctor facing us. Behind him the men stood in line, with the women in the background. In a corner was the band, drumming away on tom-toms. We waited for a few moments, deafened by this wild music. Then some women came out of the longhouse laden with food and other things, and put some down in front of each head of a family, all in a certain order. These were offerings to the good spirits, the family's ancestors, and included everything that an Iban could wish for in afterlife: a handful of rice, some tobacco, an egg, fish, meat—and a bowl of *tuak*. The little heap of rice had a bloodstained white feather stuck in it.

Each head of a family, including myself, went and placed an offering on the top of one or other of the bamboo poles, at the splayed side. The little dish would stay there for a few days. What remained on the trays would be eaten during the day by the living; it would be a shame to waste such delicacies.

Then it was possible for the wedding ceremony to begin. Lintaü, my bride, went into the *ruaï* and took down a head. It was an Iban, and not so very ancient. When I had arrived in the village there was still some hair sticking to the temples, but the eyes had almost disappeared. Actually, it should have been a head that I had cut off myself, to present to the family. Alas, time had been too short, and besides, I had no enemy in view. According to custom, before the wedding the fiancé goes on an expedition, often accompanied by a few other warriors. They lie in wait near an enemy village and return home as soon as they have a trophy. It can be the head of a man, a woman or even a child. The main thing is that a new spirit should enter the longhouse.

However, all we had today was an ancient skull, so the procedure had to be slightly modified. Lintaü left the village for a few minutes with some other girls and came back holding out the enemy head. She walked up to me and handed it over, while the drums beat louder and louder. Then I put the head back with the others in the communal verandah.

All this took place amid general good humor, the people chatting and joking together. But the ceremony was not yet at an end. Headed by the witch doctor and the chief, then Lintaü and me, the whole village—at least, all those able to walk—made its way down to the river to bathe. There was much romping and playing about, everyone took a header, and we all went back to the longhouse undoubtedly well and truly purified.

The last act took place in the chief's *bilek*. He took Lintaü's hand and mine, held them between his own for a moment or two, made a short speech, and then we were free to go—a married couple.

The whole affair had not lasted more than an hour. On coming out of the chief's *bilek* we saw dishes of food lined up all along the *ruaï*. The orgy that followed lasted no less than three days and two nights, with *tuak* flowing the whole time. Numerous boars and domestic pigs contributed to this memorable feast. Personally, I tried not to indulge too much, but I had to drink at least as much as the others; so I brought it up as fast as I swallowed it.

Lintaü proved to be much more amenable now. Seizing an opportunity, we slipped away to her uncle's *bilek,* which had been assigned to us. When we rejoined the others, our absence had already been noticed and there was a general uproar.

I was already becoming consoled to being married.

"Lintaü, niamaï bampot?"

"Dioudi? Poké Lintaü kiai jampat?"

I leave the translation to the imagination. The joking remarks and comments directed at us were enough to make a hardened trooper blush, but certainly not a Dayak.

Lintaü went across to some of her friends, and to judge by their laughter I guessed she was giving them a detailed account of our little escapade. Other women, the elderly among them, crowded eagerly around her, quite unabashed. The men, however, were slightly less inquisitive—with the exception of the witch doctor, who continued to study me with that air of cold contempt that he had shown from the start.

SEVEN

Learning All Over Again

Until the wedding I had been the guest of the Rumah
Selidapi longhouse, but now that I was married to Lintaü I was considered to be an Iban in every respect, or
almost. We were living with another family at the end
of the village. More than ever, I tried to live like all the
others. I was on excellent terms with them, except for
the witch doctor and the family of the ex-fiancé. He,
however, had gone off with all his belongings to live in
the next village of Rumah Pacou.

Now that I was settled, roped in, I reduced my evening drinking sessions as much as possible. It quickly
became obvious to me that my knowledge of the forest
and especially of hunting was hopelessly inadequate, and
that I was unable to provide for my household. Lintaü's
uncle took on the task of supplying us with game but
this arrangement could not be allowed to continue indefinitely, although the Ibans are the most hospitable
people in the world. So I went to see my father-in-law,
the Tuaï Rumah.

"Tangale, how can I get a blowpipe? I'd like very
much to go hunting."

A long blowpipe is a warrior's most precious weapon.
But to make one requires a technical knowledge and skill
that even many Ibans do not possess, and they prefer to
buy one from a craftsman for a few pigs and several
handfuls of reddish tobacco.

Making a blowpipe is a long and tedious task. The
craftsman begins by carefully selecting a long hardwood
branch that is as straight as possible. When this is quite

ABOVE The Rajang River.

BELOW A monitor lizard swimming.

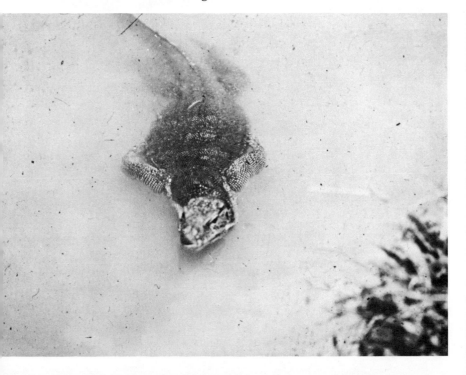

OPPOSITE TOP A gibbon makes for the river.

OPPOSITE BOTTOM My faithful Kayan guide.

ABOVE A Malaysian tapir.

LEFT A red python (*Python curtus*) about to devour a monkey.

ABOVE The Balui River. You rarely see sunlight here.

LEFT A Kayan crosses a suspension bridge. His shirt is made of bark.

The Kayan longhouse.

LEFT A woman carrying her baby.

BELOW A Kayan village.

OPPOSITE TOP A Kayan pigsty. The pigs are caged to protect them from panthers.

OPPOSITE BOTTOM Two young girls return from a fishing expedition.

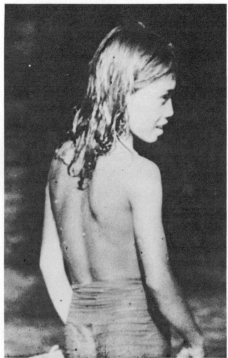

ABOVE Water carrier.
LEFT An Iban beauty.

ABOVE One of the two warriors who captured me.
RIGHT Every morning my bride delouses me: an indispensable rite.

ABOVE My wife, Lintaü.

BELOW My wife, with her sister, before the wedding ceremony.

ABOVE My enemy, the witch doctor.
BELOW Rimau, the village chief.

ABOVE My back adorned with the tribal tattoos.

OPPOSITE TOP My wife takes Totoche for a walk.

OPPOSITE BOTTOM During orgies, the indisposed vomit through this window.

TOP Making fish soup on the Baleh River.

BOTTOM First introduction to photography.

TOP I learn to be a trapper.

BOTTOM My monkey, Totoche.

LEFT Returning from the hunt. The wild boar weighs more than two hundred pounds.

BELOW The path to the river. It was here that I was bitten by the krait.

OPPOSITE TOP The terrible krait with the red head, whose bite almost cost me my life.

OPPOSITE BOTTOM This old Iban has tattoos on both hands; he has taken more than ten human heads.

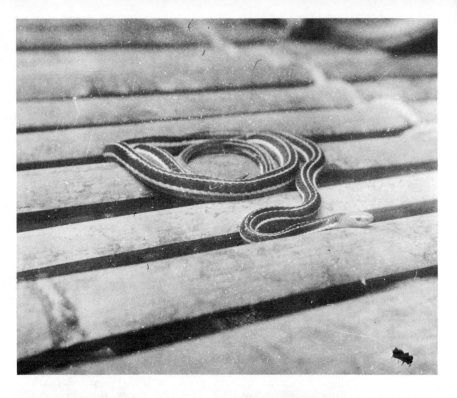

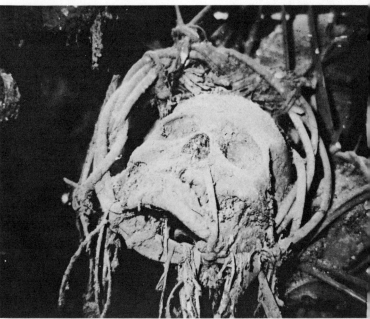

Sinister trophies.

dry—which itself takes a considerable time in such a
climate—he erects a bamboo support seven or eight feet
in height (the length of the blowpipe) and securely
fixes the branch upright inside it. Then he hollows out
the branch with an iron rod, boring into it with his bare
hands. This takes weeks and weeks of patient work before he reaches the other end and exactly in the center.
The outside is made smooth with sand and a hornstone.
The interior must of course be straight and smooth for
a dart to be shot with the greatest precision; its diameter
is slightly larger than that of a cigarette. When finished,
an iron spearhead about a foot long is attached to the
blowpipe; this comes in very useful when confronting a
charging boar or in warfare.

The darts are made of bamboo; at least, you make
them from bamboo if in a hurry or not feeling very
energetic. They are about eight inches long and very
thin, and the tip is smeared with poison at the appropriate moment. Their butts are made from hearts of elder
or a similar tree, and exactly fit the caliber of the blowpipe. A well-directed dart of this type will penetrate the
hide of the toughest boar, and can be used effectively on
monkeys and birds up to a range of eighty feet. The best
darts, however, are undoubtedly those made of hardwood; they are not only heavier but carry farther. There
are two kinds, one for hunting and the other for warfare,
the latter being made more solid and with a little iron
tip which enables more poison to be applied.

There is a tree in the Borneo jungle which has some
resemblance to a *Hevea* or rubber tree, and when a cut
is made in the trunk a white, very sticky sap oozes out.
This has to be gathered while still fresh, and from a
healthy tree; then it is boiled on a low fire. The resulting
paste is very thick and sticky, and dark brown, almost
black. You can tell the quality of this poisonous substance

by its taste—the more acrid or bitter it is, the better. Its action is effective only when it enters the bloodstream.

Every hunter has his own particular recipe. Some mix in a very small amount of the extract from the root of a certain creeper, and others add a snake's venom when possible. The latter are of course mistaken, for the venom loses its properties when exposed to heat or damp. In any case, the poisonous paste is put into a bamboo quiver, and the tips of the darts are dipped in it before it solidifies. When a dart strikes the prey, the poison enters the bloodstream and very quickly has a paralyzing effect on the nervous system.

Chief Tangale owned several blowpipes, and every man had at least two; for if a hunter's one and only blowpipe was accidentally broken he might have to wait months while another was being made. Tangale examined his blowpipes and gave me one that was very straight and strong but had no spearhead to it. However, I could add one later.

Next day he showed me how to make darts. After a dozen attempts I was able to show him some bamboo darts that were good enough for me to practice using my blowpipe. But when I went hunting he supplied me with darts at first, and with poison until I could make my own—though I never really mastered that technique.

There were often children practicing with blowpipes just outside the village, aiming at small animals or in fact anything that moved; their favorite targets were big grasshoppers, tree frogs and small birds. I joined them and soon found that shooting darts from a long blowpipe was not so very difficult. After a few days I became quite accurate and felt sure of being able to hit a monkey high up a tree—provided the monkey allowed me to get near enough. The whole art of hunting in the jungle depends in fact on the approach to one's prey. Planting a dart in an animal the size of a monkey is within anyone's capability, but stealthily approaching a group of gibbons calls for great skill and excellent eyesight, for distinguishing between a clump of foliage and a motionless monkey is not as easy as it may seem.

To become a real Iban required other skills, too: stalking a wild boar or deer without losing its tracks among others that crossed and confused them; identifying animals from their droppings or from their cries, knowing what each kind feeds on and where this or that kind is most likely to be found; and so on. I began spending every day in the forest, trying to pierce its many secrets. My companions were of little help to me, even when anyone felt lazy enough to go with me. They hardly ever took me into their confidence, or perhaps it would be more correct to say that they refrained from chattering about things which to them were so plain and simple.

The first few days were most disheartening; I couldn't get within range of any animal, yet God knows I was eager enough to use my blowpipe. Gibbons fled when I was fifty yards away; macaques disappeared just as I reached the tree in which they were perched. Birds were even more difficult. It was all very discouraging. I came to the conclusion that I was making so much noise that I scared away the most unconcerned of animals. By presuming that every bush and tree concealed game, I succeeded in walking on tiptoe even when no living thing seemed to be in sight. It made me feel ridiculous, trying to walk like a cat and looking carefully to see where I was treading, but in this manner I learned—without realizing it—how a hunter makes his way through the forest. I shan't attempt to explain this technique, which cannot be taught by correspondence anyway, but one thing is very important—never look at your feet! It's by looking where you're putting your feet that you stumble and fall and make a lot of noise. After a time you get along quite fast, while looking all around you and forgetting about the unevenness of the ground. Just as a tightrope walker cannot keep his balance if he starts thinking about his feet, so a hunter in the forest will have no success if he concentrates on his manner of walking. Once I had mastered this, the rest became much easier.

My first victim was a hornbill, the easiest game to surprise, a noisy, large bird which does not panic easily. When it does sight someone it often flies heavily off, only to settle again after a few yards. I had been observing a couple of these birds perched high above me for about ten minutes. They were too far up for me to tell which was the male and which the female, but it was easy to see that the mating season had begun. The poor things were so actively engaged that they paid no attention to what was happening sixty feet below. I chose a good dart from my quiver, slipped it gently into the blowpipe and waited for one of the hornbills to remain more or less still. Taking aim was simple enough: the blowpipe had no sight to it, but I had only to point it at the target, look along the top and blow. As the darts fit exactly into the blowpipe, very little breath is required to shoot with speed and accuracy. It is easier than one would think.

Pfft—I barely heard the dart leave the blowpipe, and it sped much too fast for me to follow its flight. Less than a second later, one of the birds gave a despairing cry, pecked furiously with its large yellow-and-red bill, then fell heavily to the ground after an ineffectual flapping of its wings. The other bird at once flew off with the swishing sound of an air fan.

Right in the center of the white breast—it was floundering about in its death throes. By a lucky chance the dart had not broken and I replaced it in my quiver, remembering to dip it in the poison again later, for a single dip acts only once. There was an occasion several weeks later when I forgot to renew the poison on a used dart, and this created serious trouble for me when I shot it into the flanks of a fine wild boar. . . .

I hurried back to the village, very pleased with my prowess.

"That's very good, Dioudi. Now you must bring back a *babi* [wild boar]."

I found the hornbill delicious, very likely because I had killed it myself, for its flesh is not considered remarkably good.

I like hunting, but until leaving home on this journey I had always abstained from killing animals, not for sentimental reasons but because everywhere I went there was so little game, or it was becoming extinct, and I considered that helping to hasten the process was downright criminal. But in India and Nepal, where there are regions with an abundance of game, I went hunting with great pleasure and without my conscience pricking me. Here in Borneo there was admittedly less game, but hunting with the blowpipe was hardly likely to upset the balance of nature.

Here one hunts to eat; it is both an obligation and a pleasure. The Ibans say that the greatest pleasures on earth are hunting, fishing and making love—in that order. I have never thought much of the modern shooting party or safari, with guns that have an ever greater range and are ever more deadly—against fauna which steadily diminish in numbers. It is not even for the meat, but solely for vanity—a photograph of the hunter standing beside the dead lion or buffalo, or the kill to be hung on the drawing-room wall. To call this a "noble sport" is something that disgusts me.

Nearly every morning I went off into the forest, but never very far. It was so easy to get lost; several times I thought I should never find my way back to the village, although I had left it only an hour before. The other hunters generally started out early in the afternoon, but I preferred leaving in the early morning; in this way I almost made up for my lack of experience.

The Ibans preferred to keep on the move while hunting, but I found it better to lie in wait, especially while still a novice. At least I made no noise and could observe the denizens of the jungle at my ease. Sometimes a band of monkeys came and romped around me; occasionally a small russet muntjac slipped stealthily past, threading its way between the bamboo thickets and the trees. You had to be exceptionally quick to shoot at one of these; it gave one bound and disappeared, and only a broken branch or two and a few crumpled leaves showed that you had not been dreaming. I usually managed to kill one of these small deer just before nightfall, when they began to come out of hiding. They are not, however, essentially nocturnal animals, for on occasion I shot at one in the middle of the day. The most common animal was the wild boar—and the most dangerous. They were in either twos or threes, though sometimes I saw a vicious old boar alone. The first time I spied one of these monsters I must admit that I just let him pass by, making no attempt to disturb him.

When I set off by myself for the day I took with me some dried meat, usually venison, some rice in a bamboo and some pickled fish in another small container. There was no need to carry water as rivers and streams were plentiful. And there grew in the forest a thick liana that held a liquid that was very thirst-quenching; you just made a cut in the pulpy stem and the juice squirted straight down your throat. It was much appreciated and had the additional advantage of being pure. There was no fear of swallowing a horde of amoebas with each mouthful, as you had when you drank from a pond. Though in these mountain regions the water is generally pure. Dysentery is rare.

But the Ibans know nothing about hygiene. Food is

left lying about anywhere, on the ground or the floor; and the women spit out their chewing tobacco, making a mucky red pool at their feet, not at all appetizing. Dogs come nosing around the meat; everyone picks about in the same dish.

A hunter never returned empty-handed, on principle; if game was lacking he filled his wicker basket with shoots and mushrooms, and perhaps came upon a durian that was not overripe and had escaped the notice of orangoutans and boars. It was as well not to be standing below a durian when it fell from the tree, for besides weighing five or six pounds this fruit has a hard prickly rind. Its yellowish pulp has an agreeable taste but the smell, to a European, is positively disgusting, enough to turn one's stomach. It grows wild in Borneo but is cultivated in Southeast Asia, and the natives consider it the most delicious fruit in creation. I like it well enough, but I'm not wild about it.

Another delicacy of the Ibans is wood lice. Some of these are very large and all have the same smell as those common to Europe. They are used for soup (foul stuff) and are also eaten raw, as and when they are caught. I tried to get used to them but never really succeeded. Dung beetles figure on the menu, too, along with other coleoptera, and their grubs have a certain novelty. As their name suggests, these delightful insects use animal or human excrement to make nests for their eggs to hatch in, and the Borneo species are no exception. Discovering larvae of dung beetles is considered a great windfall. They are found in balls of hard, dry dung— break one open and there are the fine fat white grubs —and the great advantage is that these balls can be kept intact for a long time as a reserve supply. In fact, the Ibans have a number of strange dishes, such as overripe meat in ant sauce. Ants go very well with fish, too, giving it a lemonlike taste that is not at all bad.

I was often asked about food in my own country, but I don't think the Ibans ever believed what I told them.

"How do you get your food? When you arrived here you didn't even know about the black-shelled snails, you didn't know what *paco* is . . . what do you live on then?"

"In my country there isn't any jungle. Some people grow rice or breed pigs, and other people buy and eat them. It's all very complicated."

How could they understand that it is possible to live without going hunting every day? One might as well try to explain the theory of relativity to a mule.

Fishing was a minor activity at Rumah Selidapi, but pots and nets of all shapes and sizes were spread here, there and everywhere. The best catches weighed ten to twenty pounds, a fact which would rouse the envy of anglers back home, but for this country was nothing remarkable. It seemed to me that these rivers would be a paradise for a cast-net fisherman. I was never successful at it myself, but then I've never been really interested in fishing. You need to have the knack with a casting net. The kind I saw here had a very fine mesh and were weighted with pieces of scrap iron. The fisherman walked slowly along in shallow water, being careful not to stir up the mud, until he saw a fish of decent size, then cast his net neatly.

A more frequent method of the villagers was to fish by hand, a practice which horrified me. When a tree growing on the bank fell into the river it sometimes dragged others and a tangle of creepers with it, all of which quickly became covered with fallen leaves, mud and silt, making an almost level and continuous roofing. This became a perfect refuge, with all the tunnels and cavities below, for many fish and other aquatic creatures such as lizards, snakes and crocodiles. And the villagers got into the water to grope about in such places! Some of the fish, for instance, catfish, have a very sharp-pointed backbone, and others possess a fine set of teeth. . . . One day a woman gave a frightful cry and withdrew her hand plus a fine lizard about a yard long, which seemed determined to hang on. Another time a woman dislodged a young crocodile, which almost severed two of her fingers and snapped a lump out of her calf. The little group of fishermen I was with at once dashed after the crocodile—the river was quite shallow —but it was too quick for us and got away. So there was no boiled crocodile's tail that evening after all. Crocodile meat was considered very good; some people said it was like chicken, but I found it tasted like crocodile, which is difficult to mistake for anything else.

Fishing by hand did not tempt me in the slightest, and I always found some excuse to avoid taking part. But there was another method of fishing in which I gladly joined.

"We're going *tuba* fishing tomorrow!"

This meant a day's picnic in which the whole family, children included, took part.

"Are we going far?"

"To the waterfall."

It was a delightful spot, about two hours' walk from the village. We were all up early and set off directly after the morning bathe. The women carried the food, the rice and dried meat, while the men took their small wicker baskets, parangs and blowpipes. The children had charge of the two spades which would be used to dig up the *tuba* roots. The *tuba* is a very thick, gnarled liana which often grows to a great length and coils around trees. The part that interested us was its root. This has a slightly violet color when washed. The way to determine a real *tuba* root is to twist it gently. If a very watery white sap issues from the cracks, then it is the right kind of *tuba* for fishing; otherwise it is a fraudulent variety. We had marked some of the right kind in our hunting ground, but it took an hour's work to collect the armfuls needed. When the sap is mixed into a section of the stream it has a toxic action on the fish.

We retraced our steps a little way, followed the river for a while, then plunged into the forest. We went along a big stream with many rocks and boulders in its bed, climbing over some of them, all in a leisurely manner. The children were laughing and playing, the women gathered snails from under the stones, and we collected some fern shoots and hairy leaves that make a delicious soup. But there was no question of going hunting.

Finally we arrived at the cascade. The water came tumbling down from a height of about sixty feet; nearby was a small lake with big rocks all around it, and the whole landscape was very pretty and peaceful. The children played about in the stream while the rest of us selected a suitable reach for catching fish; it had to be in a calm stretch, not too wide and easy to dam. We found one not far away; it was about ten feet at its widest part, and we spent the rest of the morning building a primitive dam with stones and branches and clumps of grass. Then each of us chose a comfortable rock just above the water, sat down and started beating *tuba* roots with a big stick. The sap soon flowed and the waters became discolored. It took about a quarter of an hour to beat a handful of roots into pulp; then you gave them a last twist, tossed them into the stream and started on another handful.

Results soon began to show. Tiny fish came floating to the surface, belly upward, and were scooped into our baskets. These would be used for pickling, though they were sometimes eaten fresh. Then larger fish appeared, swimming feebly. By then the water had the color of a weak Pernod, pale yellow. When we had all finished beating the roots we went after the fish with our baskets, and in a couple of hours had practically cleared that section of the stream of all piscatorial life. The largest catches weighed seven or eight pounds, and altogether we took nearly fifty pounds of fish back home. Most of it was distributed among the villagers, the rest was dried, fed to the domestic animals or used for pickling.

I loved these day's outings and the picnics on the sandy bank under the big trees. And, of course, there was something to celebrate in the evening.

The other occupations of the villagers, after hunting, fishing and household chores, were growing rice and tobacco, but only just enough for their needs. Most of the patches of rice were very small; they had been appropriated from the forest, which was always trying to regain its hold. Here and there around the village were sweet potatoes growing half wild, and along the verandah side of the longhouse were half-a-dozen coconut palms, probably imported by Chinese traders a few generations ago. The work of rice planting and cultivation, the felling of forest trees to make a new patch or the harvesting of rice had but slight attraction for me, and like the other village idlers I always found something else to do when such tasks were at hand. No one took exception, and in any case there were always enough volunteers, especially from the ranks of heavy drinkers of *tuak*, for much more rice was used to make this wine than was eaten.

When a big celebration was in prospect and therefore much meat was needed, or when food was scarce and everyone was hungry, the hunters stayed out for several days, sleeping under the stars. The jungle was too dense for a tent to be used. On more than one occasion I spent a night sleeping on the ground or in a tree with the rain pouring down. It was rather uncomfortable, but one managed. The usual procedure was to build a shelter of bamboo and leafy branches, and several hunters would sleep together in this, sometimes five or more if the shelter was made large enough, on a bedding of bamboo. An Iban could put up one of these small shelters in ten minutes.

A necessary precaution was to smear one's feet with a particular kind of sap that kept away insects. One night I forgot to use this preventive . . . I still preferred my nylon hammock to the uneven bamboo bedding of an Iban shelter; I just made a roof of branches and slung my hammock below it. Only a particularly vicious snake would climb one of the ropes attaching the hammock to a tree; but I was forgetting that black ants sometimes have the wanderlust.

"Ooh! What the hell—?"

I woke with a start. A few bites soon had me fully conscious. I groped around for my flashlight, which had of course slipped down; by the time I got hold of it, some ants were carousing over my arms and legs. I switched on the torch and almost had heart failure—there were millions of black ants crawling in compact ranks over the ground below and around the tree trunks. A few of the advance guard were coming up the ropes and would soon be followed by the main body.

Like everyone else, I had heard and read horror stories of adventurers being eaten alive by ants . . . this would happen to me if I let these hordes get at me. However, there was one small but important detail of which I was unaware at the time—they were not man-eating ants. So I was in no real danger, except of being badly bitten. But not knowing this, and the vegetation being so dense that I could not see how far the invaders extended, I imagined in my panic that the ants covered dozens of square yards.

It seemed safer to remain in the hammock than to attempt to flee across that sea of crawling insects. I gripped

the flashlight between my teeth and got busy crushing
the few dozen already at work on me. Then I turned
desperately on those advancing up the ropes. It was an
unequal struggle, for while I was dealing with those at
the head a whole cohort swarmed up at the foot. And
to hold the flashlight between my teeth I needed jaws of
steel. At this rate I should soon be forced to evacuate my
position, but the thought of crossing that dark wriggling
mass just below filled me with horror. A terrible smell of
formic acid was rising from the ground, where millions of
tiny legs and mandibles were working away and making
a continuous rustling sound. My pack, which was hanging up a few feet from me, was completely covered with
ants. Little would be left after they had gone. . . . But
then, what a surprise! A minute or two later nearly all
the ants had vanished; there were just a few stray ones
going around in circles. And the ground was as smooth
and level as if it had been trodden down by a platoon
of soldiers, with not a blade of grass remaining. My pack
was intact, but stank of ants.

Thank God, that kind of nightmare experience did not
happen often. Although I was told later that these ants
are not carnivorous, I never again omitted to smear some
of the anti-insect sap around the tree trunks from which
I slung my hammock.

My jungle lore increased as the days went by, though
I was still far from having the ability and assurance of
the Ibans. I was finding less difficulty in picking up tracks
and stalking my prey; admittedly, the daily rains now
meant that the tracks left by animals were always easily
discernible.

A very necessary knowledge was the eating habits of
the different kinds of game. For instance, orangoutans
are attracted by durian trees, but only when the fruits
are just ripe; when they become overripe and drop to the
ground, it is the turn of wild boars to come foraging for

them. So when you discovered durian trees in your hunting ground, you could forecast the visit of game in this order: orangoutans, macaque monkeys and finally boars. All that remained to do was to draw up a plan of campaign and arrive at the spot at the right moment.

The best places for hunting were the salt grounds, as all species of deer visited them at one time or another. The difficulty was to be there at the right moment without going too often and so scaring away the game. The location of salt grounds was a jealously guarded secret. If there happened to be one close to a village it was regarded as common ground, which meant that in a very short time no deer ever went near it by day.

I had now been living in the village for three months. The time passed quickly. I wrote less and less in my diary, partly because everything around me had gradually become familiar and partly because my last ballpoint was almost dry. I was making no plans for the moment, in fact I thought I might stay here for several years. I liked living among these people, I had a pretty, loving wife, many friends and few enemies. I was never bored—far from it, despite the many periods of inactivity.

I felt that I was slowly getting into the Iban way of life and thought. It was a hard life but easy to bear. Everyone had his or her duties, but there were no real worries; the villagers gorged themselves when there was plenty of meat and chewed plants when meat was scarce. The communal and cooperative way of living smoothed out and greatly reduced all the little personal problems that often make life impossible in our Western civilization. Above all, the law or the rule was so well made, or at least so well accepted—which amounts to the same thing —and had been for so long that there was never the slightest protest. Jealousy was unknown; the one aim of every man was to be a good hunter; there were no status symbols and no positions to keep up, for everyone knew all about his neighbors. The result of this was a very relaxing and harmonious way of life.

No one worried very much, not even in the event of illness or a wound. The wife is sick? Then it's because she has not complied with the rules of the ancestors. There were so many of these small obligations and customs and superstitions that it would be surprising if you didn't trip up at some time or other. And now it all depended on the witch doctor; if he couldn't find a cure, there was nothing to be done. . . .

"The old girl will soon be dead, her family has lots of pigs, what a feed we'll have at her funeral!"

That is more or less what I overheard on one occasion. The dying woman was only a few feet away.

If someone was accidentally wounded he suffered in silence, trying not to bother the neighbors. Sometimes the wound healed, if there were no complications, if it did not become infected or tetanus set in; otherwise death followed. Only the close relatives were anxious, but their anxiety had nothing in common with that felt by Westerners in like circumstances. No grief was felt for the dying man. Was he not soon going to join his ancestors? He had been a good hunter and a good warrior, he had cut off one or two heads, he had a wife and children who gave him presents whenever there was a festival or ceremony. No, he was not to be pitied; he would soon know a much better life. The Iban paradise is one long banquet at which the supply of boar fat is never-ending, *tuak* flows in abundance and women are available whenever you want one—and above all, you can want one as often as you like. If the wounded or sick person is in too much pain, then the remedy is to give him plenty of *tuak*. How many have entered paradise completely drunk? It is not the dying man who is to be pitied, but those he leaves behind. Who will go hunting for the family now? For how long will the widow have to go without *butua?* If she is no longer young it will be difficult for her to find a husband or even a lover. It is the living who have the problems, not the dead.

My wife explained all these customs and this Dayak philosophy to me. She also told me what a model husband ought to do, but there she overstepped the mark, for I found out later that she had burdened me with chores that were not in my province. Our conversation had been rather elementary when we first set up house, but it quickly developed and was enriched after I learned the men's vocabulary from the chief.

Lintaü did the household work, the cooking and the washing and so on. I wore the traditional *sirat* now, having made a present of my old shorts to a friend who was dying of envy for them. As a consequence he was chafed between the legs and had pimples on his bottom. Served him right! When someone is used to having a bare behind, why wear shorts which are uncomfortable and difficult to clean? Lintaü also did my toilet, by which I mean that she carefully shaved me every day, plucked my eyebrows with a little pair of iron tweezers, and kept close watch on how my hair was growing. But alas, I did not have an Iban's splendid head of hair, very dark and straight and hanging down below the neck. My brown mop was disgracefully curly; all the same, I was given a "pudding-bowl" cut in front, while my hair flopped about at the back. I must have looked like a real hippy.

When I had nothing to do, or at least when I decided that I could do nothing (because a kingfisher had flown across my path that morning—I made use of these omens and portents!), I went and chatted on the verandah or had a siesta; or else Lintaü and I went off by ourselves, insofar as anyone can go off by himself in a longhouse, for one of the interminable Iban petting sessions.

In principle, this activity took place in the evenings, but I told my other half that as I had fallen in with Iban customs it was only right for her to fall in with those of my country, and that there any time of day was suitable. As she was a good wife and far from frigid, we got on well together, like most couples in the longhouse.

Conversations in the village of Selidapi, as already mentioned, center on hunting and women—bluntly and crudely in the case of the latter.

"Linsak, why do you cry out like a gibbon when you're making love? What does your husband do to you?"

Sometimes, however, I tried to open up a new subject. For instance: "How many people are there in the world?"

I had to phrase the question a little differently, because the word "world" did not mean much to these villagers. They thought for a few moments, scratching their heads.

"It's difficult to say, Dioudi," one replied. "To begin with, there's the village of Rumah Pacou, the village of Rumah Paguma and. . . ." He named half-a-dozen villages scattered over an area of nearly two hundred square miles. "That's not counting the Punans, but no one knows how many of them there are. Like mosquitoes, you don't know where they all come from."

Everyone laughed at the witty remark.

"Well, how many people does that make?"

"Who knows? A lot anyway, perhaps more than all the fish in the river."

"You're forgetting all those who live in my country."

"Ah yes, there are all those, too. But are you sure there are as many as you say? If there's such a lot of you, why have we never seen any of them around here?"

It was difficult to make them understand that the world is not limited to a few villages scattered about in an immense forest.

The Ibans have a reputation of being daring travelers, yet those of Rumah Selidapi seemed very sedentary to me. During the whole of my stay they only once made an expedition outside their own territory.

EIGHT

Iban Initiation

One evening before we had become too drunk, the chief quietly took me aside—which immediately drew the whole village's attention to me.

"Everything all right with Lintaü? You like living in the village?"

"Oh yes, you know I'm happy here. But why do you mention Lintaü? Has she said anything to you?"

"No, no, I just thought I'd ask."

He beat about the bush for half an hour. What was going on in his mind? Now and again we had a drink of *tuak*. I could see by the way he was drawing at his big cigarette that he was nervous. I played it as cautiously as he did, giving evasive answers to his questions or replying with another question.

". . . Everyone here likes you. . . ." At one moment I had thought he was going to ask me to leave, so it couldn't be that. ". . . Except of course that you're not like us, even though you can talk like us now. You ask peculiar questions, too. I think the trouble is that you weren't born among the Ibans and particularly because you're not a *palek*."

"*Palek?* What's that?"

"There you are, you see—you don't even know what a *palek* is! A *palek* is . . . well, a *palek*. Everyone knows what that is."

"I see."

"I think the trouble is in your head. The spirits of your country aren't good. If you became a *palek* it would be much better, you'd see."

136

"I suppose so."

I still didn't know what a *palek* was, but from the way the conversation was going I would probably find out.

"So you're willing? That's good, because it wouldn't do otherwise, with all that in your head."

Here was a nice thing—now the Ibans were starting to psychoanalyze me. Whatever trap they were setting, I was certain to fall into it.

Later that evening I asked Lintaü what a *palek* was. "He's a man, a warrior," she said.

"How does one become a man among the Ibans? What do you have to do?"

"That depends. How do you become one in your country?"

"H'm. It's very difficult."

"Oh, it's not difficult here. You mustn't be afraid, that's all. Everyone goes through it."

"What about those who don't—those who fail?"

"That hardly ever happens, but they're thrown out of the village."

Ethnology is not one of my strongest subjects, but like most people I've heard of the initiation ceremonies among certain tribes. In New Guinea, for instance, young men have their foreskin cut off with a flint. Every primitive culture has its specialty, which to us often appears barbarous. I hoped the Ibans did not want to circumcise me. In any case, I was not letting them mess about with my tool, *palek* or no *palek*. There are some things that a man values.

Tangale, the old fox, had already pulled a fast one on me by getting me hooked by his daughter. What had he thought up now?

The next day Lintaü reassured me: there would be no interfering with any part of my anatomy. That was something.

The ceremony was due to take place a few days later,

but the village had already begun getting ready for the celebrations. I was to be the only initiate, as there was no other young man of an age to undergo the ritual ordeal.

Women and children went into the forest to collect red ants, digging them out of their nests with a straw stalk or just catching them in the open, then putting them into the bamboo pots. They are the most common of all ants in Borneo; they get everywhere and are a real nuisance. Any food left lying about, especially if it is sweetened, is soon covered with a heaving red mass of them, breaking it up into tiny portions to carry away to their nests. In the jungle you are always treading on these tiny creatures, which immediately inject a small drop of formic acid. It feels just like being pricked with a red-hot needle. So one of the first things to learn is to watch out for and avoid these columns of red ants, and when hunting never lie in wait near a nest of them.

The ant hunt went on for several days. When all the bamboo pots were full they were stoppered with leaves and deposited in a corner of the verandah.

The evening before the ceremony the village was decorated with little arches of bamboo and greenery; the women made the inevitable rice cakes and the heads of families got out their best *tuak*.

Gongs were booming reveille. For once the cocks had been forestalled. A few minutes later the whole of Rumah Selidapi was like an excited beehive. When the sun rose above the trees, offerings were made to the spirits of the village. Just before then I had been exorcised in a particular way. The witch doctor, holding the choicest head from his collection, which was black with soot and crowned with raffia, had walked around me and given me three taps on the head.

"Hantou kalayou."

That was to expel the evil spirits which I had been harboring until then.

He gave me three more taps on the head with his weird purificator.

"*Hantou kalayou.*"

Then I was considered exorcised; the evil spirits had gone, and it only remained to usher in the good. That was to be the most difficult part.

The witch doctor leading, followed closely by myself, the whole village went down to the river in single file. It was a cheerful, good-natured procession, with everyone talking and jostling and the kids running up and down to look for a friend.

"*Mané!*"

Everyone splashed into the river—a little extra purification. A large hole had been dug on the sandy beach, a short distance from the water. It was six feet long, about three feet wide and three deep—a little too reminiscent of a grave. As a matter of fact it was a large-scale model of an ant lion's trap.

Before it reaches the imago stage the ant lion is a shapeless insect with an ugly bloated belly ending in two disproportionately large pincers. A stomach and a pair of pincers, that's all there is to it. This monstrosity makes its devilish trap by scrabbling out the sand with its pincers, leaving a funnel-shaped pit at the bottom of which it hides. The sides are so crumbly that ants that have the misfortune to fall to the bottom cannot climb out again, not even the most agile. In any case, the ant lion hurls sand to hasten the fall of any attempting to escape, which are then sucked dry like all the others and fed to the greedy stomach.

The pit, then, looked like an ant lion's trap, but without that insect at the bottom; instead there were thousands upon thousands of ants, vainly trying to climb the sloping, crumbly sides. Those that did manage to get near the top were heartlessly pushed back by the children, who were thoroughly enjoying the game.

The villagers had now gathered around the pit. The chief had already explained to me what I must do. It was simple enough—merely to jump into the pit and lie down.

I can't say I was actually afraid, rather I was scared of being afraid. It needed no real courage, as my life was not in danger; but it called for great self-control, as once I was lying in the pit I had to keep still and let these thousands of insects, maddened by their few days' imprisonment in the bamboo pots, wreak their vengeance on me. I had thought—not being an entomologist—that they injected their formic acid by stinging, but closer observation showed that they first cut the skin with their powerful mandibles and then arched themselves to rub a drop of acid into the cut. It smarts terribly, and the aftereffects from a great number of bites are most unpleasant.

Well, it was up to me. As I went toward the pit the witch doctor told me to take off my loincloth. He must have added something like "cheating," for there were murmurs of protest from the onlookers, and the chief spoke to him sharply. I had the impression that the witch doctor would be pleased to see me refuse to go through with it. But I did not want to give him that satisfaction or disappoint the chief, who was looking at me a little anxiously.

So there I was in my birthday suit; there were a few giggles here and there. The pit had no steps to it and I had to jump down. The ants went into action at once.

The initiate is required to lie stretched out and remain still, and he must not show any signs of pain. When the warriors decide that he has passed the test, they tell him that he can get out. It lasts only a minute or two, perhaps a little longer; in that situation it is impossible to tell. Without a doubt, it hurt; it was very painful, but bearable. After the first few seconds I hardly felt anything. The most painful, almost unendurable, was the aftereffect. The formic acid quickly entered the bloodstream, and by then my whole body was one vast sore from the thousands of ant bites, though they were very superficial because the mandibles are so tiny. The itching became quite unbearable. When my time was up I had to be helped out of the pit, for my head was swimming and I couldn't see a thing. Then some women wiped away the little beads of blood covering my body, using rags that were not very clean, and dabbed fish brine all over me.

The salt ought to have made me smart, but I felt nothing at all. I had no idea whether the object of the brine was to add to the pain or to disinfect the sores.

For some minutes I felt as bad as ever; the acid continued to enter the bloodstream as though I had been given an injection. I think I must have passed out for a minute or two. When I became aware of my surroundings again I saw that I was alone on the beach. Everyone had gone back to the village. There were only a few dogs prowling around or sitting looking at me.

The *hican*, or fish brine, gave off a horrible smell and, strange as it may seem, that is the only distinct recollection I have of those moments.

I then had to go off into the jungle, far from the village, and keep away until my sores were healed. During this period the initiate—usually a lad of fifteen—is considered to be *hantou*, or cursed, untouchable, and anyone meeting him can kill him to avert the evil spirits. In no event must I return to the village before being completely healed, for my arrival would inevitably bring down the wrath of the spirits, and then of men.

It was nearly midday. I was just able to get up and make my way slowly toward the forest. I could hear sounds coming from the longhouse indicating that the feasting had already begun.

I had previously chosen a place where I could hole up during this convalescing period. It was four or five hours' walk from the village at the limit of its territory, below a weird and rugged mountain that looked as if it had been carved out by a mighty parang. There was a small, clear stream running between a steep slope covered with luxuriant vegetation and a high, smooth cliff to which clung a few trees and twisted creepers.

It was a quiet spot, where no one ever went. A village's territory is never very extensive; its border can usually be reached in half a day's walk. The territory is subdivided into family "concessions," in each of which the members of one family have the exclusive right to fish, hunt and gather poison. It is very important to know all these areas and the taboos pertaining to them, or one is likely to run into serious trouble.

I had to keep stopping and evening came before I had reached my haven. I was too exhausted to make myself a bamboo shelter; as I had no knife it would have taken me several hours. The leaves high above my head began to shake violently—it was going to rain in a few minutes. Apart from that rustling, the forest had grown very quiet. All the animals except the batrachians had hurried back to their shelters. The first big drops began to fall, then it pelted down. I tried to get some shelter under the roots of a huge tree; they came high out of the ground, spreading from the trunk like a ring of props. They did not provide much cover but it was the best I could find.

Night fell quickly and chilled the air. There I was, naked as the day I was born, without fire or a weapon, not even a parang, and to make matters worse my poor raw body burned with fever. This was the real testing ordeal; the ants were only the preliminary.

It was, of course, impossible to sleep, what with the cold, the rain and the fever. All night long I heard the frogs croaking. By dawn the situation was really serious. An icy, penetrating mist had followed the rain, and I was chilled to the marrow. I wanted to go on, but in the thick mist it would have been madness. In all probability I would get lost, and in addition I ran the risk of a bad fall; this part of the jungle abounded in boulders, streams with banks seven to ten feet high and, as everywhere in central Borneo, steep cliffs and deep ravines. One could be following a track and suddenly it would vanish at the edge of a rock face thirty or three hundred feet deep. Actually, accidents of this kind rarely happened as no one was stupid enough to walk through the chaotic jungle in a heavy mist. So I had to wait for the sun to break through, but of course the clouds remained low that day. Through the few mean openings in the canopy of foliage I could see only a dull gray sky. I would not even be able to warm myself in the sun when I reached the stream where I intended to camp. I had chosen that place just because it was the only one for miles around that was slightly open and received the sun. This was very important for survival because dry kindling is needed to light a fire and the dense jungle is no place to dry the mushrooms that are used for tinder. So heavy is the humidity in the jungle that a perfectly dry object becomes damp all through in a few hours if it is not given some protection. The humidity can almost be felt.

It is not easy to live in the jungle even with a good gun, the means of making a fire and a shelter at night. To live in the jungle without a gun but with clothing and the means of making a fire is what the army calls a survival test—and is a little less easy! Without any of that, without anything at all, ill and in grave risk of infection, only a "primitive" can possibly survive.

I should certainly not have survived very long without

my few months of learning about the jungle, which now served me well. In these hostile surroundings a man who has lost his way soon weakens; after three or four days hunger drives him to take a chance with the first plant or fruit that seems edible, only to be writhing in agony a few minutes or a few hours later, having eaten something poisonous. Three-quarters of what grows in the jungle is poisonous, and much of the remainder is too revolting to eat. In fact there are so few edible plants that one ignores the taste; there would otherwise be too little choice.

There are several ways of making fire, but they are possible only to the initiated. Only Australian aborigines and a few other primitive people can achieve any result from rubbing two sticks quickly together. In the first place it is quite hopeless without the right kind of sticks, and then there is the proper way of rubbing them together. I've tried striking two flints together hard, several times, and only succeeded in raising huge blisters on my hands. However, I did know how to make the famous Iban lighter. This is a piece of bamboo with a flint attached to the end. A tuft of very dry tinder made of mushroom fibers is placed close to it, and by striking the flint with another you raise sparks which set the tinder alight.

By the third day I had everything necessary to make fire. Until then my main food had been shellfish hidden under stones in the rivers; in some places they were very abundant. They were difficult to get out of their shells, so I smashed them between two flat stones. Most of the plants I ate had a nasty taste uncooked. But raw meat, as I already knew from experience, is far from being unpalatable.

That first morning I was lucky enough to catch a squirrel just as it was disappearing into a hole in a tree.

It was of the species *Dremomys everetti,* which lives near the ground and is usually found in mountainous regions. This one was a good size and provided me with about six ounces of meat, enough proteins for a day. I ate it raw; it was not very nice, for these creatures live chiefly on insects, as one can tell from the taste and smell. But in the circumstances it was a godsend.

I looked for something to eat throughout the day, when not building a shelter or getting together the material for a lighter. I nibbled insects as I caught them. As I had no knife I was unable to cut into rotting tree trunks or prize off old bark, which conceals larders of food for both animals and men, and had to satisfy myself with catching grasshoppers and wood lice.

Each evening I laid dozens of simple little snares for the numerous jungle rodents and gallinaceans. Squirrels abound in the daytime, but rats are undoubtedly the most active at night. At least thirty different species are known to exist in Borneo, and there are probably as many that are unknown. Some are tiny, like the *Haeromys* which weighs only one-third of an ounce, while others are large enough to make a good stew for two people; the giant rat (*Rattus infraluteus*) is one of these and is very common in central Borneo. The Iban name for it is *tikus bukit.* A good specimen weighs more than one pound. When I had discovered the knack, I caught one nearly every day at sunrise.

Sometimes I got my ration of proteins in the form of a snake, which would not be a gourmet's choice when served raw; but when they are boiled or grilled on hot embers some species can be really delicious.

To give some idea of how I spent my time, I will describe my second full day in the jungle, when I had reached my haven by the mountain stream.

I got up a little before sunrise. I had eaten practically

nothing the previous day and I was very hungry after the two bad nights I had spent lying on the naked earth, in the cold and the rain and plagued by hordes of mosquitoes. For breakfast I had to make do with a few mouthfuls of cool water. I waited until the dew had gone before starting to build my shelter. The bamboo canes had to be twisted around and around before I could break them off, and while choosing them I came across a few fern shoots; they tasted bitter and left my tongue feeling very disagreeable for some time afterward. I also ate three or four large hairy leaves, which gave me a nasty attack of diarrhea. I thought I'd better go easy on the greenery after that.

Suddenly a chestnut ball dashed from a thicket and disappeared in a couple of bounds, giving me just time to recognize it as a ground squirrel. I heard it make two or three more bounds, then there was silence; it could not have gone into hiding very far away. If it had been a tree squirrel I would not have bothered, but I knew there was just a chance of catching this one. A few yards away I noticed a fallen tree trunk covered with bright green moss; the branches had disappeared and one side had a dark, gaping hole in it. That was certainly not the squirrel's nest, for it was too obvious; but the squirrel in its panic could well have taken refuge there. The long bamboo cane I had in my hand was too thin to stun the squirrel, so I ran to the stream to get a heavy stone.

I poked into the hole with the bamboo cane—and something moved! Whether it was the squirrel or not, it meant food. With the stone ready in one hand, I poked about the hole again—and out shot the squirrel like a cannon ball. I just managed to catch it a blow on its back. It was still able to move, but couldn't get far, and I finished it off with a second blow. I used a long sharp splinter of bamboo to open and skin it, and ten minutes later it was hanging up nakedly pink, a pitiful sight. As

I had not finished making my Iban lighter, there was nothing to do but eat it raw.

By midday I had gathered a good supply of black-shelled snails. When eaten raw they are rather tough but quite tasty. However, there are few better ways of getting all sorts of intestinal complaints.

My "house" was finished long before nightfall; it was made of a few bamboo canes and leafy branches bound together with thin but very strong creeper. At least I had no fear of the rain now, but the mosquitoes were still a great problem. I kept away other insects with the wonderful sap the Ibans use, as I have already described; I used a sharp stone to cut the trunk to collect some.

I felt tired and feverish so put aside making the lighter. I only hoped that my bites would not become septic, for that would really mean the end—a horrible end, too. All I could do was to eat well and not stay too long under the trees, where it was much damper than on the tiny beach where I had my shelter.

My sores were far too extensive for me to apply herbal poultices, as is the native practice. My back hurt most; every time I made a sudden movement the newly formed scabs broke, and this attracted flies and mosquitoes. In the beginning I felt the most pain in my armpits and between my legs, but in fact there were few places that did not hurt, so that it was very difficult to find a position for sleeping.

I was usually treated to a good downpour toward the end of the afternoon and another in the middle of the night. But now that I had my shelter it did not matter so much. I gradually established a routine. When I knew my surroundings and their possibilities well I was able to eat better; and once I had completed the lighter and could make a fire, feeding was not a great problem.

The fever left me after a few days, but there were still oozing scabs on my stomach and back. I hoped that gangrene would not set in or worms lodge there. I had an idea that my return to the village was not yet imminent.

Each morning I added a stone to the little pile that showed the length of my stay. The number of times I counted them to be sure I was not mistaken! That did not help very much, as it was not the length of my solitude that mattered but the time it took for my skin to heal, for all traces of the bites to disappear.

In the end I stayed there twenty-one days; and despite being continually on the go searching for food, I was bored to death. If only I had had Totoche with me! Each day I seemed to sink further into a dull lethargy, though I did not have the lightheaded periods I had feared. Although my mind kept drifting I could always pull myself together when the occasion demanded. To prevent myself from succumbing I tried to keep my mind active, to concentrate, to talk. I tried to remember passages I had learned by heart, speeches from *Esther, Athalie* and *Othello,* but I realized that I had not retained very much apart from the first act of *Les Plaideurs.* I took a tree to witness—"Last year a judge took me into his service. . . ." When I could not remember a line, I made one up. At other times I said the multiplication tables. But you soon get tired of that. I played endless games of *pétanque* (a sort of bowls) with smooth pebbles, and this more than anything kept me alert. I made a great effort to take up my observations of animal life, but I had neither the heart nor the will power to persevere. But a desire gradually took hold to improve my equipment and thereby my food. I made a rough sort of stone ax, but the bamboo handle was not very good and came apart; I couldn't even reach the Stone Age. Then I made a stake to defend myself against any large animal that might come investigating, wrenching off a straight branch and hardening its sharp end in the fire. But I

didn't have to use it. I tried making a bow, but I did not
know the right materials to look for, and the weapon I
produced was unlikely to do any living thing much harm.

But with a harpoon I made, the tip being the bones of
a jungle rat, I eventually managed to spear a few fish.
Tuba fishing, however, easily gave me the best catches
and provided me with some wonderful moments when,
with a hollow feeling in my stomach, I sat watching
half-a-dozen fine catfish and some fern shoots cooking in
two hollow bamboos. There was a large handful of snails
being boiled, too, and the whole was seasoned with red
ants. What a pleasure it was to crush those detestable
insects between my fingers!

I could not see all of my back but I thought that the
sores had all cleared up; I had resisted the temptation to
pick off the dry scabs, for this would have delayed the
healing process. There were just one or two pink marks
where there had been a slight infection.

On the morning of the twenty-second day I set off in
good spirits for Rumah Selidapi. When I reached the
village there was no one about; it was mealtime, and
they were all in their *bileks* or on the verandah. So there
was general and complete surprise when I made my entrance—and I could hardly have been looking spick and
span after living rough and with a three weeks' beard.

"Dioudi! Dioudi!"

They all crowded around me. Lintaü ran out when she
heard my name, pushed everyone aside and threw herself into my arms. The chief appeared a few moments
later, examined me thoroughly on all sides and seemed
satisfied, and then the three of us went into his *bilek*. But
before I was allowed to eat I had to get rid of my beard.

How good rice and pork are! To finish off the meal I
had a bowl of *tuak* and then a thick, strong cigarette.
Home, sweet home!

So now I was an Iban warrior. At least, that is what

they said, but I was under no illusion. I would never be a real Iban. It is quite obvious that no European could ever become one.

One evening soon after my return, the chief came and sat by me during a little party. "We can start the tattooing tomorrow, if you like."

"What for?"

"Well, you've passed the test, so now you ought to have the tattoos."

"Must I really?" I wasn't at all keen on being turned into an art gallery. What would people take me for if I returned home with complicated designs on my back, chest and shoulders? "What designs were you thinking of doing?"

"We'll do *tanabaous* on your shoulders, so that the spirits of the jungle will protect you. On your back we'll do tattoos showing that you're married. You'll have others for hunting later on, probably."

Enough doodlings for me not to pass unnoticed on a French beach!

The tattooed designs are a kind of graduation certificate, marking the transition from adolescence to manhood. They are, so to speak, the identity card, visiting card and military service record of a Dayak. His life history is thus indelibly inscribed on his body for all to see. It's as good a way as any of knowing at first sight whom you're dealing with.

In view of my humble position in the clan I was entitled only to the two *tanabaous*, the two flower designs, for having passed the test; these, with a tattoo on the chest, are the distinctive marks of the Iban warrior. All the men in the village were thus decorated.

Early in the morning I was settled comfortably on the communal verandah, lying on my back with a cushion under my head, near the light from the doorway. The evening before, Lintaü had collected some soot from above the candle. This, with a little sweetened water added, made a very dark, thin paste. A hardwood needle stuck in a little stick was dipped in the paste, and the stick was struck sharply with a small wooden mallet so that the needle pierced the skin to a depth of two or three millimeters.

I waited patiently for work to begin. Father-in-law had got out the wooden blocks that were used to mark the designs. They were smeared with candleblack and then pressed hard on the part of the body to be tattooed, thus imprinting the design on the skin. This avoided mistakes which would undoubtedly have left the victim with an inferiority complex.

Tangale made sure that the paste was well mixed, then dipped the triangular needle into it and started to trace the design on my skin. He gave a sharp tap with his mallet and the wooden needle penetrated slightly. Tap, tap; tap, tap . . . two or three taps a second. After a score or so he took a dirty rag and wiped away the blood and any black smudges to check the design. Then he went on again. The first design, on my left shoulder, was a crude representation of a flower with five petals and had a whorl in the middle. It was about four inches in diameter, and the tattooing of it took tens of thousands of pricks and sixteen hours of suffering.

It was quite bearable to begin with, hardly worth making a face. Besides, the Ibans would have taken a very poor view of that. The patient had to keep a serene countenance; there must be no moaning and groaning. That would have stopped operations at once and left the unfortunate Iban with an unfinished tattoo—an inconceivable disgrace! Once the outline of the flower was completed, the five petals had to be blackened evenly all over, which meant that the same places were gone over again and again. These thousands of pricks set my nerves on edge until I nearly screamed. Each time the operator wiped the tattoo with his dirty rag he looked to see if there were any light patches left. If so—and there often were—he went over the places yet again. When the man who was tattooing got tired, another took his place. But there was no respite for the patient.

Right at the start, little drops of blood had begun to ooze. At the end of the operation I had a splendid sore which had every chance of becoming infected, considering the hygienic conditions prevailing. For instance, instead of using boiling water to clean the tattoo, they always used the piece of old rag which had been lying on the floor.

The following day a fine scab had formed, and pus oozed out everywhere. It could stay like that for ten days or for months, depending on one's constitution or the virulence of the germs. I must have had a good supply of antibodies, for after only seven or eight days the Ibans were able to proceed with the final stage of insuring that the blackened parts of the design were evenly colored. After the "drying out" there are usually some patches that are lighter than the rest, and these have to be gone over once more. So I had a few more hours of suffering.

Without waiting for the first tattoo to heal, they started on the second, on my right shoulder. The procedure was as before, except that we did have a break for the midday meal. Again men took turns at the tattooing. Some were fairly rough and tapped hard on the stick, while others were gentler. The hours dragged past, long and dreary, punctuated by the irregular tapping. I smoked a lot to pass the time and also to explain the tears that welled up now and again; I found it very difficult to keep a hold on myself. This second tattoo became infected and I was feverish for some days. However, it was nothing serious.

Now that I had *tanabaous* adorning my shoulders I was supposed to be under the protection of the spirits of the jungle. No misfortune could happen to me—unless, of course, I failed in my numerous obligations to those spirits. There still remained two similar designs to be tattooed on the lower part of my back; these related to my family and conjugal life. As that part of the body has particularly susceptible nerves, I found this tattooing even more painful.

When I had fully recovered I went out hunting again. I longed to make a really big kill—a four-hundred-pound boar, for instance, which would entitle me to an Iban "decoration" and to a well-embroidered tale.

I had been out since early morning and was returning with just one squirrel, having missed a monkey. My dart had probably glanced off a leaf; and the monkey had leapt away, giving the alarm to the whole band. After that I had not even sighted a wretched gibbon, just heard one or two in the distance. When I reached the spot I found a few squashed fruit on the ground, still moist, but not a sign of a gibbon. However, I was not on piecework, thank God, so I chose a place that was not too damp and was devoid of ants, and got out my picnic lunch—some dried meat and a hollow bamboo containing sticky rice which had been cooked the day before. To get at this I split the bamboo with my parang and then scooped out the rice. It was delicious. The heat of the day had warmed the water in my gourd, so I emptied it on the ground and went to a clear stream that was gurgling a little distance away.

I had a quick bathe, filled the gourd and started back, whistling happily. As I parted some ferns I suddenly heard a terrific growl, and stopped dead. There facing me was a splendid Malaysian bear, erect on its two short legs and baring its teeth at me. I remained motionless. Like a fool, I had gone off to the stream unarmed, leaving my blowpipe and parang near my wicker basket. It was a stupid, unforgivable thing to do, which could have cost me dear. It is very difficult to stop a charging, determined bear—and they usually are determined, especially when disturbed while eating. And this black plantigrade was eating what remained of my rice and meat! To turn and run would have been useless, for despite their clumsy appearance these animals are quick off the mark and very speedy. It would be equally useless to try and climb a tree, for they are expert climbers, too. The best tactic was to stay quite still, but not to look the bear in the eyes, contrary to the advice given in popular tales. In fact to stare at a wild beast is the last thing one should do; it is like bringing a positive and a negative charge together— a single look causes a spark. That is one of the first lessons to be learned in taming animals.

The bear dropped gently onto all fours and looked at me out of the corner of its little dark-brown, expressionless eyes. That is another characteristic of these animals; one can never tell what they are thinking, and it is almost impossible to know whether they are going to charge or turn away. With a panther, lion or tiger there are definite indications: the tail begins to wave, the ears flatten and the animal crouches. . . . An experienced hunter can tell what is going to happen and, above all, when the animal is about to spring. But bears give practically no sign of their intentions. They rarely stand erect to attack, as is often shown in drawings or described in adventure stories; they charge on all fours at a speed surprising for their size, and they usually go for the lower part of the chest and then work toward the victim's head. They use their paws only to hold the victim or to tear at him, not to deal blows. In my experience with caged bears I have seen these notorious blows with the paw given only when the bear was not sure of its superior strength or was afraid. It is more a means of defense, and a very power-

ful means considering the strength of these animals—
greater than that of a tiger, in my opinion.

However, as I stood there tense and wondering—what
a surprise! The bear suddenly turned and bolted into the
undergrowth. There was a cracking of branches and then
silence. What a relief!

It was certainly the last time I would go anywhere in
the jungle without taking my blowpipe. I had missed a
fine opportunity of taking back many pounds of excellent
red meat, which is delicious in a stew or with sauce.
Bear's liver is used by the Ibans in a number of medicines, and with the bile they make a very potent poison.
This fright had brought me to my senses and I felt in
good form again. I set off, walking as quietly as possible,
fully alert and keeping a keen eye on the trees and
thickets.

A little later I heard a rustling of leaves and went carefully toward the sound. A few yards away a sapling was
shaking in a most unusual manner; then I saw that a fine
stag of uniform color (*Cervus unicolor*) was nibbling at
the leaves. Although rather dry and tough, venison was
not to be scorned; besides, when smoked and dried the
meat would keep very well. The animal before me had
a fine pair of antlers, or at least as fine a pair as could be
expected for his natural surroundings. His brothers that
roam the uplands of Southeast Asia have huge antlers,
but in the jungle they would not get very far with such
attire.

This stag seemed a good size for the region. When it
stretched its neck toward a branch I caught sight of its
forequarters and judged it to stand about five feet from
the ground. But I couldn't manage to get into a good
position to use my blowpipe; there was still a screen of
ferns and branches between me and the stag. I waited
until it pulled at the sapling and its head went behind
a tree trunk, then I got within a dozen feet of it. My

presence was still unnoticed, but I had to shoot quickly as the stag would soon move on; there were no more leaves left on the sapling, which was just a stem pointing skyward. Taking great care not to touch any branches with my blowpipe, I eased myself into position to take aim. I was so near that I could almost have pricked its haunches with the spearhead. I scarcely heard the dart leave the blowpipe and even less the impact. The silence was suddenly shattered by the bucking and kicking of the stag. I had hit it in the neck, close to the jugular vein I had aimed at; as there are plenty of blood vessels in that area, I knew the stag could not last long. I've never enjoyed sights of that kind; I don't like seeing animals suffer, nor men either. I went up to it to finish it off with my spearhead, but it was writhing about so much that I misjudged my first two stabs and struck it in the chest, but at my third attempt I pierced the neck. I twisted about in its throat, and a few seconds later it was still.

It was a very big one! The Borneo rusa averages about two hundred pounds; very occasionally one reaches four hundred pounds. This stag was nearer the latter than the former weight. I admired its dark-brown coat, which blended so well with the surroundings, but I was not there to go into raptures. I cut up the carcass, hoisted the forequarters, legs included, onto my back, attaching it with some strips of bark, and set off back to the village as fast as I could. I would return later with a member of the family for the rest of the carcass; I was not cut out to be a hefty meat porter. I had a heavy enough load as it was, and slithered about several times. I was soon breathless and sweating profusely, and leaned against a big tree to rest. The stag's blood trickled down my back and legs, attracting swarms of vindictive gnats. However, I had to press on to the village, as it was still a good hour's walk for an unburdened man, and I wanted to go back and fetch the remainder of the carcass before nightfall. It would be stupid to lose so much good fresh meat.

As I straightened up I heard a short growl some distance away, which I could not at first identify. Then I saw a boar, much nearer than I had thought. It was gnawing at an overripe durian and had its back to me, absorbed in its feast; it had not even heard my approach. Without waiting to unfasten and put down my burden, I slipped the blowpipe from my shoulder (the usual position when walking) and, keeping my eyes on the boar, I fumbled for a dart. The animal was only thirty feet away—which must be a record for getting within clear range of a boar in this jungle. It was a fine target for a blowpipe.

Pfft!

In reply came a loud growl. The animal spun around and sighted me at once. Something had gone wrong; it ought to be rolling on the ground and writhing in agony, until I finished it off. Instead it charged at me. I could see only its narrow chest and yellowish head, still smeared with pulp from the durian. In such an event, according to the Iban hunter's manual, the thing to do is to put one knee to the ground and point the spear-tipped blowpipe at the charging animal, just like a wild-beast tamer; not forgetting, of course, to jump aside at the last moment. That is exactly what I was unable to do, laden with the stag's forequarters, which must have weighed eighty or ninety pounds, and weary as well.

Everything happens very quickly in that kind of encounter. One needs to be very experienced or have very quick reactions to do the right thing. I obviously had neither, for I received a violent blow and before I realized what had happened was sent flying several feet into what is called a bearded palm—a small tree covered with inch-long prickles. Another of Mother Nature's fine inventions which abounds in some parts of the jungle. However, at that moment I was far less interested in the flora (in spite of the pricks) than in the fauna. Luckily, the boar had "swallowed" the spearhead, had run full tilt onto it and was literally impaled on the blowpipe; this had gone through its neck and was sticking out just above its ribs, which did not prevent it from flailing about and kicking up the devil's own row. I could have put an end to its sufferings with a stab or two of my parang, if only it had allowed me to do so. But instead, despite this awful wound, it managed to get to its feet and prepared to charge at me again. Just then the end of the blowpipe got caught in the foot of a tree and broke off. The boar fell to the ground and stayed there, blood bubbling from its mouth. I tried to get at its throat, as I had with the stag, but these animals have a thick hide and I had a job to make the kill.

A bear, a stag and a boar all in one day! I would never see anything like it again. A triple encounter like that does not often happen, I hasten to add, in the life of a Dayak.

It does not often happen either that a hunter makes so many mistakes without paying for them. First, I ought never to have left my blowpipe behind, not for a moment. Second, the boar charged me because I shot a dart at it which had already been used on a squirrel. Third, before shooting at the boar I ought to have freed myself of my burden. Those were oversights which could have had serious consequences, and I had the firm impression that luck had been with me.

There were great rejoicings that evening, with an unforgettable blow-out. The stag was said to be the biggest brought into the village for a very long time.

"Hey, son-in-law, we must drink to that!"

The chief never lost an opportunity to tipple. I could not avoid following suit, and at this rate I felt it would kill me off sooner or later. There were some days when their confounded *tuak* lay heavily on my stomach.

Not only did Tangale lose no opportunity of getting drunk, he did not miss any for making my life difficult either.

"This is a great thing! For a very big stag like that"—at this rate the stag would soon be an elephant—its size had already doubled—"we can do another tattoo. A large one this time!"

The men sitting around greatly approved. *"Niaï rusa."*

They got out the wooden blocks to choose an appropriate design. There was one a foot long, very decorative in its way—but how many hours of suffering was it going to cost me? Before I left France, nearly two years ago, I would have leapt to the ceiling at the mere idea of having one small tattoo on my forearm. Now these blasted Ibans were doing their best to turn me into a walking picture, and I was letting them. Worse, I was even giving them my opinion on the choice of a design. "I don't like that one . . . this isn't bad. . . ." If this sort of thing continued, I would go off hunting one fine morning and come back with a freshly cut Punan head in my game bag.

It was decided to start the tattooing session the following morning. That evening Lintaü collected some soot in a coconut shell hung over the lighted resin candle. In view of the large design, the session began very early in the morning. I lay on my stomach for this one. But by evening only the outline had been completed. The artists took turns throughout the day, and each had his own way of tapping on the needle. But it would not have done for me to make any comment, even when some of them struck a little too hard.

I was given a rest the following day; no work could be done on the open sores or the scabs that were forming.

The tattoos for the initiation and my family status had taken more than sixty hours. This one and the next—making seven designs in all—would take about one hun-

dred and twenty hours. During the process my friends
kept me company, and that helped to pass the time and
make me forget the pain.

"How's it going, Dioudi, not too bad?"

"*Nadaï saket!* Can't feel a thing!" (What a hypocrite!)

"Ao! Would you like a cigarette?"

"Yes, it's a bit boring."

I was not even aware of the operator stopping to put
more blacking on the needle, for the pain continued all
the time. Moreover, the ceaseless tapping and very likely
the cigarettes I chain-smoked gave me a terrible head-
ache. I have since calculated that a well-decorated warrior must have spent about six hundred hours—say, fifty
days—of his life under the needle.

Chief Tangale was literally covered with designs, some
of them very complicated. They were certainly pretty,
but a little loud for my taste. I felt that I should be
embarrassed later on, when back home and strolling
about in swimming trunks on the beach. I could imagine
what people would say:

"Do you see that man over there? Where on earth did
he come from?"

Or perhaps friends would say to me: "I hope you don't
mind my asking, but where did you get all those tattoos?
Were you in the Foreign Legion?"

"No," I would answer, "and I haven't been in prison
or in the navy. They're just souvenirs I brought back from
my travels."

"Oh, I see," would be the puzzled reply.

I wouldn't want to tell them the whole story, not from
any modesty on my part but because it is rather long
and most people would suspect that I was distorting the
truth.

The days slipped past, one often like another but rarely
dull. It must not be thought that life among the Ibans is

one long round of fantastic adventures, countless dangers and one accident after another. Admittedly, the unexpected probably occurs more often than it does in the life of a ticket puncher or an office clerk, but certainly not frequently enough to supply material for an adventure serial. In the first place, one soon gets used to the unexpected; and at the time it does not seem so important or of such an adventurous nature as it does when one is thinking or writing about it later.

I looked through my notebook occasionally and found entries such as: "That fool Palak has fallen out of a tree and fractured his tibia. The witch doctor put it in a splint. I don't know where he learned this, but it's not bad at all." And a little further on: "It's a week since anyone killed a boar, and I'm getting fed up with a diet of bamboo shoots. I'd give anything for a good steak."

All around me there were children growing up, others coming into the world, and a good many leaving it to join their ancestors. The mortality rate was frightful. A warrior as strong as a horse would die quietly, when a few antibiotics could have soon put him right. The saddest case of all perhaps was that of the very likable ironsmith, who was being eaten away by leprosy. He was literally dropping to bits, utterly rotted; not at all a pretty sight, and he smelled bad. He still went on working, however, and even went hunting occasionally. The disease seemed to progress very slowly, and to me that was the most awful thing about it. He ate with the rest of us, naturally, with his one good hand; but unfortunately that was the hand he used to scratch himself. I couldn't help giving a shudder when I saw him picking a morsel from the common dish. Poor old fellow, he never suspected that he often prevented me from enjoying a fine slice of pork. When he joined our group I took care never to help myself after him.

There were other sad stories. Two little girls were

drowned in one day; a lad disappeared in the river—no one ever knew whether he was drowned or eaten by a crocodile. One of my ex-girl friends died after less than a week's illness—was it from malaria or what? Then there were the hunting accidents. An Iban with slow reflexes was gored by a vicious boar and remained a whole afternoon and one night alone in the jungle, only an hour's walk from the village, with half of his guts hanging out. Another hunter died in similar circumstances. Yet another had his feet nibbled at by a Malaysian bear; gangrene set in and he died soon afterward. The same kind of mishap happened to another, but he recovered, although he would walk splayfooted for the rest of his life. There was no epidemic while I was living in the village. My health remained good, so the climate must have suited me. I wasn't attacked by any parasites or germs; at least, not that I noticed.

I may not have mentioned how the Ibans answer the calls of nature: they just squat over any of the many gaps in the floor of the longhouse. The pigs clear up down below. Nothing very special or harmful about that; but when I had to eat some of those pigs I began to feel queasy. The evil-smelling morass must have been swarming with disease-carrying germs.

One evening the village elders had a grand meeting on the verandah; with all the gravity and dignity of a town council they deliberated over the choice of the warriors to take part in an expedition outside their territory. It was a matter of great import. As everyone could not go, decisions had to be made as to who should stay behind, which brought to the fore petty intrigues, family rivalries and personal influence. However, it was all arranged without coming to blows, although the selecting of the men to form the expedition took all night. As I expected, I was one; they had to show off their mascot.

We would not be leaving until ten days later—days of

feverish activity, not quite that of soldiers going up to the front, but more than that of countryfolk going up to the big city. The members of the expedition got out their best garments and carefully packed them in wicker baskets, and polished up their weapons. The object of the expedition was to barter dammar (vegetable resin) and boars' tusks for blocks of salt. I tried to find out more about the expedition but it was difficult to get any precise information. I could not even discover where we were going.

"It's in that direction, about ten days' walk" was the most I could gather.

I understood that we would be crossing the mountains and were going to visit Ibans who did not speak quite the same language; but a very important fact was that our route would take us through enemy territory. Perhaps the enemy were *panjamon?* I hoped not, for I was not at all keen to do battle, not even to defend the honor of the village.

"Will we see any Punans?"

"It's possible, though they usually keep out of sight. The only time they come to the village is when they need tobacco. They're very frightened of us, as we're apt to cut off their heads if they arrive at a bad time." (That's a good one! No wonder the Punans don't come very often.) "They don't even make *tuak*." (Certainly the most severe criticism an Iban could make. I had told them that a great amount of *tuak* was drunk in my country, that we even had a reputation for it, which had pleased them very much.) "They live only by hunting. No one can stalk an animal as well as they can, and they can walk without stopping for days on end. That's why it's difficult to kill them. They always get away; they cover up their tracks and sometimes they even set traps. But they're not really bad men, they're more like animals."

NINE

Resin for Salt

We set off at a very early hour, after a memorable fare-well party the previous evening. There was no woman in the expedition. Those we left behind looked rather sad, the men as well as the women. The members of the expedition consisted of Chief Tangale, the witch doctor, two or three greatly decorated warriors and a dozen men much esteemed by the council of elders.

There was no difficulty the first morning as we were passing through the clan's territory and everyone knew the way. But toward the end of the day it was a very different matter; we had to follow the guide, the one man who had made the journey before. It completely beat me how he picked the way to go. We were passing through a sea of vegetation in which I could make out nothing whatever to serve as a guiding mark. It was very odd—there we were in the same forest, with trees and mountains so similar to our own, and yet we no longer felt "at home."

Despite being burdened with many pounds of goods to barter we went at a fast pace, without a single halt, not even for the midday meal. When anyone felt hungry he pulled out a handful of rice and a few slices of dried meat and ate on the march. There was little undergrowth to hinder us, though now and again we had to show our gymnastic ability to get across a tangle of lianas as thick as our thighs or to pass through a copse of thorny bamboo, which meant that the file of men had to crawl on their knees for fifty—or five hundred—yards between the slender, elegantly curved stems. Occasionally, too, there were huge fallen tree trunks to get around, some of them rotting away. But these were all minor hazards, common to every tropical forest. The real difficulty was the slippery ground, so slippery in fact that the one great problem, the only problem, was to remain on one's feet.

I was not alone in slithering about on the slopes and slipping on the tangle of thick lianas forming a natural bridge across rivers and streams, and on the dead branches carpeted with moss which were worse than a frost-covered pavement. On many occasions it would have been easier to ford a river; but no, rather than take a little more time and get slightly wet, we had to cross by these wretched bridges. Anyone would think we were out to beat some cross-country record. It was not that I was frightened of falling—there was little danger even if I had—but I would have felt ashamed at holding up the march by my inexperience. So for the first day or two each difficult crossing was absolute anguish; the fear of falling completely cramped my style. However, I got over this after a few days, and then things were much better with me, except that I found each day's stage a little too long and the pace too fast. My leg muscles were soon as hard as rock, and when we stopped for the night I had cramp badly in my calves; this woke me up several times and in between I had nightmares in which trees kept slipping past, trees and more trees, and I yearned for a rest in my comfortable hammock.

As I had feared, we began to follow the beds of small streams more and more frequently, over slippery pebbles and stones. How I hated that! And now and again we had to climb cliffs, scrambling up great falls of rock and around huge boulders twined together by thick creepers. We met no one. But probably we were deliberately avoiding the villages on our line of march.

On the fifth day there was a halt to go hunting. While half of us stayed with the goods, the others went off in

twos in various directions. They were all back in good
time, without ever losing their way. It was a mystery to
me; just native instinct, I supposed. Artful old Tangale
was the first to return with a good bag—a young boar.
There was not much of it left by the end of the meal. I
had enjoyed a good slice of the heart and some fat grilled
on the hot embers of the fire. I noticed some of the others
baking fish wrapped in leaves; the ingenious thing about
this was that when the fish was cooked and the wrapping
removed, the skin came off with it. There was no *tuak* to
drink, but we were a happy party nevertheless and the
joyful atmosphere almost made us forget our sore feet.

A few days later we crossed what seemed to be unfriendly territory, for we walked at an even faster pace
and well strung out, each man carrying his blowpipe at
the ready. In these circumstances the Ibans behave like
animals on the prowl, constantly peering about them,
ever watchful for traps in their path. We were sure setting a pace! I didn't know where we were going, but it
was quite a way! We had been on the march for a fortnight, and at our rate of progress we must have covered
a good many miles. Each day's stage, except when we
took time out for hunting, lasted at least twelve hours.
We started at about five in the morning and did not stop
until the end of the afternoon, giving ourselves just time
to build a shelter before nightfall. We had crossed several mountains and every one of us was ready for a rest.

Finally, one fine afternoon we came over the top of a
rounded hill and there before us was a rice field in the
forest. A couple of miles lower down the roof of a longhouse showed between the trees, and just beyond was a
shiny stretch of water, probably a small river.

It did not take us long to get down to the village,
where we received a friendly welcome. How pleasant it
was to have a roof over one's head again! One of the first
things I noticed was that the woven garments were not

of local make but almost certainly of Chinese manufacture, and I wondered if there was a town within reach. I had no idea at all of where I was; I had taken no notice of the direction in which we had been traveling, and I could equally well be in Indonesia as in Sarawak, for all I knew.

I found out in the evening that the river on which the village stood was a tributary of the Kapuas River, and that there was a small army post at less than a week's journey by outboard pirogue. I didn't like the sound of that. If the famous bamboo radio went into action the army post would soon learn that a very odd European was living up-country—probably a parachuted enemy agent, a spy. . . .

This village was an outpost of civilization. It was visited once or twice a year by Chinese traders bringing cloth, glass beads, cheap jewelry and, of course, salt. "My" Ibans were going to barter their precious dammar and other goods for such shoddy products, including Aji-No-Moto, a kind of powder made in Japan used for heightening the taste of soup. The one worthwhile commodity they obtained was salt—but at what cost! A pound of it, weighed against stones supposedly correct, was bartered for ten times the amount of dammar. This resin is used by the Chinese for making lacquer, and I knew that the amount the Ibans were exchanging for salt was worth a small fortune. I also knew how difficult it was to collect, having helped to do so, climbing fifty or sixty feet up trees with the risk of a spectacular fall.

I suddenly felt deluded. I had never imagined that my Iban friends could have succumbed to the demon of commerce. And at this rate they would soon be completely taken in by civilization. Their tribal brothers in this village had already learned how to rob them—having been themselves robbed by the Chinese. A really vicious circle. . . .

The following evening, when we were all sitting and chatting after the meal, I tried to get my bearings. I asked my neighbor, one of the locals, if he could tell me where I had come from—where Rumah Selidapi was situated.

"Where do you come from?" He looked puzzled. "But you know that better than I do, since it's you who have come here."

Such logic ruled out any further attempt to obtain information.

"Tangale, how much longer are we going to stay here?" I asked.

I had no desire to hang about in this longhouse with an army post comparatively near. If a patrol came this way I would find myself in custody.

"We'll just stay for the feast, then we'll start back," said Tangale. "The village will be expecting us."

That was a relief. It was not that the people here were antipathetic, but I didn't feel safe; this made me uneasy and spoiled everything.

The feast was soon polished off; it seemed to me not nearly as good or as jolly as the most ordinary of our own orgies. Most decidedly I was not feeling at ease. It was time for a change of air. My companions, moreover, were of the same opinion. We had a last meal with our hosts— strongly flavored with Aji-No-Moto—and started on our way back.

It was a pleasure to be in the forest again. And to think that only a week before we had had more than enough of all these trees! We kept up a fast pace, faster even than on the outward journey, for there was less to carry; the salt weighed not nearly as much as its worth in resin. The time spent in hunting was reduced to a minimum, and we ate rice and fern shoots much more often than boar's fat. Consequently, the evenings in the shelter were rather dreary.

It was during this return journey that there occurred

one of the awful hunting accidents I mentioned earlier. One evening a little before sunset we dispersed into the jungle with our blowpipes for a short period of hunting. We usually went in couples, an elementary precaution to take, but this evening one man was delayed a little and rashly set off alone. When we gathered together again at the camping site, one man was missing. Night had fallen, and there was no question of getting an Iban to budge once it was dark. I plunged back into the jungle but did not search very far, as I had no desire to get lost. When I returned I asked for someone to go with me, but it was hopeless.

In the morning we all went to look for the missing man, cautiously though, for it was not beyond the bounds of possibility that he had fallen into an ambush. Eventually the man was found not very far from where we had camped. He was horribly wounded: his stomach was split open as though by a sword and at least six feet of his intestines were hanging out, grimy with earth and covered with ants. Apparently his guts were still whole; nevertheless, I didn't think much of his chances. For he was still alive! Even more incredibly, he was still conscious after twelve hours or so in that condition. We carried him carefully back to camp, but as we had expected he died soon afterward.

It was not difficult, from the torn-up ground at the place of the accident, to imagine what had happened. He must have surprised a sow with her young, and before he could place himself in a defensive position with his iron-tipped blowpipe the sow had charged and caught him in the thigh, knocking him down. She had turned and charged again, and split open his stomach with a terrible thrust of her snout. Then she had collected her young and hurried off into the depths of the jungle.

This fatal accident weighed heavily upon the morale of the expedition. Fortunately we were only three or four days' march from Selidapi and were all eager to be back.

Everyone was anxious about his family, and at the long-house they must have been worried about us. So it was with obvious joy and relief that we entered village territory. We trotted along, the bundles of salt bumping on our shoulders, and reached the village as night was falling, to receive the most delirious welcome I ever saw. Our wives and children flocked around us, all talking at the same time and looking to see if we were unhurt.

It was a happy moment for everyone—except for the poor woman who had lost her husband. She was pitiful to look at, sitting in a corner and weeping silently, her two children playing around her, too young to understand the tragedy that had befallen them. She was later given a large share of the salt, and many friends took rice and chickens to her; the chief, who was the richest man in the village, presented her with one of his largest pigs. It was an example of spontaneous solidarity that was a pleasure to see. A widow was always helped out by her relatives and neighbors, by the whole village in fact, and she had no great problems of a material kind. No one was ever left destitute. The aged and the wounded, the sick and the idiots, all were members of the community provided they behaved as Ibans, and community life had a real meaning here. It was not a competitive society; there was no "I'm all right, Jack" but rather "All for one, and one for all."

The long communal verandah soon looked like a fairground with all the goods we had brought back spread out on matting—the manufactured cloth, the blocks of salt, the beads and shoddy jewelry (which all lost its color in a week and was thrown away). The villagers went into raptures over it all, commenting with many exclamations and much laughter. No sooner had we put down our burdens and taken off our equipment than the women brought us large bowls filled to the brim with *tuak*. Lintaü, whom I had greatly missed during the expedition, brought me a calabash holding at least a pint.

The returned warriors could hardly wait to tell of their adventures; certainly they had no need of a stimulant to make their tongues wag. To hear them talking about the feast given by the other village, which had seemed to me nothing out of the ordinary, one would have thought it was the celebration of the century . . . hundreds of men drunk, mounds of pork eaten, girls abounding, all pretty and very willing . . . O happy Ibans!

"And how about here? Anything happen?" the chief asked.

Batou, the warrior who had been left in charge of the village, remained silent for half a minute before replying. He obviously had some bad news for us.

"Men from the next village"—he pointed in its direction—"came hunting. We saw their tracks. They killed a *babi* [wild boar] in our territory."

Silence fell. In a moment the atmosphere had completely changed; eyes narrowed, bowls of *tuak* remained poised in midair, halfway to mouths.

Batou slowly emptied his own bowl, looked at the chief and then at the silent crowd, all in a very theatrical manner. He turned his head and nodded toward his *bilek*, and said in a flat voice, though he must have been bursting with pride, "*Dua kepala* [two heads]."

He looked down with false modesty and helped himself to some more *tuak*.

The men's smooth faces shone in the light from the smoky candles; they went on drinking again and continued their talk as though nothing had happened. Yet all the returned warriors were dying to hear Batou's story.

A little later Tangale asked him in an offhand way, "You weren't wounded?"

"*Nadaï*," was all he replied, still playing for effect.

After a few minutes Tangale had to put it to him more directly. "Where and how did it all happen?"

Then Batou began to tell his story, calmly and almost

coldly at first, but warming to it as he went and gesticulating, and he ended by acting out the final scene. This
was his account:

Two hunters from another village, taking advantage
of the absence of many of our warriors, had intruded into
our territory. They had left quite clear tracks, perhaps
in defiance, and these were found very soon afterward
by a young man of Selidapi who was hunting in the
vicinity. He hurried back to give the alarm. The acting
chief happened to be taking a siesta in his *bilek;* he
called for all the available warriors and they set off on
a manhunt, the idea being to lay several ambushes.

The two intruders were believed to be from the nearest village, that is to say, the one only three days' walk
away. Relations between this village and Selidapi were
not of the best, but I gathered that an incident of this
kind was nevertheless exceptional. The forest is quite
large enough for there to be no need for anyone to tres-
pass into another's territory. So very likely it was a pro-
vocative act.

Although the forest is vast, hunters prefer to take certain ways through it rather than others, especially when
in a hurry. Batou laid his ambushes along the way the
two intruders were likely to take, posting himself at the
most likely place of all, a ford that was very practicable
and often used. And, sure enough, the two were spotted
approaching the river at this point.

They looked warily about them—but not keenly
enough—then entered the water. One was carrying a
young boar on his back. Batou had craftily concealed
himself on the far side of the river, which was outside
the village territory. He waited until the two were in
midstream, where the water came up to their waists,
then took aim with his blowpipe at the man without a
burden, the more dangerous of the two, and hit him with
a dart. The man gave a yell, tried to pull the dart out,

lost his footing and, paralyzed by now, went under and was drowned. His companion dropped the boar he was carrying and took his blowpipe from his shoulder as he made his way to the riverbank as quickly as possible.

Batou shot a dart at him but missed in his hurry; however, the other had not noticed the dart. An eight-foot-long blowpipe is a weapon difficult to handle, and taking a dart from the quiver, slipping it in and aiming require a certain amount of time; and much can happen during this period. So Batou wisely stayed still to avoid being spotted. The other, thinking he was out of danger now that he had reached the right side of the river, set off at a trot but looking behind him every couple of yards. Thus it was that he ran on to Batou's spearhead. Our hero had remained hidden until then; although a duel with parangs would have been more noble, it had the distinct disadvantage of placing the adversaries on an equal footing, and Batou preferred getting his head without leaving bits of himself on the field of battle. Before the other could recover from his surprise, Batou had stabbed him again, in the chest. And a few seconds later off came his head, with two or three furious slashes from Batou's parang.

That was how Batou had got the two heads, a double seldom achieved. They were considered to be two fine trophies, and still smelled. In fact, for a day or two I wondered how the inhabitants of the longhouse could put up with such a stench.

I took a couple of photos of them. Unfortunately I had no flash and hoped for the best as I took a time exposure by the poor light of candles, leaning against a post. One head still had its hair, and there were hundreds of white grubs seething around the mouth, which hung low—awfully low. A grim object altogether . . . and the flies! A grim custom, most definitely. Well, that was their affair. They could cut off whatever heads they liked, so long as mine was not one of them to make the longhouse reek. The story of these two heads ended on a gruesome note. When the last eyeball fell out it was found on the floor by a young child, who, probably not liking the smell of it, threw it into the cooking pot; and it was recovered by his mother during the next meal—from a mouthful of food. This happened a week after the two heads had been chopped off.

It was not improbable that the men in the next village would seek to get their own back and send a small expedition to recover the two souls which we had stolen. According to Iban belief, the village had been deprived of two spiritual forces, and the only way of retrieving them was by capturing two other heads. However, nothing happened, so very likely the two intruders had told no one of their intentions and their deaths were attributed to a hunting accident.

The incident led me to wonder what I should do if Selidapi ever found itself at war with another clan or tribe. If I had not been chosen for the expedition to barter for salt I would certainly have accompanied Batou to ambush the two enemy hunters, and in that case what would I have done? I find it difficult to answer. Which party was right in this matter? Is it important to know who was in the right or the wrong? Has anyone the right to kill a man for stealing a wild boar? By Iban standards and customs, yes. But however much I tried, I could not become an Iban 100 percent. Yet the question remained. A year or two previously, if I had been asked to take part in an expedition which might include chopping off someone's head, I would have firmly declined right away. But now I was not sure. . . .

The problem never arose and I had no need to debate with myself. There were no more intrusions into the village territory and no punitive expedition took place during the rest of my stay there. Which was just as well.

TEN

How to Catch
a Poisonous Snake

My ball-point was finished, I had no paper and I could take only half-a-dozen more photos. I had carefully stored the exposed films in their little aluminum cases but I doubted whether they would be much good after six months in such a damp climate.

However, that didn't keep me awake at night. I had become one of a world apart, where I was happy and where such little worries had no place.

Still, all was not for the best in that best of worlds. At least, not always. I had had several clashes with villagers —nothing serious, but a little unpleasant all the same. The Ibans are very hospitable people, perhaps the most hospitable in the world, but unfortunately they are very touchy about their innumerable customs and taboos, and become quite annoyed if you break any, even inadvertently. From the very first the witch doctor had taken a dislike to me, quite unjustifiably, I thought. Later, my marriage had set a whole family—the hapless fiancé's— against me. Their hostility was more understandable, but I was by now very pleased with the outcome.

Everybody was supposed to know the law, all the rules, here as anywhere else, and the Ibans made no allowances for me and my rather special circumstances. Since my initiation I was considered a warrior like the others, and the spirits I had been harboring had fled to make room, in theory at least, for the good spirits of the tribe.

One day when I was two hours' walk from the village I came upon a splendid *tuba* liana, the sort whose roots kill off fish. This was a great find! Very pleased with myself, I started digging up the roots with my parang and soon filled my pack with them. This meant a picnic by the river for all the family next day, so I gave up hunting and went happily back to the village.

Although the *tuba* was not a very rare liana, there was always a warm welcome for anyone who brought some back, especially as it meant a pleasant picnic and fish in store. I emptied out some of the roots on the bamboo floor of the verandah and rolled myself a big cigarette while Tangale inspected them.

"Where did you have the luck to find such good *tuba*?"

He had little hope that I was going to tell him the exact spot.

"Oh, you have to look hard, and it's some distance away—just behind the hill where the *musangs* [tree-dwelling civets] are."

"Not in Maché's territory?"

"Certainly not. It's at least two hours' walk beyond the hill."

The men sitting around were looking ugly. The chief said nothing more but seemed very annoyed. An uneasy silence had fallen. Two men got up and went into a *bilek*. Then Maché arrived. He was a nice fellow and we'd often drunk *tuak* and had a good laugh together; but at the moment he did not seem at all pleased.

"Why did you steal my *tuba*? The witch doctor's right, you're not a good Iban."

The argument was becoming embittered, and I made the mistake of standing up for myself. Everyone around joined in, taking sides, but I must admit that very few spoke on my behalf. Nevertheless I made a last attempt to calm down the furious Maché.

"Look, I admit I'm in the wrong, though I didn't know I was in your hunting territory. So take the *tuba* and I'll give you some more if you like, and let's stay friends. I'm truly sorry."

And I was. But the idiot was not satisfied with that. He angrily seized my pack and emptied out the rest of the *tuba*, also the gibbon which I had killed earlier, and he took the lot. I didn't mind about the *tuba*, but the gibbon was another matter. To the Dayaks one thing is sacred above all else—the products of hunting. Game is willingly shared, but no one lets it be stolen without protest. Of course, Maché was trying to provoke me, or rather to make me lose face. It was a tricky situation. I couldn't care less about the six-pound monkey, but if I let this pass I would never be able to open my mouth again.

"Take the *tuba*, Maché, but leave the *ouak-plaio*."

He gave me a spiteful look and turned away. I wasn't particularly angry with him but I had to make a show. And without thinking how he might react I jumped up and drew the hunting parang I carried at my side.

There was a general "Oh!" of startled surprise. The men moved aside and a few women hurried off into their *bileks* with their children. The chief ordered us to desist —but instead Maché dropped the *tuba* and the gibbon, sprang back and pulled out his own parang. It is quite a formidable weapon, with its sharp, two-foot blade and well-balanced handle.

My action had taken Maché by surprise—it had me, too. I had acted on impulse and stupidly found myself on the spot. If I had used my advantage I think I could have drawn first blood. But before we got to grips the chief, red with anger, came between us and ordered us to drop our weapons at once. There was complete stillness all around for a moment or two. I was certainly not keen on fighting a duel but neither was I going to back down before this stupid fool. I had had no idea that the *tuba* was in his territory, and he must have known that I meant no harm in digging it up; besides, I had just offered to compensate him. It was he in the end who had put up his parang first, muttering threats as he did so. I just turned my back on him and went to my *bilek* where Lintaü was anxiously waiting, seizing the gibbon by the arm as I passed but leaving the *tuba* where it was.

This was a serious incident, and the council of elders was at once summoned to a meeting in the chief's *bilek*. It lasted a long time, and while I waited at home my wife did nothing but sulk. A fine day this was turning out to be!

Two or three hours later I was called to Tangale's apartment, where a dozen elderly warriors were sitting in a circle, each with his bowl of *tuak*. Maché was already there. We sat down at the end of the room, not looking at each other. No one offered us a drink, which was a bad sign.

We were given a proper dressing-down. When Tangale got going he did not mince his words. Then sentence was pronounced: Because I had started a fight I was to give a half-grown pig to be killed for the next village ceremony; and for the theft of the *tuba*—they still considered it a theft—I had to give a grown pig to Maché, return all the *tuba,* and apologize. Maché had to present the village with a half-grown pig, too, for having taken part in a fight; and he would have to give me a grown pig for having taken the gibbon, and apologize to me for that. I was taken aback at first, but there was nothing to be said against this truly impartial judgment. I shook hands with Maché and we drank a big bowl of *tuak* together. But all the same, we were never really friendly again. That was not my fault, as I bore him no ill will and readily admitted I was in the wrong in some respects.

I could not help admiring the clever way of cooling

down a couple of hotheads, by fining each of us to the benefit of the whole village. No one had any cause for complaint. If we had gone too far we would have been tied to a post, back to back, and left there all night, and the fines would have been heavier.

When I returned to the family *bilek* Lintaü kept her back turned to me; I supposed that was part of the punishment. I seemed to have let everyone down that day, which was what saddened me most.

Another day there was a "diplomatic incident." I unfortunately cut across a part of the forest that was sacred. I had done so at least a dozen times before, without anyone's knowing. But this time someone saw me, and just as I had killed a monkey. There was of course nothing to show that a part of the forest was taboo. But everybody knew it, they said. Everybody except me. When I tried to get some information out of them on the subject they shrugged their shoulders or burst out laughing, gave vague answers or said that three hours' walk in that direction it was taboo to fish in the river, that no one must go hunting over here, a tree was haunted over there, and so on. There were so many haunted places, sacred corners of the forest and other prohibitions and taboos that you could hardly avoid running foul of ancestral law now and again. And each time you had to make an offering to appease the wrath of the spirits. Complications sometimes arose because the spirits were not always sure who was the culprit, and the whole village might have to pay for one person's mistake.

There were, however, ways of getting around these innumerable pettifogging restrictions, otherwise life would be quite impossible. For instance, when kingfishers were seen flying the wrong way but you really wanted to continue, then you just turned your back on them; though never when with a party, of course, only when alone or with one other man you knew well.

The taboos were sometimes useful, especially to lazy men. There was one villager who stayed firmly in the longhouse for more than a fortnight, sitting about and drinking, because he could not go hunting. A sign from the gods always prevented him. And he never stopped moaning about his bad luck. "Whatever can I have done? At this rate we'll starve to death. I can't understand it."

I understood easily enough and had no difficulty in diagnosing the complaint—acute indolence.

Apart from making blunders I specialized in catching snakes, including cobras, as was becoming well known at Selidapi; and that, anyway, did not meet with too much disapproval. What astounded the Ibans was that no harm came to me, for as everyone knew, a *ullar sindouk* (cobra) bites everything that comes within reach and death follows in a matter of minutes. So some of the villagers were beginning to be suspicious of this "supernatural" gift.

In France I had already had a taste of the consequences of an unusual hobby. My small collection of reptiles was housed in a dovecote in the solidly middle-class town of Angers, and this had drawn upon my head many double-edged comments from my neighbors—and these were taken up by the whole population when my favorite python went for a stroll in the prefect's gardens, an incident which set in motion the police, the fire brigade, tracker dogs and journalists, including a TV team. It was somewhat the same here at Selidapi, except that I did not keep my captures, thus avoiding a good deal of unpleasantness.

The first time I caught a snake with my bare hands the Ibans were quite impressed; the second time made them feel anxious, and after that they began to wonder about me. However, they appeared to have become used to my strange habits and took little notice. The ability to catch snakes must have seemed some sort of magic to them.

I had already noted more than twenty species, some of which were very interesting, but on the whole I was a little disappointed. These creatures were not very abundant, or rather there was not a great variety. More often than not I came across one or another of the same half-a-dozen species: ringed krait, python, green viper, *Natrix piscator*, etc. A very ordinary sample.

However, there came a day when I really thought I was going to capture a rare and beautiful species—a *Bungarus flaviceps borneensis*, a krait with red head and tail.

That evening, like any other, all the village went down to bathe in the river, for the traditional *mané*. And as on every evening I joined in a little friendly horseplay with the girls, splashing and jostling amid shrieks and giggles. Then I stayed behind because I had to fetch water for "her ladyship," who was busy cooking. I was being the indulgent husband, goodhearted soul that I am.

The fairly steep path was only just wide enough for two people to pass, and the clay soil had become so trodden down by villagers carrying water that it was very slippery. Suddenly this splendid krait darted out of the bushes only a few feet in front of me. There was no mistaking it, not only because of its bright skin but also from its swift movement, for others of the species are mainly nocturnal and have lazy habits. I lost sight of it for a moment or two, then caught a glimpse of it on the other side of the path. It seemed to be going toward the river. I dropped my two calabashes and looked around for a stick or a cane, but there was nothing handy. In desperation I went to catch it with my bare hands, a procedure not to be recommended, especially when one is not quite sure of the habits and reflexes of the quarry. Just as the snake reached the water I managed to grasp its tail, but it was a very lively snake and I let go only just in time, before it got my thumb. Its fangs missed by very little. It immediately darted into the water, making for the bamboo landing stage where the pirogues tied up and women did their washing; it enclosed a small bathing pool made of stakes, six feet square, where children were safe from crocodiles.

While the krait was twisting about in the water I had time to find a length of cane. In the meantime the snake had got on to the landing stage and hidden in a pile of laundry, but stupidly left its tail sticking out. The landing stage was deserted; the women and a few men were watching me from the bank.

I poked my cane into the pile of laundry as near as I could judge to the snake's head, then carefully lifted the top of the pile. There was the krait writhing about like a fish; I had its head firmly held by the cane. I grabbed it by the neck between my thumb and forefinger and started back with it, up the path to the village. As it twisted its head about, trying to bite my fingers, I caught a glimpse of its short, thin, curved teeth in their sheath of pink flesh.

Kraits, like cobras, do not have the long poison fangs of vipers; the Gaboon viper (*Bitis gabonica*) can dart forth veritable daggers two inches long. Its venom is therefore injected deep under the skin; whereas cobras and kraits inflict only superficial wounds and so make longer bites to allow their venom to penetrate. A krait in fact usually grips the flesh and chews savagely into it to spread as much poison as possible; this quickly enters the bloodstream and causes a very painful death in a period varying from twenty minutes to several hours, according to the amount of venom and the position of the bite, the snake's fitness and whether it has just eaten or not, and also depending upon the time of year. The season has no effect upon the species found in Borneo, but in the tropics a cobra is more dangerous in the rainy season, when it eats a great amount. In the dry season it is more likely to be in a state of torpor; its store of venom is smaller and is more diluted. The victim's morale and reaction to being bitten also affect the action of the venom; a person who panics increases the rate of his circulation and so causes the venom to spread more rapidly —and even more does the person who runs about shouting and gesticulating. I am not a great expert on snakebites, as I have been bitten only five times; but I knew a Thai at Bangkok who had been bitten about thirty times, once by a king cobra. I hasten to add that he worked at the Pasteur Institute at Bangkok, where the serum is prepared.

I was very pleased at having captured this krait and tried to recall the scaly formation of its species. This is useful for checking whether or not you have captured an interesting subspecies. Afterward, when I had finished with the snake, I would give it to my family to eat, if they wished. Personally I find kraits very tough and almost inedible, especially the black and yellow ones (*Bungarus fasciatus*).

The path up from the river was most slippery, and in my haste to reach the longhouse I skidded and nearly fell. I just managed to recover my balance but as I flung my arm up I unfortunately stepped on the snake's tail; its head slipped through my fingers and it fell to the ground with me, taking advantage of this situation to bite me just above the knee. I didn't realize it immediately. A woman's scream made me look down, for I thought I still had a hold on the snake. But the brute was still hanging on to me. I snatched it away and threw it as far as I could before it had time to return to the attack.

I was well and truly bitten. I could clearly see the tiny punctures where its two poisonous fangs had chewed into my flesh. My immediate reaction was to press hard around the bite to squeeze out as much poison as possible, then I tried to clean the spot with a little water. But I was under no illusion; the poison was well in and nothing could now stop its having effect. Yet I felt no fear, no more than I had when bitten before by poisonous snakes. I can't explain this phenomenon; I value my life as much as anyone else and I'm frightened when I'm in danger—but not when bitten by a poisonous snake. I have complete control of myself, my mind remains clear and I don't panic. It is difficult to believe, but I am never so much master of myself as in the moments following a bite.

It is part of my profession to study the effects of snake venom. I have carried out many experiments on these reptiles and, as already mentioned, I have had the honor of observing on myself the consequences of the bites of the Egyptian cobra (*Naja haje*), the Indian cobra (*Naja naja*) and the sand viper (*Cerastes cerastes*), this last one just before leaving on this Asian trip.

So I knew quite well what would happen to me now, although there are sometimes atypical effects. The bite of this *Bungarus flaviceps* is strongly venomous, and without the right serum I would soon be in a serious condition. But I refused to envisage the worst, which seemed highly probable, however, in this case.

The village was quite near, nevertheless I asked two sturdy men to carry me there. The news of my accident had spread like wildfire. At that time in the evening everyone was back in the longhouse after the day's activities, and soon the whole population of Rumah Selidapi was gathered about me. Poor Lintaü was very upset; she was convinced that I would die. Her father tried to console her, while everyone gave his or her opinion. A good many openly declared that there was no hope for me and that I should soon be with the ancestors in the land of everlasting orgies.

At that moment, about five minutes after being bitten, I had a slightly uncomfortable feeling in my knee, but that was all. I could still move quite easily. I joked with the men standing around and told them not to worry. They laid me down on the floor of the communal verandah. Seeing my cheerfulness, they began to wonder if I was something of a witch doctor, too, whether I had some philter to immunize me against snakebites. Alas no, for now the venom was starting to take effect. I was suddenly overcome by a great weakness, and could no longer move my left leg. These symptoms I was expecting had developed rapidly, and I was really worried The development is much slower in the case of cobra bites. So before I lost the power to speak, I asked the chief to come near.

"Tangale, in a short time I shan't be able to breathe. What I want you to do then is to sit on my thighs and press your hands on my chest as hard as you can. When you are tired, ask someone else to take over. It's a remedy used in my country. I've been bitten by *ullars* before, and I know what has to be done. Now see if you can do what I said."

I was trying to teach him artificial respiration, as a krait's venom induces death by asphyxia.

"Yes, that's right. You press in time with your own breathing. It isn't difficult."

"Dioudi, why are you always playing with snakes? I told you you'd get bitten one day. Now you see."

"*Ullars* can't kill me." Alas, I wasn't nearly so sure as I tried to make out. "If you keep up the movements just as I've shown you, there isn't any danger for me. But don't give up, even if you think I'm dead. Lintaü, you heard what I said, make sure it's all done just as I've asked your father."

Paralysis was beginning to set in, affecting the neck muscles first. My head waggled about, so I had a couple of cushions packed under it. Cases are known of people having their neck broken by these sudden convulsive movements.

I no longer felt like joking. Now and again my arm or leg gave a jerk, then fell back limply. Next came stomach contractions and occasional vomiting. About an hour later (an approximate estimation, as I had no watch) my respiratory muscles were functioning irregularly. Each intake of air was a great, exhausting effort of will power. "Breathe, breathe." But breathing became more and more difficult, weaker and weaker, and more irregular. I felt that my eyes would start out of my head with the effort. I could not have been a very edifying sight. The crowd around me were nodding their heads and commenting quietly on my condition.

What the hell was the chief doing? Why didn't he get on with the artificial respiration? I tried to speak to him, but could make no sound. Fortunately he caught the imploring message in my eyes, and with a hopeless air he straddled my body and got into position. His action was a help, but nowhere near as good as normal breathing. I remained perfectly conscious, which served only to increase my anguish; I could see and hear everything that was going on around me. I felt that every moment would be my last. I urinated and defecated, and my stomach seemed filled with razor blades and red peppers; it was like being burned with acid. Now and again my body gave violent jerks, reminding me of death throes—which was no doubt what the people standing around took them for.

The chief told Lintaü to go to the *bilek*, but she refused, and three women dragged her away. I wanted her to stay, but I was incapable even of motion. Most of the time there was a fog in front of my eyes, although I had moments of perfectly clear vision. The pain in my stomach became agonizing. I vomited and kept pissing and shitting. Two old women cleaned me up.

Then the witch doctor arrived and set out his paraphernalia. He opened a leather bag and produced half-a-dozen smooth, colored pebbles, as round as peas. He put one on my lips, blew on it and then returned it to his bag. He repeated this performance with each of the other pebbles. Later, of course, the whole village would believe that he had saved my life. In fact their faith in him was almost the death of me, for they concluded that there was now no need to continue the artificial respiration. But Lintaü—who had come out of her *bilek* again—made such a scene that they kept it up. Thank God!

Throughout the night I was drowsy but lucid and in continual pain. My brain functioned intermittently; I had no real sleep but had waking dreams rather psychedelic in character, with strange shapes and colors. But predominant was the dread of not being able to breathe.

By some miracle, men continued taking turns at pressing on my chest. I owe my life to the chief and above all to Lintaü; whenever one of the men looked as though he was going to stop, even for a few seconds' rest, or said that it was useless to go on, she cursed and reviled him in a way terrible to hear. I would never have thought it possible for such foul words to issue from that pretty little mouth.

In the middle of the night the paralysis began to recede slowly but perceptibly. The following day there was no change in my condition but I was able to breathe unaided, though with difficulty; my chest felt as if there was an enormous weight on it. I must have brought up everything I had in my stomach, yet I was still subject to convulsions. On the other hand I was far too weak to move even my hand.

I was also worried about any aftereffects on my health. I had known from the very beginning I would come through, and the worst was now over. But I was concerned about side effects on my nervous system, which could be extremely serious; cases were known of permanent lesions. It would have been better to pass away than to be left impotent or a dotard.

On the morning of the third day I felt some strength returning, and my muscles began to respond to commands from my brain. In a few hours everything started up again, beginning with my stomach. I was hungry. As my appetite improved, so did the family's morale. Nevertheless, several days passed before I was able to stand up. The ordeal had been a great shock to my nervous system especially, and I was quite unable to control my emotions; I would suddenly burst into tears or have fits of laughter.

I had had the devil's own luck, for a krait is the most venomous of snakes, equaled only by the African mamba. Very few people have survived a bite from the latter. I know of no cases of bites from a *Bungarus flaviceps*, but research has proved how strong its venom is. The large proportion of neurotoxins it contains does not give the victim much chance of survival, and when no serum is available he usually dies.

It would be very nice to say that it was my excellent constitution which enabled me to fight off and overcome most of the venom's effects. But the true reason for my escape was that when the krait sensed it was about to be caught it bit into the washing it was hiding under, thereby wasting some of its venom. When I was holding the snake, it had tried to bite me; and while I was examining its mouth, tickling its teeth with the end of my cane, a little more venom had escaped. It is impossible to know just how much venom remained for the snake to inject into me, but it was quite enough to kill me off if I had not been helped by artificial respiration.

For several weeks afterward I was unable to look at a snake, even a dead one, without being seized by convulsive movements. But I got over that surprisingly quickly.

ELEVEN

Hunting Stories

At certain times of the year the wild boars of Borneo, for some unknown reason, migrate in large herds, straight ahead, rather like the lemmings of the Arctic. They gather in defined places and then, suddenly, off they go. It is a mystery to zoologists—and a delight to the Ibans, who don't ask themselves vain questions.

On a day like any other, with most of the villagers out hunting or fishing, a young warrior came running back, sweating and gasping. *"Paraga babi, paraga babi!"*

In a second, all the men who were taking their ease jumped to their feet, seized their parangs and blowpipes and hurried down to the pirogues.

The one place where the boars could be killed in large numbers and without danger to the men was where they crossed the river. But it was quite narrow at that particular point and quick action was necessary to achieve good results. When we reached the place one herd of boars had already crossed, leaving a confusion of tracks on the muddy bank to mark their passage. Half of us took up concealed positions near the bank, while the others crouched in their pirogues behind a flimsy screen of leafy branches; and we waited for the arrival of the next herd.

The men on land spread out their poisoned darts on large leaves, so that they were more readily at hand and could be shot off in quick succession. The men in the boats—of whom I was one—were going to use their blowpipes as spears.

Several hours passed without a sign of a boar. These

migrations lasted only a few days—had we missed our
chance? No, for there came a snuffling sound and then a
distrustful snout poked out from behind some leaves
about thirty yards in front of us, and was followed by a
second snout. The first boar came into view, sniffed the
ground, and raised its massive head, and its deep-set
little eyes peered about in a wide semicircle. After another sniff at the ground it entered the water and was followed by the herd, which had been waiting just behind
the leader. I counted a score of them, and there were
still more to come. It was time to act.

The leading boars had just reached the opposite bank
when a show of darts fell among the herd, and at once
the water seethed as the animals floundered and strug-
gled. We in the pirogues rowed quickly toward them.
Some boars tried to turn back, while others continued
on; and those that had not yet entered the water realized
the danger and took refuge in the forest. The air was
filled with savage grunts, men's cries and the hoarse
groans of dying animals. It was an awful carnage—spear-
heads being thrust into flesh, darts piercing thick hides;
in some places the river was slowly turning pink. We
killed more boars than we would ever be able to eat,
even by drying the meat. We were intoxicated by so
much blood, slaughter provoked yet more slaughter; dead
boars were drifting slowly away, and many of them were
left to feed the fishes and the crocodiles. We took more
than a score of carcasses back to the village, and they
looked quite sinister when lined up along the verandah.

There was a festive atmosphere to the longhouse that
evening, but without any music or dancing. We worked
hard nearly all night cutting up the carcasses and divid-
ing the best portions, and eating and drinking as we
went. Most of the fat was melted down and stored in
pots, while we ate as many slices of it as we could there
and then. The lean meat was cut into thin slices and

cooked over a glowing fire, then it was smoked and dried. As the night wore on we staggered off to bed one after another, drunk with *tuak* and bawdy songs; some collapsed on the spot, as though stricken by a sudden weakness. For once, everyone was late getting up in the morning, to be greeted by the sight of meat hanging from the beams and offal strewn about the floor of the verandah; dogs bloated with food were sleeping it off and others were scavenging again; and a few men were still sprawled among the remains of the butchery. It was the kind of wild and brutish orgy that prehistoric man must have known, after killing the great bear or stampeding wild horses over the edge of a steep cliff.

The large animals hunted by the Ibans were chiefly wild boars, panthers and bears, occasionally a rhinoceros (to my regret I never saw one) or a banteng, a big horned animal. Nearly all hunting accidents were due to boars or bears. The Ibans rarely hunted the orangoutan, and the stories I've heard on the subject seem much closer to legend or myth than to truth.

Tangale had a good story about a panther. He had killed several in his time, but the one whose tanned skin he wore draped over his behind when in ceremonial dress had given him a lot of trouble.

The evenings were sometimes long, and when we did not start drinking too early everyone liked listening to stories of hunting or ghosts or of love. Sitting around the fire, with a few smoky, flickering candles or torches dimly illuminating the room, there was no better way of passing the time. Someone would tell a fantastic tale of evil spirits and sorcery, and someone else a fabulous hunting story with so many frills and so much imagination that it was difficult to know truth from fiction. But that mattered little, so long as it was an exciting story.

There were several good storytellers among the vil-

lagers, each of them able to keep the company listening
eagerly and sometimes in suspense for hours on end. They
were not necessarily the best hunters or the heroes of
their stories, but no one minded about that; the essential
thing was to tell a good story well. My father-in-law was
one of this little band of poets, for they were indeed poets
in the way they chose their words, used vivid expressions,
heightened their tale and played for effect.

One evening after the meal, Lintaü went to see some
friends and I settled down with a few other men sitting
by the chief.

"You killed anything lately, Dioudi?"

"No, I haven't seen a thing for three days, although
I've been a long way. No luck at all. How about you?"

"Only a monkey, but I've seen the droppings of a
rimau [panther] quite near the village. It must be old.
For it to hang about near the village isn't natural. It'll kill
and eat a dog soon, or a pig."

"Does the *rimau* attack men?" I knew the answer but
I wanted to see what they thought.

"No, it's frightened of men. When it sees one of us it
retreats higher into the trees. It's not an easy animal to
kill, for you have to climb up after it, and that's dangerous. If a *rimau* isn't killed by your first dart or spear
thrust, it might attack you then."

Tangale was already itching to tell his panther story,
waiting impatiently for a break in the conversation. Apparently it was well worth hearing. So I gave him a lead.
"Has anyone in the village killed a panther?"

"Several hunters of Selidapi have killed one. The Tuaï
Rumah . . ."

All eyes turned to the chief. Every other man there,
except me, must have heard this epic a dozen times at
least, but never mind, they were all ready for a revised
version.

Taking his time, Tangale refilled his calabash and took

a drink before beginning his story. At first he spoke in a flat voice, like someone tired of telling the same thing over and over again, but gradually he became animated, his tone livened, and toward the end of his story he was gesturing and playing out the kill, even to imitating the angry growls of the animal.

"It happened a long time ago," he began, "before you were born perhaps. A panther ate one of our dogs. We heard it howling one evening, as the *rimau* carried it off to the forest. That *rimau* was not afraid of us, for it ate the dog alive quite close to the village. The children were crying, the women were scared and the men were uneasy, for it's a very bad sign when a *rimau* eats near a village. That means he'll seize a pig next time. . . ."

Tangale paused now and again for a drink of *tuak* or to roll himself a cigarette. We put questions to him, but he never replied straight away; the answers came at the appropriate moment in the story. Now and again he stopped to ask if he was boring us or to pretend that it was getting late and as we were going hunting early next morning . . . the old humbug. Then, having been assured of how interested we were, he deigned to continue.

For ten days no more was seen or heard of the panther. It had probably found prey more to its taste, prey that lived in the trees, far from the scent of man. However, hunger set in again, and the panther's muscles were not so supple as they had been, the gibbons had good ears and long arms, and it was not easy to catch them; or perhaps the panther's sight was not what it was at night. So the beast came down to the village again and seized a pig from under the longhouse. The dogs woke up too late to give the alarm in time. The unfortunate pig made all the noise it could, but more than that was needed before a panther would drop its prey. And it ate the pig in a tree near the village, as it had the dog on the first occasion.

By the time three pigs had disappeared in this way, besides an unknown number of dogs, the villagers were greatly worried.

The panther became more daring. Sometimes it ate only part of its prey, leaving the rest to rot in the tree—which scared the superstitious Ibans even more. If they had had the courage to go out at night they might soon have put an end to the panther, but it was common knowledge that all the evil spirits and ghosts gather together in the forest after the sun has gone down.

A trap was set, but this devilish panther was as cunning as they made them. It even managed to take the bait without letting itself be trapped (which was something other animals succeeded in doing fairly often). The trap was a tunnel about six feet long made of hollow bamboo, with a door that fell as soon as the bait inside was touched. But the panther had more sense than to get at the bait, a large piece of pork, by going into the tunnel. By poking between the bamboo with its claws, it succeeded in sliding the piece of pork along to the entrance. As all the village dogs had been shut in for their own safety, the panther was able to take its time removing the bait.

A feeling of insecurity spread through the village, and every evening at sunset there was a flutter of panic which prevented the men from enjoying their *tuak* and the women from dancing. The dogs added to it by howling at the slightest suspicious sound and so giving at least a dozen false alarms every night. Of course Tangale, in telling the story, exaggerated and let his imagination run loose; nevertheless it was all highly probable. Panthers have been known to commit far worse depredations, even carrying off several men before being caught and killed.

This panther was finally sighted one day by Tangale—who was not then the village chief—and his brother. They came upon the animal asleep in a tree less than twenty minutes' walk from the village.

"What's that up in the tree there?"

"I can't see properly, it's too high up. Just leaves perhaps, or a big snake."

"I think it's the panther."

"H'm, I'm not so sure. Wait a moment."

While they watched, a long thick tail slipped from a branch and dangled down.

"*Rimau*," Tangale confirmed softly. "I'm going up after it. You stay here. If it wakes up, try to see where it goes."

To try and follow a panther you need to be a great optimist and have a good pair of legs. The only way for a man without a gun to get at a panther is to approach when it is asleep. If the animal wakes and sees you approaching, there's a growl, a flash of movement in the foliage and then nothing more. But if you get within attacking distance the panther begins to back away, climbing higher all the time, until a point is reached when it can go no farther; it is then forced to overcome its fear—either to confront its attacker or take a leap into space.

Two possibilities are said to be open to the hunter, depending on his courage and—this is my own feeling—whether or not there is anyone to witness his act. He can attempt to kill the panther with poisoned darts when he gets within range, or he can go closer and spear the beast with his iron-tipped blowpipe. The latter method has several disadvantages, as can be easily imagined, but is much favored—especially when recounting an adventure around the fire one evening.

What can one's thoughts be while balancing on a branch more than a hundred feet above the ground and facing a panther? It seems a lot of risk for a fleeting glory. Anyway, one needs to be very sure of oneself.

Tangale climbed the tree slowly but steadily and very quietly. He had taken off his bamboo quiver, his hunting parang and *sirat*, in order to climb without hindrance; but he still had his spearheaded blowpipe with him. I have often watched Ibans climbing trees and have always admired their facility. It's a tricky business and means taking advantage of every unevenness on the bare trunk, being careful of loose bark and watchful for venomous insects, scorpions and snakes.

This tree's branches began about eighty feet up, and to reach them a climber needed horny hands, plenty of strength and good wind, not to mention a great deal of courage. There were lianas hanging down here and there, but these were of no help as even a slight touch would shake the branches above and rouse the sleeping panther.

Tangale, telling his tale, broke into a sweat at the thought of it; but the *tuak* he had drunk may have had something to do with that.

Eventually he reached a point only the length of two blowpipes away from the panther. To me, it has always seemed a mystery how anyone could get so near to such a wary animal. Suddenly the panther stood up on its short legs and gave a sharp mew of surprise and fear; its snarl revealed teeth as long as a tiger's but not so big.

Tangale was quite close now, and the animal could only back away. And here the hunter's skill came into play. The slightest abrupt movement could cause the panther to attack or, more likely, turn and flee. But if the hunter advanced steadily and evenly (remember, all this was happening some 120 feet above ground) the panther would continue to back away until brought to bay)—unless a handy branch enabled it to leap into the next tree. The hunter had to keep tormenting it with the tip of his blowpipe, distracting it so that it continued to face him.

Wild beasts such as panthers tire very quickly. They can exert great strength for a short time, but after a couple of minutes of fighting they are panting with exhaustion. So this panther had to be worn down as well as having its attention preoccupied. The branch behind it was now too weak to bear its weight and was sagging considerably. Tangale crept forward, toes outspread, until he was within ten feet of the panther, and kept provoking it with his blowpipe, making it lash out with its paws.

These feigned charges were tiring the poor panther, and it gradually exposed itself more. This was the opportunity Tangale was waiting for; the animal advanced a little way, its head slightly raised after an angry growl, and quick as lightning Tangale thrust his sharp spearhead into his chest.

Even when mortally wounded, a beast usually gathers its remaining strength for a last attack which is often dangerous for the hunter. So it was now. The panther sprang at Tangale, who was still holding the blowpipe which was stuck a foot deep in its chest. He had to let go, lost his balance and fell—fortunately only a few feet, onto a large branch with much foliage where he just managed to get a hold in time. The panther, however, went tumbling down from branch to branch, and was dead when it hit the ground, still with Tangale's blowpipe sticking from it.

Whatever frills he had given to his story, there seemed no doubt that Tangale had climbed the tree alone and had killed the panther; and he was rightly proud of it. We had heard a fine hunting story that evening. And when Tangale reached the end of it we all remained silent for a few minutes, still under its spell and in spirit out in the nearby great forest, face to face with a *rimau*.

I, too, had a hunting story, though not nearly so remarkable as Tangale's.

There was bound to be accidents of one kind or another, from the comic to the tragic, when men hunted practically every day in such a forest. It should not be thought that all hunters were on the alert all the time, nor that there was danger everywhere, that behind each thicket there lurked a wild beast or a poisonous snake. In fact, provided you respected certain elementary rules and did not defy the Fates, in principle you would be all right. There were, however, what people call the intangible factors. Of course, all this applies equally well to drivers on a highway as to hunters in the wilds of Borneo. But it is possible that the intangible factors materialize differently or occur more frequently in Borneo. Who can foresee a heavy branch or a wild durian falling on his head? Or a branch suddenly breaking when he is a hundred feet up a tree, where he has climbed to collect a monkey that remained hanging there after being killed by a dart? Numerous other examples could be given.

The rule here, unlike that for men with guns, was never to pursue a wounded beast. We hunted to eat, not for sport. What mattered most was to bring back proteins at the end of the day.

Whenever I came upon an animal that seemed vicious I left it in peace. This happened to me several times, and I'm certain I was by no means the only hunter from the village to do so. The one law of the jungle was to give way to superior strength. It was up to the hunter to make sure he was the stronger.

My profession being the study of animal behavior, specializing in animal psychology (or ethology), I had a comparatively good knowledge of animals; and over the years these studies must have left their mark on me, for my philosophy of life was similar in some ways to that of the animals I had the pleasure of observing. When in the jungle I was often frightened, and it then seemed only natural to obey this animal law of giving way to the stronger.

Sweltering heat, mosquitoes and a few leeches, exhaustion or long spells of lethargy—this was the daily lot of the hunter. Very often I went hunting in the forest more from habit, and need, too, than from conviction. One day I found myself a long way from the village, almost at the limit of its territory. The risk of an accident was comparatively small; in any case there was no more danger when five hours' walk from the village than when half an hour's. But if any trouble did occur—such as a broken leg —it was a nuisance to be so far away when alone. Difficulties arose, too, if there were a hundred pounds of dead meat to carry back.

I suddenly heard a slight grunting sound quite close at hand—a wild boar no doubt. I always found difficulty in locating an animal and then getting near enough to shoot a dart at it. If I succeeded in doing so with one boar out of five, I reckoned I was keeping a good average; with monkeys and birds I was even less successful.

A few seconds later I saw something moving behind a screen of foliage, and then part of the animal came into view. Now the great advantage of poisoned darts is that they can be shot into any area of your prey—there is no need to select a vital spot. The poison acts just as well whether the dart hits the throat or the buttocks.

Every hunter prepared his poison himself, and if the traditional method was properly followed the resulting "sauce" retained its potency for a considerable time. My own concoction was not bad, but its potency did not last for very long and the period varied a lot—from a fortnight to two or three months. This was because of the fact that I was not very good at choosing the right kind of sap to make the poison, and that I did not always boil it as I should. The chief had supplied me with poisoned darts during my early days as a hunter, but now I managed by myself.

When my dart struck, the animal gave a great leap and stood erect. What I had thought was a boar was in fact a bear! The poor light in that dense part of the forest was chiefly responsible for my mistake. But even more astonishing was that instead of the bear's rolling on the ground as it ought, after receiving a good dose of poison, it gave me a wicked stare and showed every sign of evil intent.

There was only one thing to do—face the bear and see what it decided to do. If it attacked, as sometimes happens with bears, you held it off with your spearheaded blowpipe; or if there was time you shot another dart into it, hoping the second would be of better quality than the first. Sometimes, quite frequently in fact, bears turned away and made off. In that case you wiped the sweat out of your eyes. (As the Ibans plucked their eyebrows—the very height of elegance, in their view—the perspiration trickled right into a man's eyes, which was a great hindrance.)

This bear stood there swaying a little and showing its teeth. I could see only its head and chest, the lower part being hidden by a clump of ferns. Suddenly it dropped on all fours and disappeared from my view. I pointed my blowpipe in the direction where the beast would probably appear and stood ready for any eventuality. Nothing happened. But then I heard a great bustling going on behind the ferns. A minute or two passed; still no sign of the bear. I prudently stayed where I was, on the defensive. The bustling noise died away; I waited a little longer, then cautiously moved forward. The bear was lying on the ground, still alive but in a bad way. The poison from the dart had taken a long time to have effect. The dying bear staggered to its feet, but a couple of thrusts from my spearhead put an end to it. Then I had time to see that it was no monster but in fact was below average size.

This story was not worthy of being told when sitting around the fire with the Ibans, but that bear had given me a fright.

TWELVE

On the Run

Many things had happened since I first arrived at Selidapi. There had been my acceptance by the Ibans, my
marriage to Lintaü, the initiation, the tattooing sessions,
all the hunting—plenty to keep me occupied. Yet I still
hardly knew this race, and I certainly wouldn't venture
to say that I understood them, for it would take a very
astute European to penetrate the workings of the Asiatic
mind.

In spite of a few misadventures I still found life in the
longhouse very pleasant, and my relations with the villagers were on the whole excellent. Little problems were
always cropping up, but no one worried very much—
which was all to the good. Now and again I thought a
little longingly of the past, but I can't say I was really
homesick. I liked it here, and thoughts of leaving never
entered my head. But there were times when I longed to
listen to some music, real music, not an orchestra com-
posed of calabashes and gongs. The fat pork was very
good, but I wouldn't have said no to a dozen fresh oysters
or even a plate of sauerkraut. I quite liked *tuak*, but a
bottle of vintage wine wouldn't have done any harm.
Those were very ordinary longings, which passed fleet-
ingly through my mind without undermining my morale.
In any case, it is impossible to adapt fully to a civilization
other than one's own, though if it comes to the point one
can cut adrift from it, which was partly what I had tried
to do. But what made it most difficult to become absorbed
into the Iban way of life was that they did nothing to
understand me. They made not the slightest effort to

meet me halfway; it was I who had to think and speak
as they did and to learn their customs, I who had to com-
promise for them. I must admit that understanding and
tolerance are not their most outstanding qualities.

We weren't on the same wavelength nor did the same
things spur us on. But the basic problem was simply that
they were primitive while I was civilized.

In return, however, I was having a most interesting experience. Lintaü was a great asset, and I had learned
much about animal habits, even if there was nothing remarkable in my observations. I thought of it all as having
a holiday the hard way, a sort of camping out carried to
extremes, but certainly not as a feat. Everything that had
happened had not been of my choosing, one thing had
followed another and I had just drifted along with events,
giving a slight shrug of the shoulders. For anyone who
liked that kind of thing, it was great.

Unfortunately, this sweet calm did not last. It was quite
unconsciously my own fault. Where I was in the wrong,
so far as I could see, was in not being born an Iban.
There was obviously nothing I could do about that.

Once again I had broken one of their innumerable, un-
predictable laws and taboos. It was no more serious than
on previous occasions, but I happened to be in a bad
humor and the witch doctor, who was beginning to get
on my nerves, seemed in little better mood.

My transgression earned me a gentle reprimand: "Dioudi, you mustn't hunt when the moon is . . ."

The witch doctor, however, took a more violent view
of it. He was everlastingly scolding and no one escaped
his tongue. It was not for nothing that we called him the
merekamane, the otter. This attractive little creature has
one great fault, apart from always smelling of fish: it calls
very loudly when hungry, and it is hungry all the time.
"*Ween, ween*," it goes for hours on end. The witch doctor

did not smell of fish, he was not so attractive as an otter, but his voice was raised just as much.

His dislike of me had already resulted in one or two squabbles, but this time it was more serious. I was sharpening my hunting parang on a flat stone by the river when he came up to me. It was a peaceful spot, not at all the place for quarrels.

"Was the boar you killed good?" he said.

"You ought to know. The whole village had some."

"It is forbidden to hunt when the moon—"

"Shut your trap. No one refused to eat it, not even you. It can't be so forbidden as all that."

I went on honing the blade without looking at him. But he persisted.

"It was forbidden. You're not a good Iban."

"Go away and let me get on with my work. I must have a parang that's really sharp. I might need it soon to cut off a head."

"What did you say?"

"You heard."

"You want to cut off my head?"

"*Nadaï*. I didn't say that, but if you keep on annoying me, it might happen. And I shan't need any *sapo*."

The *sapo* is a mushroom that induces hallucinations and is used to incite warriors before they go on a punitive expedition.

I ran my thumb along the blade of my parang; it was sharp enough to shave the toughest beard. Then I looked up at him and our eyes met. I caught a glint of hatred, and there could not have been any friendliness in my glance either.

"I haven't seen you out hunting very much," I said. "Do you know how to use a blowpipe and a parang? I know you can talk."

He was about to reply when two men came along.

They looked at us as they passed, said something to each other, went on a little way and then turned back. They could sense there was trouble in the air.

The witch doctor made no move, and his black, scornful eyes gave no indication of what was going on in that smooth head. He was not very big, quite thin and bony in fact, but he could carry heavier loads than I could. It was difficult to say what the outcome would be if we came to blows. But one thing was certain—I had a real enemy.

"From now on, don't speak to me, or it'll be *panjamon.*"

It is always a mistake to threaten anyone, for you only put him on his guard, and it's often just a form of giving way. I would have done better to take him on there and then; we could have had it out in some quiet spot, and one of us would have been left in peace afterward. But as it was . . . a little later he almost finished me off.

It was rare for villagers to come to blows, and it was never encouraged. However, when two men had some real reason for wanting to fight, and if they had had time to think it over and were sober, they were allowed to have it out, but not in the longhouse or in public. There was often a bit of playacting in these disputes and friends arrived on the scene in time to separate the two. The Ibans always shouted a lot before coming to blows. If the two were so furious with each other that no reconciliation was possible, usually one moved out and went to live in another, friendly village.

One night we had eaten well, talked and sung a great deal, danced a little and drunk too much. A typical longhouse party. I was tight but nevertheless realized something was not quite normal. To feel queer after drinking a few pints of *tuak* was not unusual, but to have a burning sensation in my innards was another matter.

I woke up in the night feeling that I had a bad attack

of dysentery. Odd things were going on in my stomach.
I had always been scared of falling ill here, especially
with that kind of complaint. In the morning, however, I
had come to the conclusion that it was not dysentery.
I've no medical knowledge, but it was obviously not
cholera (very common here), nor was it malaria or jaun-
dice. Probably one of the unrecognizable diseases that
flourished here. But what?

My head was swimming and I kept vomiting, nothing
but bile, and I felt very weak. I would rather have had a
good bite by a cobra or even a krait, for then I would at
least have known what to do. As it was, I seemed to be
suffering from the effects of a drug that inhibited all my
faculties. I had practically no energy, mental or physical.
I was as limp as a wet rag.

"Have some rice soup, it will do you good."

"No thank you, Lintaü, not just now. I'll have some
later if I feel better."

She put down the bowl and went off to serve other
members of the family, in the next *bilek*. Lintaü was the
only one, just then, who knew I was ill, and felt as worried as I did. She knew only too well how easy it was to
die here.

The more I thought about it, the more fishy this business seemed. The symptoms were very odd and fitted no
illness that I knew of; although my brain was sluggish,
I could not help wondering. . . . By the end of the afternoon there was a distinct improvement in my condition,
and I had a little food that evening, eating by myself in
the *bilek*. During the night it started again—pains in the
stomach and everything else, just as before. Could it be
possible that I had been poisoned? The suspicion gradually gained ground, but I still couldn't really believe it.

The following day I ate nothing and felt slightly better in the late evening. While I was alone in the *bilek* I
emptied all the soup down a gap in the floor.

"Did you finish it all up? That's good. You see, you're better this morning."

"It's probably because I ate nothing at all that I'm better!"

I thought I might as well confide my suspicions to her. At first she didn't comprehend, she thought I was criticizing her cooking.

"Don't be angry, that isn't what I meant. Look, I was feeling better the other afternoon, but after I'd had that soup I was ill again. I think someone is trying to poison me."

She was explosive about that.

"Quiet, you'll have the whole village here. I've never thought it was you or anyone in your family. If I had, I wouldn't have said anything to you."

We discussed it for a long time, often interrupted by people coming and going. In the end she agreed to keep my suspicions to herself, but I got the impression that she thought I was imagining things.

"You're feverish. That's why you've got such ideas into your head."

There was always a lot of visiting among the *bileks*, neighbors dropping in to borrow something or to have a chat, and so on. It was real communal life. Anybody could have put his little mixture in my bowl, especially as it was left in a corner and kept separate from the others; since falling ill I had not been eating with the family group.

Before I went to sleep I asked my wife to give me some rice, meat and fish from the family cooking pot. I had quite a good night afterward, though I was still far from well.

Lintaü had a great surprise for me in the morning. "A pig died in the night. They say it was from *ratgun* [a poison made from roots], because when they cut up the pig they found its entrails in a bad state.

"Ah, I threw the soup down there last night. At least one pig ate some, because I heard it."

I was feeling much better, but I took care not to show it. I reckoned that someone had been giving me doses of poison of increasing potency, and the last one—the one swallowed by the pig—was intended to be the final dose. Even I knew at least a dozen plants more poisonous than *ratgun,* and I did not at all fancy having them tried out on me. So far the poison had been administered to give the appearance of a serious illness, but there was nothing to show that more drastic methods would not now be applied.

I had no proof, but I'd have staked my own head that it was the witch doctor playing one of his tricks on me. It was just the sort of thing he would do. I thought hard about it all night, and ideas went round and round in my head, some more cunning than others. By morning I had decided on my plan of attack, which was actually a plan of withdrawal. However, until I was fit and well again the safest thing was to go on pretending that I was ill.

Only a week earlier I had been thinking of staying in the village indefinitely. But now I would have liked to be somewhere else, in France for instance, in a society with less liking for late-night soup. Homesickness comes upon one suddenly and for a variety of reasons; often something quite incidental will set one's thoughts turning that way—a word overheard, a face seen in a crowd, an anecdote. In my case it was a dose of *ratgun.* A good reason if ever there was one. And once homesickness gets under way it can no more be stopped than a herd of charging elephants.

Moreover, I was in a state of panic, real panic, which was very difficult to curb. For the first time in my life I felt all alone, desperately so, even more than when lost in the jungle. There was Lintaü, of course; but it is very difficult, exceptional even, for a Westerner to arrive at a communion of thought with an Asian woman. On the other hand, she creates very few problems, if we except one or two Asiatic types that shall be nameless. There is no need to psychoanalyze her before bedding her, and provided the husband observes two or three elementary rules he will have a faithful and loving wife. But it is a different matter when life gets tough.

There could be no question of taking Lintaü away with me, although I seriously considered it. I had done plenty of stupid things already. Here at Rumah Selidapi she was very attractive with long slits in her sarong and with her naked breasts, and the demure tattoos on her forearms were quite elegant. But in Paris? Even if I did not feel embarrassed, how would she feel? There's quite a difference between Borneo and France, between the Bamboo and the Atomic Age; and the gulf is more difficult to bridge in the Selidapi–Yffiniac (my home town) direction than in the opposite. There were many other reasons, all quite valid; and as if those were not enough, I thought up several more. It was not exactly a nice thing I was going to do, but at the time I sincerely thought it was for the best.

After I made my decision, the main thing was to go on playing a part and to stay alive. But pretending to be ill was not easy. I spent the long days and interminable nights evolving my plan of escape, for that is what it was. I could not confide in anyone.

The chief suspected nothing, though he was worried at seeing me still lying there when I was looking better.

I had moved again and was living in the chief's apartment, so all my photographic material was already packed. My hunting parang was always at my side and I had my blowpipe handy; luckily I had a good supply of darts. But that was about all. My flashlight had been useless for months and I had given my hammock to one of the storytellers, an impulse I now bitterly regretted.

So my baggage would not be heavy to carry. I thought of myself more than two years before, plodding out of Angers with my huge pack on my back, imagining all kinds of danger ahead, crossing wild countries and virgin lands, meeting "savages"—in short, adventure with a capital A. And I had indeed found adventure, but not as I had imagined; it had appeared on tiptoe, with no sounding of trumpets, no glorious Technicolor—it had just cropped up. I had got so used to its tame appearance that I never thought of it as such.

The sacred flame was not burning so brightly now. I had kept my record fairly clean, with just a few small blots here and there, but I had never done anything to be ashamed of; and now to have come so far and slink off with my tail between my legs— For that is what it amounted to. And yet there was a simple way out: to take my parang with a long straight blade, specially made for cutting off heads, and go and look for the witch doctor. That would put an end to it all.

It was all very well having tattoos everywhere on my body, but I had still not become an Iban and never would. Better for me to let them be; they were all right as they were, even the witch doctor. It was I who had come and upset things in the peaceful longhouse. What was the good of having fine principles and railing at half of humanity, the missionaries and teachers among the blacks, if in the end I did as they do—perhaps worse. But there is one thing that cannot be said against me. I never poured scorn on the Ibans' customs and I did not corrupt them. I was about to tiptoe away even more quietly than I had arrived. All they could say was that white-skinned Dioudi had no guts. And they would not be far from the truth.

It is a principle of mine (that sounds pompous, but never mind) never to have regrets, or at any rate to start all over again from the point where things have gone wrong. As in the circus, you finish your turn. If there is an accident, you mount your horse again or climb up to the trapeze again or get the lions back into place, and you carry on to the end.

In the depths of the Borneo jungle I failed to live up to that excellent principle, and I took to my heels. Flight is never glorious except in history books, where retreats are heroic. A pity that my story ends in flight.

It was night, a cloudless night, and the toads and bullfrogs had been serenading for some time. Everyone seemed to be fast asleep. There had been a good party that evening, the first one I had missed since my arrival, and the men were sleeping off their *tuak*. Even the dogs were replete, sleeping on their backs. I have never seen that anywhere except in Borneo. The dogs had not only eaten too much, they were all alcoholics as well.

There was hardly any noise in the longhouse now. Poor Lintaü was sleeping curled up and I could only just see her flat little face between her hands. I felt a pang; I should have liked to make love to her for a last time.

The rest of the family were dead to the world. My gear was close at hand, and in a moment I had my pack on my back, the blowpipe in my hand and the parang at my side. I hadn't too many regrets; at least, I was too anxious to be off unnoticed to waste any tears.

I was familiar enough with the *bilek* and the *ruaï* to avoid tripping on the shaky floor and knocking my head against the low beams. A few yards away a rectangle showed in the darkness—the doorway to the outside verandah. Another twenty yards and I would be on firm ground. Just then the moon disappeared behind a solitary cloud. I hurried forward and a dog barked, then fell silent. At last I reached the end of the verandah. There remained the steep tree trunk with its crude steps to negotiate—a real danger. But I knew all its tricks, having

been up and down it hundreds of times. I knew that the
fourth step was missing and that all the others were as
slippery as soap. When I reached the ground I felt safer,
as there was no longer any fear of the squeaks and creaks
from the bamboo flooring. The spongy soil deadened the
sound of my footsteps as I crossed the open space to
the edge of the forest. Then I was in the relative safety
of the trees and the night—and the ghosts. For once, the
spirits were of help. Even if the Ibans discovered my
flight there and then, they would not dare to pursue me.
I was safe until morning.

I hurried down to the river, down the steep little path
where I had been bitten by the krait only a month or two
earlier. A dog barked, others started up and then cocks
joined in. I heard a stream of oaths, then gradually silence returned.

The river was shimmering over the pebbles and stones.
This was the first time I had seen it at night. It was low,
for there had been no rain for two or three days, but it
could easily become a rushing and even dangerous tor-
rent from one day to the next. A dozen pirogues were
moored to the exposed roots of the big tree on the bank,
most of them lying on the shingle. I chose the best one,
a long, slender, well-balanced boat, and dragged it down
to the water, making a terrible din. A few dogs started to
bark again. I took advantage of the noise they were making to drag all the boats down and rope them to the stern
of mine. I had no desire for the Ibans to pursue me. I had
an idea that some of them would not be at all pleased at
my leaving, so I preferred to get a headstart on them and
not give them the opportunity to tell me as much.

I have never been very good at paddling a canoe but
it was easier to tow this flotilla than I had thought, especially as the river was very calm. The only difficulty was
that I had to go upstream, and I made slow headway.
Fortunately the place I had chosen to scuttle the Iban

fleet, a wide loop in the river, was not far away. Before they could refloat their boats I would be well on my way. Sinking a pirogue is not at all difficult, but for the moment I was having a job to keep them afloat, as they were so narrow and wobbly. They had been hollowed out of strong, heavy wood, and after a few years on the river they easily sank if they filled with water.

I stood astride the first pirogue and started to rock it; water slopped into it and I jumped onto the next. Alas, results did not come up to expectations. Two or three boats did sink completely but most remained wallowing low in the water. It was no use wasting time; I left them and swam to the pirogue I had chosen, in which I intended to paddle upstream as far as I could. As I swam the few yards I said a little prayer. There were never very many crocodiles in the river, and they were quite small; I was in little danger, but nevertheless accidents occurred from time to time. . . . When I reached the pirogue I was in a state of near-panic. Darkness does not help one to be reasonable, and once I had begun to think of the crocodiles it was difficult to keep calm.

Long before dawn my arms were aching from paddling, and to save my strength I kept as near to the bank as I could, to avoid the current. It was hard going; I could see very little, as the moon did not shine through the overhanging foliage. I brushed past thick creepers and kept bumping into roots of trees; I grounded on pebbly shallows more and more often, and each time had to jump out and push the pirogue a few yards, then set off again. All this was very tiring and cost me a lot of time.

I had a notion that the sun was coming up somewhere behind the screen of millions of trees, themselves enveloped in a thick mist. I could still not see clearly but the gloom was not the same. Then it began to drizzle. These early mornings were always very cold, but I was sweating like a pig.

"How glad I'll be to start walking!" is what I thought while paddling. And yet I would regret the easy progress on the river; it was quicker and really less tiring, clean and safe, and free of mosquitoes except when passing close to low branches.

The time came for me to leave the river, as it turned away from the direction I wanted to take, which was a pity. I was going to head northwest, keeping the rising sun on my right. I could have used a compass, for I caught only rare glimpses of the sun; and the few tips on direction finding that I had been taught in the army were of little use in these latitudes. There was no glade or even a clearing in I don't know how many square miles. The only means of getting your bearings was by the pale glimmer of the rising sun, which you guessed at rather than saw; for the rest of the day you had to try to keep going in the right direction without any landmarks to guide you, climbing steep hills and following twisting riverbeds. So it was very easy to lose your direction without knowing it. Fortunately I could allow myself a wide margin of error as Sarawak, which I was making for, is very long and comparatively narrow. If I went too much to the west I would skirt the frontier and reach the sea, and if too much to the east I would arrive in Kayan territory, and with my Iban tattoos I was not at all sure of my reception. There was also the possibility of going around in circles, which happened to hundreds of Japanese during the war.

I tied up the pirogue and filled my gourd before leaving the river, as I might go half a day before coming upon a stream, especially if I had to climb a mountain; and I could not be sure of finding a "traveler's liana," one of those long, thick lianas containing a cool, sweetish, uncontaminated liquid. I drank some water and then fastened the gourd to my shoulder with a length of bark, which was strong and supple but which made a red stain on my skin. Usually, when carrying a heavy load, you fix the bark strap around your forehead, after the manner of the Sherpas of Nepal.

I attached my blowpipe on my left side and the hunting parang vertically, in the Dayak way. I was wearing only a small, workaday *sirat*. The ceremonial one was in my pack, not because I wanted to dress up but because I wanted to use it as a blanket at night. It was very wide and at least eight yards long. I walked as fast as I could through what was a "nice" area of the jungle, that is to say, there were no prickly bushes, hardly any bamboo thickets and very little undergrowth—just tall, thick, smooth trees. The ground sloped steeply and I made for the ridge, as keeping to that would save me a great deal of effort.

I pushed steadily on, not even stopping to eat, but chewed a few strips of dried venison as I went. There were ten pounds of rice in my pack, which would last me a good time. It was a very hilly area but easy going underfoot and I made good progress. I hoped this would last, so that I could put a good distance between myself and the Ibans. In terrain of this kind I could travel quite as fast as they could, perhaps even faster. But in dense areas, especially where there was much secondary forest or bamboo thickets, I could not keep up with them; and as for walking along riverbeds, over slippery pebbles, I was quite hopeless; whereas the Ibans could keep their balance with astonishing ease and hardly ever fell.

Thinking of that had me worried, for they would gain on me by following the streams. However, I doubted very much that they would pursue me for more than two or three days; in fact they might not even stir from the village.

The pleasant cool of the morning had given way to a stifling heat. The sweat was trickling into my eyes and blurring the one remaining lens in my glasses. I was plagued by mosquitoes, gnats, red ants, leeches—all the usual penalties for taking a stroll in the region, plus grazes from falling on my knees or my behind, according to the slope of the ground. But I was used to it, and to keep going I had only to think of my late friends who might be hot on my trail.

If they had decided to come after me they would know by now the direction I was taking. I had no time to cover my tracks, and in any case it would be pointless on this spongy, often clayey, ground. However, they must have lost time in picking up my track when I left the river. Each time I came to a stream I thought of attempting to throw them off the scent by wading a few hundred yards; but that would have lost me half an hour and delayed my pursuers no more than five minutes. I had seen them at it one day when a band of Punans had crossed their territory: While most of the pursuing Ibans stayed where the tracks disappeared, two went scouting quickly up and down the stream to find where the tracks started again. Not the slightest sign escaped their keen and practiced glance.

Just before nightfall, however, I made an attempt to delay them. I had come to a river more than sixty feet wide and the current was flowing fast enough to wash out my tracks in the mud. A huge tree trunk had fallen across, some fifty yards from where I was standing, with its head lying well forward on the opposite bank. These huge trees have practically no roots, and when one falls it drags down with it a small forest of tangled lianas of all sizes, some as much as three hundred feet in length. I half swam, half waded, laden as I was, to the recumbent tree trunk and hoisted myself onto it. When I reached the head of it I was able to step onto another fallen tree, still with its leafy branches. I was then about thirty yards from the river and so had made a clean break in my tracks. It would take the Ibans some time to pick them

up again. I was under no illusion that my little trick
would throw them off altogether; but if it held them up
for only an hour or two, that was something. They would
have to scatter widely and search hard.

I reckoned that I had a lead of five or six hours. But it
occurred to me only then that I could have made my
escape more intelligently. If I had let it be known that I
was going hunting for the day, and had left very early
in the morning, I would have gained a lead of a day and
a night instead of only half a night.

When darkness fell and I had to stop I was at the top
of a hill, so in the morning it would be much easier to
get my direction from the rising sun. The fear of going
around in circles was still with me. However, I felt that
I had been going in the right direction so far; the morning would show. I did not have the courage to build a
shelter for the night; instead I packed myself between
the exposed roots of a big tree, wrapped the *sirat* around
despite the heat, and dropped straight off to sleep. I
wasn't hungry. Several times during the night I was
waked up by the blasted mosquitoes, which always
seemed to find a little place to sting.

In the morning I was very stiff but it passed off after
about half an hour's walking. I had not had any exercise
for a fortnight.

That day I had to climb a great deal, and often my
way was blocked by huge granite boulders piled one
upon another, covered with moss which had vegetation
clinging to it. I had to search along the foot of these
grotesque crags for a long time in order to find a way
through, for it was impossible to get back far enough to
have a wide view and pick out a route. I had to retrace
my steps half-a-dozen times. But my pursuers would
only have to follow my tracks to find the way through,
which had taken so much of my time.

When I did reach the top I was rewarded by a won-

derful spectacle. It was simply superb, at least for anyone who likes green colors. Below me were trees, nothing
but trees in an infinite variety of shades of green, a great
wide, dense mass without a single gap or the slightest
sparkle of a river. I could see for miles around, and yet
there did not seem to be a space even to sit down, not a
patch of grass in the sun. It was certainly very impressive. It looked as if any human being who ventured
down there would soon be stifled. And to think that
under the blotchy blanket of green were millions of
creatures great and small . . . and perhaps a band of
Ibans looking for me. That probability brought me back
to reality. I had no time to stand and stare, enraptured,
lost in thought; I had to get a move on.

All day I pondered the chances of their having given
up the pursuit or even of not having left the village at
all, just happy at being rid of me at last. And yet, if
there's one thing I have complete and almost blind faith
in, especially when I am in the jungle, it is my intuition.
I have put my trust in it many times and never regretted
doing so. It is not infallible, but I often prefer to rely
on that rather than on logic. So although I tried to tell
myself that there was no danger, I sensed that the Ibans
were behind me, and not very far behind either, as I had
lost a lot of time finding a way through those crags. The
feeling was so strong that it lent me wings; yet I would
have liked to stop to hunt, for I had eaten nothing but
some dried fish and salt meat since the day before. I had,
however, drunk innumerable pints of water, which had
at once been taken from me as sweat.

I could easily imagine who made up the band of
pursuers. The witch doctor for sure, I'd stake my head
on that; he would have been the one who had harangued
and worked up the others. The rejected fiancé for another, with his brothers and cousins; and probably
Maché, though I was not sure of that. They must be

angry, but pleased, too—this was real hunting. Craft against craft, pick up the tracks and follow a trail and . . . *pfft!* No doubt they could already see my head hanging from a beam. "That's Dioudi's head up there."

Don't be too sure, my boys! A few days earlier I had been feeling low and full of pessimistic notions, but now I was back in form and in good spirits, and I wasn't going to be caught if I could help it.

For the rest of the day it was downhill nearly all the time, a gentle slope from the top of the mountain, and I made very good progress apart from a few falls. In the evening I came to another river, just before stopping for the night. I debated whether to cross at once or wait until morning, and decided to cross; if it rained during the night they would not be able to see where I had reached the opposite bank. That would be something gained.

I had time only to build a rough shelter, in fact I finished it in the dark. I was hungry and thought I'd cook a little rice; I needed something substantial. The banks of this small river were fairly clear, and I thought that even in the dark I could gather a few dead branches to make a fire. The forest wall was so thick that there was no risk of being seen.

I had walked about fifty yards when a gleam of light suddenly appeared in the darkness on the opposite bank. My God, a fire! My heart missed a beat. It could only be Punans or Ibans from Selidapi. This part of the Borneo jungle has no more inhabitants than the Sahara.

My first thought was to turn around and put as much distance as possible between myself and them, whoever they were. However, I went a little nearer to try to identify them and find how many there were. I soon recognized a few voices, but it was impossible to tell the strength of the party. Some must have been lying down or were hidden by the undergrowth. I watched them for

about half an hour and then moved away. I had seen
enough. I dared not think of what would have happened
if I had remained on that side of the river or had lit a
fire. There was no question of setting off again at once,
in the dark. I spent the rest of the evening thinking
things over, which was of no great help in the circumstances. All that emerged from my long cogitation was
that I had to get the hell out as early as possible in the
morning, which was hardly a brilliant conclusion. Later
in the morning I could try to throw my pursuers off the
scent, but that would depend upon the terrain. I had to
think of something, otherwise they would catch me.

I had little sleep as I was afraid of not waking early
and then finding myself surrounded by a lot of gleeful
faces. As soon as it was light I packed my things and set
off, leaving a dart planted in the ground by my shelter—
a language used by all primitive people, including Ibans,
to let strangers know that they are unwelcome.

For a moment I had thought of facing them across the
river and shooting at them, but a blowpipe takes time to
reload and before I had hit two of them the others
would have got across and captured me. I might also
have surprised them while asleep and tried to cut their
throats—except that they have excellent hearing. And
besides, I would not have liked doing away with half-a-
dozen men while a chance of escape was still open to
me. But if brought to bay, I would not have thought
twice about it.

Wherever possible I jogged along at a slow trot, a
pace that can be kept up for a long time; but this is not
often possible in the forest. After an hour of it I was all
in; my chest was on fire and my legs were like cotton
wool. The blowpipe kept getting caught, my pack
bumped about uncomfortably and my glasses fell off two
or three times. I continued half trotting, half walking,
but by midday I had to sit down and rest for a little

while. I wondered where the others were. Certainly not far off. I was dismayed at the speed they must have traveled. A start of six hours shouldn't be so easy to catch up on. I obviously still had plenty to learn from the Dayaks.

As the time passed I became aware of my chances growing fewer, and I felt the wind of panic. I couldn't possibly go any faster, and it would be senseless to try to ambush them on my own; I would be the one to pay for that. Another possibility came to mind, a hazardous one, for if it failed I would have lost a lot of time. But the idea gradually gained ground, and it would show them that I was still thinking of them. The Ibans had at least taught me how to set a trap, and very good teachers they were, too. I looked about me for a suitable place, taking into account the nature of the ground and especially the surrounding vegetation.

At the time I did not think of the consequences of what I was planning, though even if I had . . . I was fleeing, I had been forced to leave the village, attempts had been made to poison me—that's what counted more than anything else. But why look for excuses? I had the wind up, it was as simple as that. Those people were after me, and I had no wish to be caught.

Only a few days before we had been eating together, we were friends and we slept under the same roof. We had eaten together, yes, but not the same food. There had been *ratgun* in my soup. And now we were enemies. This story did not seem to have a very moral ending, but in the jungle there are some words that do not mean very much. I had no desire to keep harping on the point, but I did think they were wrong to treat me as a foreigner. I wasn't completely an Iban, admittedly, but a good bit of them had rubbed off on me. As I tried to find excuses for myself, I got worked up and became bad-tempered. I regretted having warned them that morning by planting a dart in the ground.

Now and again one finds a run in the secondary forest, and almost certainly it has been made by wild boars. A neat little path, used by many other animals. That is the best possible place for setting a trap. The game that uses such a run is not so wary there, though the trapper has to be careful not to disturb the natural surroundings. Normally he places a handful of grass in front of and behind the trap to warn anyone passing that way—a sign that plainly says, "Look out! Trap!"

But I did not intend to leave any such sign.

In a way it is more difficult to trap a man than a boar; although the former may have no flair and not such keen eyesight, he has a far more effective weapon—intelligence. But it is a double-edged weapon and can be guided in a desired direction.

I had found a very nice run, better than most, and I followed it for about a dozen yards. All around was the secondary forest—saplings already reaching for the sky, sturdy ferns as tall as a man. The sun gleamed fitfully through, and it was very hot. Quite a number of old trees were still standing, but I could see some fallen trunks all covered with moss and fungi.

In that thick undergrowth it was impossible to go off the path without leaving traces which would be visible for several days. Luckily there was an old tree trunk lying just on the edge of the run. I left my pack and blowpipe on it but took my parang with me, stepping onto the part of the trunk bare of moss and then over the ferns growing just beyond, leaving no trace of my passage that I could see. Now that I was away from the path I could freely look for bamboos and a *pohon raqué*, a tree with very pliable young wood.

The trap I intended to make was normally used for stags and boars; one or more spiked bamboos were securely fixed to the lowest branches of a *pohon raqué* growing by a run.

I cut some solid bamboo and nicked and sharpened

them at one end; they could penetrate any hide, even a boar's—so when it came to a man's skin. . . . When the creeper holding them back is touched by an animal, they spring forward and pierce its belly.

I returned the same way ten minutes later and in order to avoid leaving tracks near the tree trunk I crept under the ferns to reach the run; and to prevent the footprints in the run arousing the suspicions of my Ibans I poured a little water on the trunk—then they would think I had just stopped to take a leak. A few yards away, just at the end of the run, was a tree I was looking for; this *pohon raqué* was just in the right place, had plenty of leaves and almost horizontal branches. I took the three sharpened lengths of bamboo and tied two onto a young branch at the height of a man's navel and the third onto another at chest height, then bent the branches well back.

I had to be careful not to move around and leave a lot of marks, but with everything at hand it was possible to work without changing position. It was not very difficult and did not take long. When the two branches were in place I took a step forward, holding them back with my blowpipe—one false move and I might have got my device slap in my own stomach—and tied the two branches together and joined them to a thin liana which crossed the run. On the other side I pegged the liana down with a forked piece of wood. Then it was all ready. I spread a few fern leaves over the strand of liana—it looked all right to me, but I took the extra precaution of dropping a piece of dried meat a few feet in front of the trap. That would probably attract the attention of the leading Iban and he would not look under the fern leaves. In any case, they would not be expecting that sort of surprise from me, despite my warning that morning.

When someone had the misfortune to touch the stretched liana it would jerk out of its peg and at the same time release the two branches. The spiked bamboos would strike the victim less than a second later, just as he took a step forward and so placed himself in the right position. This sort of trap rarely killed at once, but the profuse bleeding left an easily discernible trail and the animal could be tracked down and finished off.

It had taken me more time than I had expected. If they discovered my trap before it did any damage, I was done for. But on the other hand, if one of them got caught in it I did not think the others would go on, especially as I intended to plant another dart in the ground a little farther on, though I would not set another trap. But they would not know that, and if they did proceed it would be much more slowly, for fear of another man's being impaled.

I felt no regrets over setting the trap, but a few hours later my conscience was troubling me a bit. The devil had got the better of me.

The rest of the afternoon was uneventful and I carried on until nightfall. I slept on the ground, but after an hour I was wakened by a cohort of insects who had taken my body for a parade ground. I couldn't think what it all was at first and got out my lighter; but the night was so humid that I had a job to make it work. I just groped along to a place a few yards away and then I lay down again. But I couldn't sleep for thinking of my pursuers. When constructing my trap I ought never to have fixed a bamboo at chest height; the leading man would probably die at once or in a very short time. I ought to have been satisfied to make the trap with just one pointed bamboo at the level of a man's stomach—to wound him, but no more.

It was rather like modern warfare where small-caliber rifles are used more and more. A dead man is no trouble to anyone, but a wounded man requires the attention of a great many people—two stretcher-bearers, nurses, a doctor, an ambulance, perhaps a helicopter, not to mention antibiotics and bandages. Moral—don't kill, strike hard.

I had no idea whether I had been traveling for a week, ten days or twelve. It was a long time since I had kept a diary. I was very tired but not nearly so frightened. I made myself a shelter every night, and now and again I hunted. I had not seen or heard anything of my pursuers. I wondered if they had even crossed the river; but if so, had they discovered my trap and turned back, or had one of them been transfixed? I would never know, and it was just as well.

By now I felt that I was practically out of danger, and my only worry (and it was a big one) was to keep on course and not to run into trouble with animals. Fortunately I made a lot of noise, scaring them all away, which reduced the risk of accident. Internally I was still going strong; it would have been stupid at this stage to come down with dysentery or sprain my ankle.

I gathered a lot of insects and ate about half a pound of them, keeping as many for next day. These little creatures come in very useful, as they can be kept for a long time; you just nip off their legs and put them in a hollow bamboo. No need for a refrigerator. When I was hungry, all I had to do was to get out a handful and nibble them. It's a good tip for survival.

I was walking along a sandy strip by a river and smoking a big cigarette. It was dark, but I could just see where I was stepping. In any case, I wasn't going very far, as all sorts of creatures gather on these riverbanks and I had no wish to tread on the tail of a crocodile or a krait.

A whole squadron of fireflies traced graceful, glowing patterns in the air; they gave off a very pretty, soft, bluish-purple light. Then something else caught my attention. At first I thought it was a number of other fireflies that had settled in the same place, but as I went near I could see that it was a fire tree—a promising name and one which has given rise to a good many legends in Africa as well as in America and Asia. These fire trees are old tree trunks that have been eaten all over by termites or other insects and become sodden and covered with tiny fungi, which emit this eerie light. Sometimes it is the wood itself which contains phosphorus. This particular tree was not a very good specimen; still, I could understand natives' weaving a legend around it.

It was a beautiful river, the Natibas River, and there was an Iban village on it, but one where the inhabitants wore shirts and some of them could even answer "Yes" to questions. In the evening there was a celebration, with dances! I was safe at last.

"That's my daughter," the old chief said to me. "Isn't she pretty?"

"*Na badas.* Oh no, she's not at all pretty!"

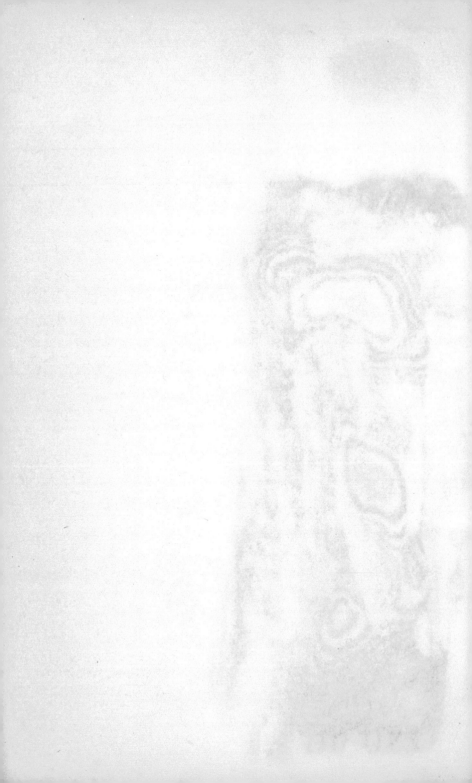

DATE DUE		
MAY 25 '78		
MR 21 '88		
MY 9 '88		
JUL 0 9 1990		